CW00520171

Jobe

THE BEGINNINGS OF A LIVERPOOL LEGEND

John Thompson

Published by RedPaintPublishing 2017

Copyright © 2017 John Thompson

John Thompson asserts the moral authority to
be identified as the author of this work

A catalogue record for this book
is available from the British Library

ISBN: 978-1-5272-1018-9

While some of the events and characters are based
on historical incidents and figures, this novel is
entirely a work of fiction.

Cover Design by Sion Morris
www.cinnamondesign.co.uk

All Rights Reserved.

No part of this publication may be reproduced,
stored in a retrieval system, or transmitted,
in any form or by any means, electronic, mechanical,
photocopying, recording, or otherwise, without
express written permission of the author.

To an Angel, a Monk, a Frog and
a Queen

I Love you All

Chapter I

The dockers paused periodically, catching their breaths as they wiped away beads of sweat that ran down their foreheads and stung their eyes. Those that had them used crusted and filthy handkerchiefs to stem and dab away the rivulets; those that didn't used their forearms, leaving a smear of soot and dust across their brows. They looked at the crowd of idlers who had gathered around George's Basin and muttered their resentment towards them before once again losing themselves among the barrels and crates being unloaded from the three-masted barque.

"'Ere, you don't wanna be putting your foot on *his* block sir!" A small boy emerged from the shadow cast by the Church of Our Lady and Saint Nicholas, took a battered orange crate from under his arm and set it down.

"I'll warrant he told you he'd shine your shoes for a copper, didn't he?" He chirped as he efficiently pulled at an arrangement of threadbare brushes and cloths secreted around various parts of his person. The bespectacled captain looked from one boy to the other, confused by the sudden complication.

"Oh he'll black 'em and he'll crack 'em but he'll never get a shine on them, all he's got is soot and vitriol, vitriol and soot, his father's a chimney sweep you see," he continued as he meticulously spread out the tools of his trade. He took a lavish step back to survey them and finally satisfied, looked towards his competitor for the first time.

"Deny it if you can Johnny, protest to the good captain here." The boy bristled but remained mute and the captain removed his foot from the block.

"That's it sir, you come over here. I'll give you somewhere to see your face without need of a looking glass and all for the aforementioned copper." The captain shrugged at his initial choice, who could do nothing but stand in forlorn defeat, and moved over to the effervescent boy whose chatter didn't abate as he rubbed, scrubbed and spat at the captain's left shoe. He leaned back on his haunches admiring his work.

"There you go sir, now let's have the other one and I'll do it for sixpence," he said, a grin spread over his face. The captain pulled back his half-cocked right leg.

"Sixpence, why you said you'd shine them for a copper; the boy there was charging me a penny!" He bristled.

"Well he'd have blacked them for a copper I can believe, but if it's a matching shine you want it'll cost you sixpence. You wouldn't expect to catch a weasel asleep now sir, would you?" The captain begrudgingly handed over the small coin and placed his foot on the crate.

Albert watched the whole scene play out with a smile on his lips. The smile twisted into a grimace and his body froze as he thrust his hand into his trouser pocket with instinctive sharpness and, with a vice-like grip, held on to the small hand he found already in there. Jobe, sitting astride the broad shoulders, was jolted forward as his father craned to peer at the imp who owned the hand. The urchin, snared and with no chance of escape, flapped and writhed with the shock of a hooked fish. Albert immediately relaxed his grip, relieving the bone-crushing pressure. He looked into the boy's face and was shocked at the features, which had been sharpened and chiseled by hunger.

"Your hands would be better employed helping the stevedores over there or perhaps scavenging cotton from under a scutching machine my lad, wouldn't you agree?"

The small boy stopped jerking at mention of a cotton mill and looked mutely up at his captor, an anxious defiance etched across his prematurely wizened face. Albert looked away from the accusing eyes and scanned the outskirts of the crowd. Jobe was involuntarily twisted and turned at the mercy of his fathers movements and placed a hand on his cap to stop it from falling to the ground. Albert found what he was looking for and again addressed the boy.

"What is your name?"

The boy, guessing that the man holding his hand had spotted a copper, remained mute. Albert fished around in his pocket with his free hand.

"On the edge of the crowd there's a woman selling penny pies; here, go and fetch three. Attempt to cheat me again and there'll be a consequence, do you understand?"

The boy, slack-jawed, nodded at Albert and took the offered threepenny piece in disbelief. Albert released his hold completely but the boy remained in place rubbing his liberated hand.

"Off you go then! Three penny pies!" stated Albert, waving the boy away.

The boy blended into the crowd in a daze. He turned back in case the man thought better of his leniency and was pushing through the crowd in order to re-apprehend him. He was assured that this wasn't the case, as he could still see that the boy with the best view on the dock remained stationary.

Although Albert hadn't reconsidered his show of compassion a witness to the exchange had taken offence. He approached Albert and addressed him with a well-practised air of superiority.

"Do my eyes deceive me? Am I to believe that you have just released that scoundrel to go and prey on some other poor unfortunate?" Albert looked down at the squat, well-heeled man addressing him.

"No, I've released him with orders to fetch myself and my son a penny pie," he replied blithely. Jobe was again forced to lean backwards to safely retain his perch, such was the extent Albert was forced to look down in order to converse with his accuser.

"Have you taken leave of your senses, man? I must say I find it an outrage, nothing less than an outrage, to release such a fiend into the crowd - and with a tuppence reward to boot," stated the man, his high-pitched voice corresponding perfectly with his small stature. Albert remained nonplussed.

"It was thruppence actually, and I assure you he'll return with my pastry." The man became exasperated, confusing Albert's light attitude with some hidden weakness of the mind. He began to wave his hands at the taller man, revelling in the spectacle he was creating.

"Return! Oh I'm sure he will, sir, and with a multitude of his High-Rip brethren. Why, once they hear that there's a fool at the dock who rewards attempted robbery and impertinence with thruppenny bits I'm sure there'll be a veritable horde." Albert remained a picture of composure and again fished around in his pocket until he felt the familiar shape of a threepenny piece.

"Well congratulations, my good man, although I could not accuse you of attempted robbery your impertinence has certainly earned this!" Albert flicked the coin at the man causing him to flinch.

"Now good-day, sir," he said looking at the man squarely. The man, sensing he had made a misjudgment, melted into the crowd with as much dignity as he could muster.

Jobe had not paid the slightest attention to either of the affairs his father had been engaged in. The bustle and confusion around the dock made no impression on him. He unconsciously shifted his position allowing the blood to flow through his haunches for a second before he settled back on his perch and re-impeded the arteries' flow. He was oblivious to the buzzing sensation of paraesthesia building in his already numb legs. The throng of people around George's Basin, comprised of people from every conceivable walk of life the city had to offer, shared his single-mindedness; as necks craned they marvelled at the hot air balloon floating high above the Mersey.

Silky slunk and threaded through the spellbound crowd with ease. His unconscious mind scanned and spotted half a dozen well to do targets in as many yards. Easy pickings were galore. His brush with capture hadn't slaked his appetite. He'd made a mistake, that was all. He rebuked himself, why on earth had he attempted to dip the giant? He'd been on his tiptoes just to reach his pocket! He'd had a lucky escape an' no denying. His initial fear hadn't lasted though. He'd been confident of a reprieve as soon as he had met the giant's stare; there was a twinkle in the unusually green eyes and a twitching of his neatly trimmed moustache, as if he were trying to stifle a smile.

This lot would be different, dipped and flipped within the blink of an eye as they stood around George's Dock gawping up at the balloon in the sky. Silky didn't know what all the fuss was about. An over-inflated pig's bladder bobbing above the Mersey. He knew it was there to allow some Nancy a bird's-eye view to produce a painting of the city. He imagined the rich toffs marvelling at the finished article hanging on a wall in a fine gallery as they slapped each other on the back, congratulating themselves on constructing such a fine town, the majority of which, they failed to notice, chose to ignore or avoided like the plague every day of their lives. But he wasn't arguing. He'd heard it was going to take the Nancy another two days to finish his drawing and if the balloon attracted crowds like this one he wouldn't be going hungry for a while.

He made his way to where he knew McGhee would be with her tray of mutton pies. Silky's unconscious brain, which was every bit as forceful as that of his conscious one, screeched at him to continue dipping the cluster of snobs as he made his way out of the crowd and back up Chapel Street with the gift of a threepenny bit and a good story to share at the corner. Instead he reached McGhee and ordered three pies.

"'Ere, how about four for three Missus McGhee?"

"Penny a pie," came the stock reply from the barrel of a woman. Silky handed over the threepenny piece and cradling the pies like new born babies entered back into the crowd to his liberator and, Silky assumed, his son. He was tormented by the smell of the hot pastry but enjoyed the warmth of the pies against his perpetually cold hands when a heavy gentleman, who couldn't quite crane his neck back far enough to view the balloon to his liking, took a step backwards and landed heavily on his bare left foot. Silky let out a scream and, acutely aware of the pies, attempted to stop his arms from fulfilling their natural reaction. He had partial success and kept two of the pies cradled but watched in helpless horror as the third and topmost pie somersaulted in mid-air before descending and splatting on the ground. He looked up at the owner of the heavy foot in anger. He was a tall but vastly rotund man with a crimson complexion caused by a fondness for claret. His bulbous, vein-ridden nose, which was if anything a deeper red than his face, twitched in revulsion as he realized what he had stepped on. Silky was incensed.

"'Ere, if you didn't have so many chins maybe you'd be able to look up in the sky like everybody else. Why don't you go up Everton Brow, you'd be able to stretch your neck enough to see from there!" The man bristled at the laughter that came from a majority of the surrounding crowd and responded by planting his foot firmly into the fallen pie, his turkey neck trembling with the effort, ruining its pathetic contents.

"Ahh, that must've hurt you, trampling on good food." He turned his attention to those who had dragged their gaze from the spectacle in the sky. "Keep an eye on this gent! I'll give you a silver shilling each if he's not on his hands and knees snaffling that pastry down his big fat gullet the instant you next look up at that pox-ridden balloon." There was more laughter from those in the crowd. The working men, whose employment usually depended on them treating such a gentleman with a well-measured deference, ensured they added an extra element of derision.

Silky cut further into the crowd as the man took a step towards him. He was crestfallen. This is what you get for being honest he admonished himself. He considered eating the remaining two pies and getting back to dipping. Maybe he'd have a go at the fat toff with the big foot. But something about the man with the boy on his shoulders drew him back and he knew it wasn't the promise of a penny pie or the threat of consequences.

Albert wondered whether the irate stump of a man at the dock had been right. He had to concede that the fellow certainly had a point. Had he done the right thing, not only releasing the little street Arab but also rewarding him with a pie and sixpence? Was he one of the High-Rip who were spreading so much fear throughout the North End of the city? He thought it unlikely. The heel imprint on the boy's dirty bare foot had certainly proved testament to the unfortunate fate of the third pie. Added to that, the boy looked as if he had not eaten that day or possibly the one before. He had split the two pies between the urchin and his son and also given the boy a tanner, warning him to get home before his good fortune was spent.

Although around the same age as his son, probably a little older, Albert reflected, Jobe's expression of infancy and inquisitive innocence was one that, in all likelihood, had never had the luxury of gracing the other boy. The two were of similar stature and physique but where Jobe had the healthy glow of an eight-year-old, the boy was stunted and starving. Albert decided he was correct to afford the boy his liberty. It would do little harm to those in the crowd wealthy enough to own pocket-watches and silk handkerchiefs to be relieved of them in order to help fill an empty stomach.

The noise of Jobe still sucking remnants of the unfamiliar grease from his fingers interrupted his thoughts.

"Jobe, there can't possibly be anything left of that pie. Now remember, no mention of it to your mother." Jobe continued to turn and stare back at the balloon lingering above the Mersey as they rose through the rolling hills of Everton. His father had eaten up the three miles from the waterfront to their home, stopping only to place him on the ground in order to brush the pastry crumbs from the baggy knee pants of his grey knickerbocker suit. As the blood flow had been restored to his legs he had suffered terribly from the pins and needles that afflicted him. His legs seemed to be on fire. His father advised him to stamp up and down while he massaged his son's legs with huge hands, explaining to him that the pain was only caused because his blood was rushing to where it was needed. That had made him feel better. Now he was back in his favourite place in the world and the view he had was astounding. The roofs of Great Homer Street, Scotland Road and Vauxhall stretched all the way to the docks in a black confusion, punctuated here and there by the outlines of churches and chimneys, ending with the radiance of the Mersey, sparkling like a jewelled ribbon as the sun reflected from it. The river was crammed from north to south with shipping and goods from all over the world. Looking down on it all was the magical balloon. Jobe wondered if the artist could see him and his father. His father being a giant, Jobe thought it likely and gave a wave. He looked forward to seeing his father and himself when the painting was finished.

Jobe pushed down on his spinning top and watched in wonder as it blurred before his eyes.

But still failed to rise. He knew if he could just get it to spin a little faster it would take off and hover like the balloon he had seen with his father down by the river. He grabbed the top and put his full weight on it, attempting to induce as much power and speed as possible. The top's handle snapped under the pressure and Jobe watched as the device skewed off on its side across the small foyer and into the dining room. His mother entered the drawing room with the broken top in her hand. Although she had been baking and was wearing an old pinafore, Jobe thought she was beautiful. She was forced to continuously blow a loose strand of dark hair from her deep blue eyes as she spoke to him, her elfin face contorting as she did so.

"Jobe, d'you know how many children in the street I grew up in would kill for even a single spin of this top?" Jobe sensed his mother's genuine emotion and wondered at it.

"You must be careful, toys like this are precious. You need to be aware of how lucky you are."

"I wanted it to fly, mother," Jobe said by way of explanation. This seemed to turn his mother's sadness to anger.

"So you threw it up into the air is that it? You need to learn to appreciate what you've got and how lucky you are to have it." Kitty proceeded to collect the toys that Jobe had scattered over the floor, and once returned to their box, she put it on top of Albert's bureau.

"You shan't be having these back until you learn to respect your belongings," she chided him. Jobe heard the front door close and a second later his father entered the room. Albert immediately sensed the strained atmosphere.

"What's all this, have my two angels had a falling out?" he asked, bemused.

"Oh Albert, I'm worried he's becoming spoiled. He's broken his new spinning-top. He's no regard for his belongings. I want him to know the value of the things he has."

"Well, that's certainly not like you Jobe. Let's have a look at it, maybe it was faulty." Albert looked around the drawing room floor.

"Where is it?" he asked.

"It's up on your bureau with the rest of his toys. It's not faulty; he's thrown it into the air to make it fly. I've taken them all away until he learns their worth," explained Kitty. Albert located the box and reached up for it.

"Come now, Kitty. Haven't we agreed we don't want him to be deprived or to know want?" Albert nodded towards Jobe quietly sitting on the floor.

"Just look at him, not once has he interrupted or attempted to plead his innocence, and look at the rest of these toys, they're immaculate. How did he react to you taking his things? There was no tantrum or beseeching, I'll wager." Albert was on his knees now sorting through the box of toys. He took out the top and its broken plunger, fingering the sharp metal where the break had occurred. He looked at Jobe.

"Can you tell your mother and me how it broke, Jobe?"

"Mother is right, Father. I was trying to make it fly," he confessed.

"I didn't throw it in the air, though," he quickly added. Jobe knelt forward and took the two parts from his father, explaining his aim as he provided a reconstruction.

"The top spins so fast that I fancied if I could make it spin just a little faster it would take off. So I pushed down on it as hard as I could, but it snapped instead of spinning faster." Jobe released the broken top to the floor and knelt back sadly. He looked at his mother.

"I wasn't trying to make you sad, Mother. I'm sorry. I love all my toys." Albert brought his hand to his forehead.

"The boy is a genius," he said, more to himself than his wife or son as he scooped Jobe up and spun him in the air.

"Eight years old! An absolute genius!" This time he did address his wife.

"Don't you see, Kitty? He was trying to create enough downward pressure to enable the top to hover." He noted his wife's total bafflement.

"Never mind," he smiled. He kissed his son on the forehead as he placed him back on the thick rug before standing and taking his wife in his arms.

"We've created an absolute genius," he said again as he bent and kissed her. Jobe looked happily at his mother and father, glad that everything was harmonious again. His mother looked down at him, smiling now.

"Well Master Genius, just be more careful in future, that's all."

Albert took his pocket-watch out. The hands had barely moved since the last time he had checked. He was well aware of the hungry glances his watch was attracting but for once discarded his caution. He had more serious concerns. He scanned the bar again. Being at least a head taller than the rest of the clientele in the poorly renovated parlour he was in no doubt that Potter wasn't in the room. Potter was never late. The onset of worry began to gnaw at him, an odd sensation that he didn't enjoy. He drained his glass flinching at the hot unfamiliar liquid burning his throat. Why did people drink? The question became more pertinent as he opened the heavy door to find a man lying prone in the doorway. Albert bent and was about to heave the man into a more comfortable position but noticed the vermin that crawled over his body and instead stepped over the obstruction. Without a word being said, three men standing around a hogshead barrel drained their glasses and followed Albert out of the pub.

Although the sun shone brightly above neither warmth nor light permeated into the dank and narrow canyon that remained in constant shadow. So high were the black tenements on either side that the air itself was inert, causing a noxious atmosphere that Albert could almost feel pulling against the exposed flesh of his hands and face. His mind spun as he navigated his way through the refuse, sewage and uneven cobbles with a dexterity that belied his ignorance of the street. Albert wondered if he had misread Potter's note but Kitty had also read it and indeed directed him on how to reach the venue named on it.

Potter, as tall as himself but even broader, enjoyed their clandestine meetings and wrung all he could from them by insisting they use a different public house for each of their monthly rendezvous. It seemed to Albert that the pubs had grown seedier and rougher over the course of the years, each one located deeper in the courts and entries than the one before. Albert had wondered how he carried out his reconnaissance and could only venture that Potter remained in the localities long after Albert had left.

He couldn't blame Potter for attempting to wring maximum excitement from what must otherwise be a mundane existence serving Albert's parents on the Wirral peninsula.

Albert's usually reliable and self-preserving powers of observation and awareness were heavily diluted by the tumult of anxious and apprehensive thoughts cascading through his mind. He failed to notice as mothers ushered their protesting, emaciated children out of the gutter and into the cellars and tenements on either side of him.

The shock of the heavy thud to the back of his head caused an instant explosion of stars before his eyes. His knees buckled and he was on the verge of sinking to them but on some unconscious level he was still aware of the filth that covered the street and it was his desperation to avoid falling into it, rather than self-preservation, that caused Albert to shuffle forward and remain on his feet. He spun around and, again more through instinct than sense, threw a heavyweight of a haymaker just as the lead pipe was about to make contact for the second time.

The wielder of the pipe was bewildered that the toff, big as he was, had somehow remained on his feet. He prided himself on his strength and ability to fell an opponent with a single blow of his two-pound lead pipe. It always fell to him to land the blow that got the job done. The kicks and punches that followed, thrown by all three of them, as their prey lay prone and penniless, were purely for pleasure, fuelled by spite and hatred. For one of his victims not to collapse instantly into the gutter was nothing short of miraculous, especially when he had the element of surprise on his side. These thoughts raced through Bernie's mind as he trotted forward the couple of paces needed to deliver the second, and surely, killer blow. They also served to slow and weaken the strike that was aimed at the same spot on the back of the head but never reached its destination. Bernie was helpless to avoid the crashing blow from the huge right hand that ceased all flow of thoughts through his head.

Albert leant forward and retched the fiery liquid he had just consumed on to the cobbles, adding to the plethora of human waste that already festered there. With both hands on his knees he looked up at the two remaining assailants.

"I'd give it a bit more thought if I were you," he managed to croak. The two men looked at their fallen comrade face down in the filth and then back at the colossus in front of them who was straightening up to his full height, wiping his mouth with a handkerchief as he did so. They glanced at each other for an instant and, decision made, ran full pelt back to the safety of their abandoned hogshead.

Albert, unsure, of his legs waited for a second before approaching his assailant to pull him out of the filth he was quietly drowning in. He was a dead weight and it took all of Albert's diminished strength to prop him against the soot-covered wall.

"Yer wanna leave him in the gutter where he belongs, nothing but shite anyway." Albert slowly turned in the direction the voice came from but the movement was still too quick for his aching head's liking. It felt as though his attacker had found his way inside it and was hammering away with his lead pipe. Albert retched again, but this time nothing came up and his stomach and ribs ached with the exertion. An old woman stood in a doorway, her shape and face hidden by a swathe of black rags that seemed to hover around her. Something about the woman affected Albert more than an army of assailants, and his heart sank. Children who had been dragged indoors by their mothers now flooded into the street and approached the unconscious ruffian cautiously. On seeing that he was no threat they descended on him and in a silent frenzy tore at him, removing anything of value including the lead cosh. His earlier dexterity and demeanour forgotten Albert half ran, half staggered to the end of the dank entry, bursting out of it into the relative security and sunshine of Great Howard Street, shocking a match-seller who stood on the corner into dropping her basket of wares.

Kitty had just finished basting the roasting piece of meat and was flushed from the hot stove when she heard Albert come in. She entered the parlour where her husband was sitting before the unlit fireplace. A wave of relief flooded over her whole being and her nerves ceased their continuous jangling. She understood the necessity of his monthly meetings with the mysterious Mr Potter but couldn't for the life of her imagine why they took place in such surroundings.

"Kitty, do you know where this public house is, dear?" Albert would ask, unfolding a luxurious piece of paper in front of her. Kitty would take the paper and although the scrawled street name would cause her stomach to lurch, and more often than not provoke a flurry of memories, she couldn't help but marvel at the exquisitely fine paper.

As often as not she knew of the pub, or if she didn't was always at least aware of the court, street or entry it was in. The meetings were always in the worst parts of her old parish or even less desirable neighbouring ones, and she would blanch as she gave him his answer and then directed him on how to arrive there by the safest and least unsavoury route.

She had stopped trying to talk him out of having his rendezvous in such areas for fear he would stop asking her advice.

"Well Kitty, if you're going to worry so I shall have to stop asking your advice and not share my whereabouts with you," he had told her.

She instead mollified her anxiety by forcing Albert to repeat her directions at least three times which would, please lord, negate the need for him to spend longer in an unknown area, going deeper into the depths until he was lost in the honey-combed labyrinth of tenements, alleyways and courts. Still she couldn't help trying to curtail Potter's risk-taking.

"It's just common sense, Albert. Why not meet in the town? Why can't your father's man just come here?"

"It's Potter's prerogative, dearest, and if anyone were to see us...If mother found out he'd be in as much trouble as father. More. She can't sack father!"

Kitty put down her tea towel and looking at Albert noticed that his face, usually so rugged and robust, was pale, clammy and his breathing shallow. He sank further into his armchair. She went over and sat on the arm stroking his head.

"Albert, are you hurt my love, whatever's the...?" Kitty tailed off as her hand traced the huge lump on the back of his head.

"Oh my..." This time it was Albert's interjection, a raised hand, which caused her to trail off. She fell to her knees in front of him, hands in his lap, waiting for him to speak.

"I'm fine dear, I promise, physically at least. I'll let you fuss over me all you want in a moment or two but first please hand me Potter's last envelope from the bureau in the drawing room." Kitty, although shocked and with a hundred questions that needed answers, got up and carried out his request. She returned with the envelope her husband had brought home a month ago containing the precious pound notes. Now all that it contained was the beautiful paper with a pub's name and street scrawled on it in a terrible hand. It reminded her of Jobe, although even at eight his writing was better. Thank God he was at school now and couldn't see his father in this state.

"What does the note say, dear?" asked Albert. Kitty knew from memory, having given Albert directions at the beginning of the month and again that morning, but looked down at the note anyway.

"It says Nonpareil, Luton Street," she said. She brought it over to Albert and again sat on the arm of his chair.

"You see, Nonpareil, Luton Street," she repeated as she held the note in front of Albert, who held his hand up to his eyes.

"Yes, I knew already, and it's the one off Boundary Street, just under the railway," he said, his hand still massaging his eyes. Kitty's nerves began to jangle again but she forced herself to stand, tall and bright.

"Yes, that's the one Albert. Now c'mon, I want a proper look at this head of yours, and to know where and how you got such a coggie, although I can well imagine. Didn't I warn you they call the place Sebastopol on account of how rough it is!"

Kitty flinched on numerous mental levels. The sheer size of the man was cause enough, he was bigger than Albert even, hugely tall, long-limbed and broad in the chest, though none of his intimidating size was portrayed in a face that shone with geniality. The greatest shock was that this was obviously someone from, or sent from, Albert's family over the water, and he was addressing her as Madam.

"May I speak with your husband, Mr Albert Warburton, please Madam," the big man said again. Kitty, to an extent, recovered herself.

"Yes, that is, I'm sorry. Please come in." Kitty stepped back and opened the door fully. Although the doorway was large enough to accommodate him the man stooped in order to enter.

"From habit", Kitty thought, then mentally rebuked herself.

"C'mon now Kitty, get a grip of yourself girl, this is important." Kitty had entered into the habit of mentally chastising herself soon after being estranged from her family. Although she had never been wantonly scolded by any of them, her habits always left room for minor chiding and as nobody was around to do it for her, she did it herself. Out loud when she was alone or with Jobe but inwardly at all other times. She saw the man in the hall looking at her, awaiting direction.

"God! Now c'mon Kitty will yer!"

Potter sat facing Albert. His sympathies were obviously genuine and Kitty found herself liking the man. Albert held on to the china cup in his hand so tightly that Kitty feared for it. Even though she shared the full pain of her husband's bereavement she couldn't bear to see something so delicate and precious damaged. Her prudent nature took over.

"Here my love, let me take that for you." She gently removed the full but cold cup from Albert's grasp. He looked at her as if waking and then looked at Potter.

"And the funeral was last month!" He looked at Potter but spoke to no one.

"I'm so sorry, Albert. Your mother has ensured I remained busy, which wasn't difficult given the circumstances. She knows I was your father's man and has always had her suspicions that we met on his behalf. He always spoke about wanting to accompany me..." Potter tailed off as Albert stared into the fireplace. He could only speculate at what was going through Albert's mind. He wondered if the anguish of the news had given way to pragmatism. If not the grief of losing his father must be accompanied, if not outweighed, by the worry of losing his regular stipend.

"I can't believe she never let me say goodbye." Albert's words interrupted Potter's musings and he saw that Albert was addressing his wife. Potter took the opportunity to study Kitty unobserved. Her beauty was startling. He had been taken aback by it when she had pulled open the heavy front door. Only his ingrained politeness and years of service had allowed his face and voice to remain unaffected.

Potter had been well aware of what enticed Albert back to the Merchants Coffee House on Water Street; and he knew it wasn't the quality of their beans or the panoramic views across the Mersey. Potter had heard of the serving maid's beauty but hadn't witnessed it personally; he fully expected that, either the sating of Albert's lust or the continual rejection of his advancements would bring the visits to an end. Potter was as shocked as anybody when Albert announced his marriage plans to his distraught parents.

He now appreciated Albert's decision to defy his mother's authority in order to make the serving girl, Kitty, his bride. Albert's mother, as always, had been unwilling to have her totalitarian habits queried and responded brutally to her only son's deviation from the path she had prepared for him. Her decree that Albert be ostracised by the family and deprived of the benefits of belonging to it, had met opposition, but when it was learned that his intended was a Catholic cellar-dweller from Liverpool, even the boldest opposition, that of his father, melted away. It was a heavy price to pay.

Potter cleared his throat, not knowing any other way to intimate he had something further to add. Albert and Kitty both looked at him. Potter returned their gaze. Unwilling to add to their burden but having no other option he looked Albert in the eye.

"I'm afraid the will has been read, Albert. Your mother was the sole beneficiary."

Fergus's permanently stooped back became even more pronounced as he tackled the steep brow. His knees screamed in protest with each step of his threadbare but heavy hobnail boots. The impact of the gradient on his physical condition was equivalent to that of the vicinity on his mental state. His sensibilities grated as he travelled further into Orange territory. He'd never crossed the invisible divide between Scotland Road and Great Homer Street into the Orange enclave before Kitty, his only daughter, had been banished there. He crossed Byrom Street and followed the ever-ascending Richmond Row across its junction with St Anne Street and so on to Everton Brow itself. Fergus tensed as he crossed St Anne Street, into what he considered staunch Orange country. He was ready to defend himself against the angry horde of Orangemen, the O's, gathered to dislodge him, the Irish Catholic, from their territory. As usual the outraged mob never materialised and the people continued with the daily grind of their existence, a huge majority of which mirrored the struggles those of his own parish faced. Fergus turned his attention to the real battle ahead. Everton Brow was an unmerciful climb and given his almost decrepit physical condition it was one he was never sure he would conquer.

He attempted to observe the O's without ever being caught looking. The better quality of air and life itself offered on the hills didn't permeate to these lower reaches of the climb and Fergus only encountered the types of people he would on his own doorstep. Still they were queer fish. Sure there were the odd few Catholic families scattered in the enclave of Protestantism but to Fergus's mind their continual exposure to the O's had somehow tarnished them.

"Tinged with Tangerine," as his Nelly would put it.

Nevertheless it had been wrong to ostracise his youngest daughter and so force her into Orange clutches. He had tried to intercede on her behalf. Attempted to make his wife see sense, and so in her eyes "went against her," something she found hard to forget or forgive. That was how she viewed Kitty's marriage to a Protestant. A betrayal so heinous it could never be rescinded. Kitty didn't stand a chance. Nell had not stopped rocking in her chair for an instant, as was her wont when she was perplexed.

"But mam, if you'd just give him a chance," implored Kitty.

"A chance! A chance! Did they give us a chance when they were setting fire to the roof over our head? Did they?" responded her mother.

"But mam, what's that to do with Albert? He's never even been to Ireland. He's loving, kind and gentle," she continued.

"Ah well, isn't that always the way with the devil until he's tricked you out of what he wants."

"Well, he's had it mam. I'm having his baby and we're to be married next week," blurted Kitty. Nell's rocking stopped and she pointed at her daughter as though she were cursing her.

"Then you'll leave this house Kathleen Flynn and you'll never darken its door again! I'll have no bastard Orange in this house!"

Fergus almost collapsed against the set of railings that surrounded the pleasure gardens on Shaw Street. A group of young women with bonnets and perambulators sat inside the fenced summer seat casting the odd furtive glance in his direction. Fergus gulped in a lungful of the fresh spring air. It couldn't hold a candle to the good clean Irish air he'd been raised on but compared to the fug those in the rest of the town were forced to inhale it was an elixir. Kitty was better off up here away from the degradation and despair of the slums, even if she was surrounded by O's. He couldn't shake the melancholic feeling that the haphazard swirl of thoughts that accompanied him up the hill like an extra weight had caused in him. He dragged his calloused palm across his sweating forehead before wiping it against his trousers. He'd had to get involved when he realised the enormity of the tragedy facing his family.

"Well hang on there, Nelly. If the girl is pregnant and to be married then this is a situation that needs discussion not hot-headedness." His wife had twisted on him like a viper, her rocking regaining its momentum.

"Hot-headedness is it? Is that the hot-headedness that got us out of our burning house as they barricaded us in? Is that the one? Sure Fergus, you'd have had a hot head all right, never mind just a singed one, cowering inside as you did! Wasn't it my hot head that broke us out and lambasted the Orange!" Fergus had spent years trying to impress on his wife the fact that he wasn't cowering at all but trying to protect his youngest from the burning thatch that had begun to fall upon them.

"I'm just saying…"

"Well you'll say no more Fergus Flynn, or you'll be out on your ear with her." Nell scooped up the quart of ale from the table and after filling her pot fixed her eyes stubbornly upon it. Her rocking gained an extra impetus but she didn't spill a drop.

Kitty looked at her Da and seeing there would be no further intervention on his part ducked under the lightly laden washing line and ran from the dimly lit room.

Fergus had looked at his wife who kept her eyes averted from him. He took up the quart of ale and emptied its remains, every last drop, into a jam jar on the table. He stood over his wife as he swallowed the contents in one go. He slammed the jar back on the rickety table causing it to tremble and, confident his point had been made, which was verified by Nell's lack of protest in the face of such blatant antagonism, left the room. Nell picked up the quart jug and threw it with force against the opposite wall where the heavy pottery smashed into pieces.

There was no way Fergus would ever sever ties with any of his, let alone his youngest daughter, of that he was sure. He hadn't fought all these years to keep his children alive just to forsake them when they made a decision that went against the grain. It was true he had had to fight far harder to protect his eldest children from the grasp of death. From the very outset it had been against all the odds that any of his eldest would live. And he had to concede that without the strength of his Nell there wouldn't be one of them left.

Vincent had been born to great joy just before the first blight. Fergus, who never drank, went into the village and celebrated in style in O' Shea's that night, ensuring that everybody in the tavern, fisherman and farmer alike, shared in his joy. He stood them all at least one jar of poteen each. It would prove to be the last true celebration the village experienced. Fergus could still put a name to the face of every man that congratulated him with a slap on the back, shake of the hand or a toast to his first-born son's health that night.

The first blighted crop had been a disaster. Black stalks replaced healthy green ones overnight. There was no warning, no opportunity to rescue any portion of the crop. Fergus had experienced bad crops before, as had everybody else, but this one was different. News of spoiled crops was coming from every corner of the country. It seemed the whole potato crop of Ireland had been reduced to a pile, no, a mountain, of dry black shoots whose foul smell pervaded the entire island.

Taverns, there were always enough potatoes or corn to make poteen, were full of talk about a bad fog that had blown in and settled over the fields at the worst possible time. The optimistic nature of the locals decreed that a toast be raised to the easterly wind that would ensure the fog didn't settle the following harvest.

"Have no fear boys and raise a glass to the easterly that'll blow that accursed fog straight across the sea to the Godless English's fields."

Fergus wasn't so sure. This was something he had never experienced. It was as though there was an invisible and island-wide pestilence. He worried it didn't bode well for the next year's crop or the one after.

His young wife had not only detected his fears but acted on them. She spent every spare moment collecting and preserving every scrap of food nature's larder had to offer. She would be seen up in the hills, on the coast and in the woods with Vincent strapped to her back and a sack in her arms. Every vessel she could put her hands on was sanitised, made airtight and utilised. Everything she Salted, pickled, dried or smoked Nell would somehow preserve and then bury in the cool dark mud, sowing the earth with a bounty that had no chance of growing but would provide sustenance when so many others were starving. Blackberries, turnips, mushrooms, herring, shellfish, even roots, nettles and seaweed all found their way on to the table while others were laid with nothing but broths made from roadside weeds and grass.

"Good God Nell! Is there no end to these jars?" he would say in mock exasperation each mealtime.

"You'll know about it when they're gone, Fergus Flynn," would be her stock reply.

The situation became worse as each succeeding crop failed. The village and surrounding farms, although spared from the viciousness of the food riots and influx of English soldiers that the bigger towns and cities were experiencing, was still subjected to the hated landlords and the barbed pangs of hunger that heralded slow starvation.

Fergus and Nell, together with their neighbours, witnessed ships loaded with Irish oats and grain sailing up the coast to feed the world while they watched and starved. Then Fergus and Nell watched as the village itself depopulated daily. In the majority of cases there were only two destinations on offer. One was to follow the oats and grain into the world, namely Liverpool; the other didn't bear thinking about. And so it was either on the coast or in the cemetery, on a steamer or in a coffin that Fergus had bade his family, friends and neighbours farewell. Both were heartbreaking. In days gone by he had known people who travelled for new starts in the relatively close city of Liverpool and, those that could afford it, further afield to exotic places like America and Canada. But such was the news coming back about the degradation and disease that festered in Liverpool that he was of the opinion it would be better to stay and be buried in his local and ancestral cemetery than a strange and English one. The cost of travelling to America was so prohibitive he had more chance of taking Nell and the nippers to the moon.

In the end it was the landlord, or rather his hired mob, who forced the issue.

The opportunity to transform the hovel and potato-pit-strewn land into lucrative fields full of cattle and sheep was not one to miss for the landlord. Tenant farmers up and down the country had found themselves evicted from their land to make way for livestock.

Nell had ensured that the landlord's agent never left the Flynn door without his monthly dues. Just as she produced meals from barren coastlines and the thin air of misty hills so she conjured up pennies from out of the blue that she saved behind a loose brick in the blackened fireplace in order to ensure the roof over their head was one that would remain. The landlord, frustrated by the lack of arrears which he could manipulate to his advantage had tried to pay the family's passage to Liverpool. When that didn't work his agent employed one of the many gangs who had been sent over to Ireland from England to evict and terrorise tenants. Bigger towns had began to form their own gangs to defend their own against this threat but such was the small scale of the village and its surrounding farms there wasn't the strength in numbers or bodies to fight, such was the shortage of food. It was his Nell, alone, just as she liked to remind him, who had confronted their particular persecutors. As he cradled the three-year-old Vincent and his baby brother Bog into the protection of his body she smashed her way out of the barricaded front door with their only knife in one hand and a poker in the other and scattered the group of English, who although not wanting to come within striking distance of the flame-haired banshee had retained their masculinity by laughing and calling obscenities. The following day they were on board a steamer looking at their Ireland grow further and further away as England loomed ever nearer.

Fergus looked down on the city and traced the line of the Mersey back to its mouth. He stared into Liverpool Bay and wondered where it was that the Irish Sea began. Unaware of his vacant expression, the passage of time or the people of Everton deviating from their routes in order to avoid the bedraggled stranger, he simply stared as the events of a different life tumbled through his mind. He unconsciously licked his lips in anticipation of the pints that would numb, if not flush away, his melancholic mood, to be bought with the money he would allow his youngest daughter to force on him.

"Da," Fergus straightened as his daughter ran the length of the fence and threw her arms around him. He was forced to strain against her weight or risk falling back against the railing, such was her force. He felt her body begin to rattle as sobs shook her slight frame. Bewildered, he stroked her hair and patted her back.

"Hey now, what's all this? My brave Kathleen all of a fluster?" Kitty remained nestled in the rough fabric of his overcoat. The coat was redolent of her early years and the sobs became audible.

"C'mon now, let's have a look at you, get your head out of this stinking coat," Kitty allowed him to gently grasp her cheeks with his rough hands and look into her eyes.

"Oh Da, I'm so scared, I don't know what we're to do." She gained a modicum of control and disengaged herself from her Da, instead taking him by the hand.

"Are you ok to walk a bit, Da?" Kitty led Fergus out into the rolling pastures where the population dwindled and they could talk alone and undisturbed.

"Albert's father has died, Da." Fergus was surprised that Kitty was showing so much grief for an in-law who, to his knowledge, she had never met. Fergus removed his greasy cap and Kitty ruffled the flat hair that was pasted to his scalp. Now that it had been disturbed the gentle breeze played among his jet-black locks, which were incongruous sitting atop his worn, narrow face.

"Well God rest the man, I'm sorry for your husband's loss." He sat down in the field, his knees cracking loudly and looked up into the unbroken sky for a second marvelling at its blueness.

"I'm a little surprised that you're so upset, Kathleen?" Kitty had sat down next to her Da and, knees tucked under her chin replied,

"I am grieving for Albert's loss, Da, but it's not him losing his father that has me in such a state."

"I don't understand, Kathleen, what're yer telling me?" Kitty rested her forehead on her knees, obscuring her face.

"He was our only source of income, Da. Albert received a monthly stipend from him. It's what's kept us for all these years."

"But I thought he was a writer?" Fergus replaced his cap on his head.

"You should leave that cap off for a bit, Da, let some fresh air at your head. He is a writer but for all the money it brings in it might as well be voluntary, you'd make as much for a day down the docks. We've no income Da, all we've got is what I've put away." Fergus was still struggling to grasp the situation fully. He knew his daughter's husband came from a wealthy family over the water. He looked across the Mersey and over to the rolling hills of the Wirral.

"Am I remembering right, he's the only son?" he asked. Kitty nodded her confirmation.

"Ach Kathleen, you're worrying over nothing, he was a rich man, there'll be a will. You'll be better off than you are now." Fergus was troubled that this reduced Kitty to tears again.

"No Da, the will has been read. His mother was the only beneficiary. Albert suspects trickery but we're powerless to contest it, we could never afford a solicitor." Kitty sniffed and wiped at her eyes with her cuffs. Fergus blinked as his daughter regressed into the little girl from Vauxhall Road; he half expected her to drag her sleeve across her nose. Kitty felt the need to explain further.

"She's like mam, Da. Stubborn to the core, only she's worse, she's rich and powerful. He didn't even get to pay his respects. She's never forgiven him for marrying a Catholic, and a slummy to boot. He's in the same situation I am, Da, ostracised by his family and now his father has gone all ties are severed." Fergus had difficulty deciphering the torrent of information but was able to grasp the situation. He glanced furtively around, ensuring there was nobody in earshot. Even though the fields were empty, Fergus spoke in a whisper.

"They're a queer lot Kathleen, you've always known that." Kitty stood up in exasperation and paced around her Da.

"Oh Da, you sound like mam. Albert couldn't care less about any of that nonsense, it's what he writes about, satire he calls it. Isn't it him who's forfeited a life of luxury to be with a cellar-dweller like me? It's not us I'm worried about Da, it's Jobe, this is the only life he knows." Fergus held out his hand so his daughter could help him to his feet.

"He's a lucky man to have you Kathleen, and don't you go letting him think otherwise." Fergus brushed the grass from the frayed backside of his trousers.

"And if all he does with his writing is poke fun at the sectarianism in this town then it's small wonder he makes nothing from it! He must be the only person I've heard tell of that reckons it a joke." Fergus took his daughter in his arms and kissed her head.

"Now c'mon, will yer walk an old fella a little way down the hill. Give him safe passage past all these bloodletting O's." Kitty smiled for the first time that day and as she always did wordlessly opened her Da's hand in order to slide a few coppers in. Fergus kept his fist tightly shut and closed his other hand over hers.

"You'll be all right girl, you've more of your mam in you than you'll ever know."

Albert stared at the pile of notes and coins that Kitty deposited on the table. He began to drag his hand through it. Kitty slapped at his arm.

"Be careful now Albert, you'll scratch the surface," she scolded. Albert straightened up, taking his hand from among the money, and looked at her. Kitty immediately licked her thumb and wiped at a small scuff mark.

"But how? I don't understand!" He brought his hand to his face and played it along the length of his moustache. Kitty detected his discomfort and attempted to downplay her achievement.

"Ah c'mon Albert, you've been giving me a small fortune for an age now. What d'you think I do with it all? The house is furnished. You know I refuse to waste money on hiring help. Apart from food and fuel the only real outlay is the rent and Jobe, his school fees, clothing and such, oh and the toys you insist on spoiling him with of course. When you've had nothing all of your life it's only common sense to put a bit away for a rainy day." Albert looked at her.

"You truly are a wonder to behold, Kathleen Warburton." Albert looked at the money again, remaining utterly confounded. Kitty broke his reverie.

"C'mon, let's count it together and then we'll decide how it's best spent." Kitty fell to her knees before the low table. Albert took her hand and pulled her up and into him. He nuzzled her head as he spoke.

"I promise you now, Kitty, I will begin writing in earnest, no more of these pieces for pamphlets or newspapers, or my own vanity come to that. I will earn the money to keep us in the life we're accustomed to." Kitty looked up at her husband and kissed him on the lips.

"There's not a bone in all of my body that doubts you will, my love."

Chapter II

1888

Jobe wished more than ever that he'd found toys alongside the fruit and nuts in his stocking this year. It would be no hardship to sacrifice those toys, he told himself. The task he faced now was an impossible one. How could he possibly choose? He started the process again, knowing it was futile but feeling he had to be doing something to gratify his parents, especially his father. He picked up an engine, scrutinising it for any flaws, before putting it down and rolling it forwards and backwards. Content that its wheels ran smoothly he stroked the engine reverentially before placing it on the floor and repeating the process with another of his treasures.

Kitty looked from her son to her husband who had begun to drum his fingers on his knee, a new habit he had developed whenever he was growing agitated. She was about to kneel down and help Jobe point out some of his particular favourites before Albert urged him less diplomatically, when Jobe picked up his spinning top. An inertia-inducing memory of Albert triumphantly holding Jobe in the air like a trophy flashed into her mind. She silently stifled a sob. Albert looked at her, sensing her reluctance to interfere with the endless process.

"Come now Jobe, enough of this procrastination." The severity in his tone was unintentional but Jobe immediately aborted his mock inspection of the spinning top and sat frozen. Albert berated himself. He was aware that the boy wasn't at fault but lately he found it increasingly difficult to keep his patience in check. He knew Jobe was constantly at pains to behave in a way, he, his usually tolerant father, would appreciate but his constant cautiousness and tiptoeing around only seemed to infuriate him further which fed his guilt serving to make him even more abrasive.

Jobe placed the top on the floor. He would usually make every effort to satisfy his father, quell his new-found temper and subsequent raised voice but on this occasion found he could summon no pretence. It rarely worked anyway. He looked at his father.

"I can't choose father, I'm sorry."

Albert stood up from the rickety chair and looked down at Jobe. His interruption had only served to prolong the torture. His voice was steel.

"Look over there Jobe, that's right on the far wall. Can you tell me what is missing?" Jobe looked at the bare space and, happy to oblige his father, answered at once.

"The piano, father," he smiled nervously.

"And here where I'm standing, what's missing?" Jobe was again eager to please and his nerves fell away.

"Your armchair, father." Albert pirouetted around the room, almost dancing; as he conducted Jobe's gaze his movements serving to stimulate his son further.

"On the mantelpiece there?"

'Mother's candlesticks and vases!" he chirped.

"And here under our feet?"

"The rug, father!" Jobe was practically singing out the answers now, unaware of the path his father was leading him down. Kitty watched as Albert became almost manic, until she could tolerate no more.

"Stop, Albert! In Heaven's name, stop!" She sank to her knees on the varnished but bare floorboards. Jobe looked at her and the implication of his father's questioning dawned on him. He looked around the empty room, seeing its bareness for the first time. Without speaking he knelt and carefully placed each one of his toys into the large box he used to store them. When it was full he stood.

"I think I'm a little old for toys now, father."

Albert had walked well out of his way, travelling along Byrom Street and the length of Scotland Road, winding his way up the hill rather than taking the direct route up it. The expectant look on his wife's face plagued his every step. He felt he could no longer meet the eyes that had once captivated him such was his inability to procure a means of living from his writing. Reaching the junction of Kirkdale Road he stopped and watched as a bedraggled but sizeable crowd headed along Netherfield Road in the same direction. He walked along, remaining independent of the crowd.

On reaching Shaw Street and passing the pleasure gardens he glanced over at the house that lay positioned behind them on Westbourne Street. From here it looked the height of respectability. Manicured shrubs, spotlessly clean, heavy drapes hanging at every window. He had ignored Kitty's pleas to pawn the drapes rather than Jobe's toys.

"If we allow our façade to falter...the drapes are a defence, if that defence is lost, so too are we." His wife had followed his word but not his reasoning. He turned his attention back to the crowd but couldn't help imagining the scene playing out behind the drapes. Kitty and Jobe in the kitchen, busily concocting whatever travesty she had managed to conjure up for dinner while chattering incessantly between themselves, unaffected by the disconsolately bare floors and walls around them. Sensing an opportunity to postpone returning home to the desperation, despondency and depression that engulfed him as soon as he opened the door, he joined the crowd.

As he approached Soho Street the crowd ahead began to boo and hiss. Albert looked down Soho Street as another mob, seemingly intent on entering

Shaw Street, passed the Chapel of St Francis Xavier, the object of the jeering. Before he had passed the junction he watched as more than one missile was launched at the church.

As they passed into the shadow of the Collegiate Institution, Albert looked up at the imposing building. His stomach sank; he had harboured dreams of Jobe attending and honing his obvious intelligence at the Institute. He refused to dwell on such matters and returned his attention to the crowd. Realising that he had no idea of their intent or destination, he turned to the man next to him.

"I say, what's the carry-on?" The man responded by looking him up and down before looking away. Albert wasn't sure whether it was through ignorance or arrogance and was about to find out when a thin man wearing a butcher's apron decorated with flecks of offal and blood that didn't seem to be completely dry took it upon himself to enlighten him.

"It's that new pastor, he's holding an open air rally in the square. I've left work early to see him tell it like it truly is, not like them Irish lovers." Albert was now being carried along by the sheer weight of numbers and had no opportunity to turn back even if he had wished to.

The crush became intense at the entrance to Islington Square as other crowds of an equal magnitude to the one he travelled with converged from Brunswick Road and Erskine Street to the east, Moss Street to the south, and west from Carver Street and Islington itself. There was electricity in the air and Albert was glad that he had made the decision to join the crowd. He used his sheer brute strength to shoulder his way into the square where the multitude fanned out and there was at least room to catch a breath and look about freely. The crowd continued to surge like a confused tide and Albert, having no agenda, allowed himself to be pushed, first one way and then the other.

Spontaneous cheers erupted and the crowd descended into a fervour of jostling before a relative calmness naturally established itself. An unassuming man in his early thirties had taken to the steps of a building on the corner of the Square and Shaw Street, not far from Albert's vantage point. He stepped up onto a small platform that had been erected between the white Grecian pillars. A thick moustache covered his face. It met and combined with his heavy sideburns, hiding his jowls but leaving his chin exposed and bare. The round metal eyeglasses he wore seemed too small for his face and he looked over them as he addressed the eager crowd.

"Brethren, welcome, I thank and applaud you for your attendance here this evening." The crowd cheered and clapped and after a few seconds the man held up his arms, signalling for quiet.

"We gather together to illustrate how fervently opposed we are to the ritualistic Romanism that is encroaching on our worship! Many of you are experiencing the idolatry to such an extent that I'm amazed you don't wonder yourselves Papists every time you attend church! Is it not enough that we already have to swallow the Fenianism that we are force-fed each and every day by those who think they have a right to dictate to us...but were no more than human ballast when they reached this great port!" More cheers greeted this and the speaker continued in his alluring sing-song baritone.

"Do not wait for the Established Church or the politicians to protect you or impress your rights... for they will not. If we do not act...if you do not act, then our very church, our very society, our very moral code will be a thing of memory..." Albert lost track of the speech as he felt a hand on his shoulder. He turned around to see a smiling Potter.

"Albert, how are you?" he smiled, taking off a leather glove and holding out his shovel of a hand.

"Potter...Potter, I'm fine thank you, how are you?" replied Albert only too aware of the cold, raw hand he proffered.

"What the devil are you doing here?" A man in front of the pair turned round, his intention to tell the chattering toffs behind to shut up but on seeing their size turned around again and returned all of his concentration to the speaker.

"I'm with him," replied Potter, pointing over to the speaker. "Listen, I can't speak now, but make your way over to the steps when the crowd clears, we'll have a drink and I'll explain." Potter clapped Albert on the shoulder as he made his way to the front of the crowd and discreetly took a place a few feet to the side of the speaker, surveying the crowd in front of him as he did so.

Albert failed to notice the two men who came and removed the temporary platform or the traffic that had began to traverse the now empty square as he leaned against one of the Grecian pillars, ruminating on the points the speaker, Pastor George Wise he had come to learn, had raised. The problems the town faced had consumed Albert's intellect for a long time. The majority of his writing was aimed at ridiculing those who insisted that religion or immigrants, particularly the Irish influx, were the root cause of every problem the city, and the country itself, endured. He satirised the ignorance of the fundamentalists who believed the great unwashed were in any way perplexed by the manner in which a church service was conducted or a mass said, he chided their choosing to disregard the myriad of socio-economic problems that kept their congregations in the poverty which was, as far as he was concerned, the origin of society's ills.

Although it caused him a distinct discomfort to admit it there was a logic behind some of Pastor Wise's arguments that he could not contradict. There was no denying that he was a fundamentalist, and a fanatical one at that, but Albert had to admit to the fact that, not only was he incapable of opposing Wise's arguments, he actually agreed with the majority of them. He tended to view himself as a progressive, an enlightened soul regarding such issues, and the conflict raging within him led him to question the legitimacy of his writing. Had his personal circumstances created a bias that must pervade his work as conspicuously as a lightning bolt? The realisation evoked an unprecedented sensation of shame that emanated from deep in his gut and quickly traversed his body. He was conscious that his burning face must be a deep crimson, which only served to enhance his discomfort. The door of the building opened and Potter emerged.

"Ah Albert, you're here, good man." He surveyed the square and seeing there was nobody in the immediate vicinity beckoned out the speaker who emerged, flanked by two heavyset men. Compared to Potter and Wise who were immaculately turned out the two fellows looked incongruous in their rough and dirty clothing. They followed Potter to the bottom of the steps. Potter commenced with the introductions.

"Pastor, Albert Warburton, Albert, Pastor George Wise." The two men shook hands and Albert was aware that the pastor was conducting a surreptitious scrutiny of him. Already ill at ease he broke the handshake a little too hastily.

"An eloquent sermon, Pastor," he complimented, attempting to cover his faux pas.

"Thank you, Mr Warburton. A pleasure to make your acquaintance," replied the pastor. Albert was again alert to the fact that he was somehow being measured and his tongue evaded him.

Potter interceded.

"Until next week, Pastor, good evening." He shook hands with the pastor and then addressed the men who had remained behind the trio.

"See Pastor Wise safely home and then get yourselves off. I'll be in touch." With that he turned to Albert,

"Shall we?"

Potter led Albert down Islington as far as Commutation Row, past the Wellington Monument and on to the thoroughfare of Lime Street which was, as usual, well lit and alive. Every demographic the town had to offer was represented on the busy artery. Well-heeled gentlemen, their top hats bristling, linked arms with their immaculate ladies as they headed to an evening of dancing in St George's Hall or a show at the Royal Court or Empire Theatre. Bare-foot children, faces and hands as black as their feet, flitted between them in the hope of a few pennies, the lucky ones depositing their gains with mothers who waited, gathered around the Stebble Fountain in anticipation of the paltry windfall. A commotion broke out around the fountain as a belligerent husband arrived, demanding the pennies his wife and child had begged.

Men, those who had finished their day's work, traversed the street on their way home or to the next pub. Those who had failed to find work or the loafers that had no compulsion in doing so, idled on the corners. A good number of them emitted a casual air of threat. Clerks and other office types poured in and out of Lime Street station oblivious to the danger of the horse-drawn trams and carts that they cut between. Those who had just decanted from Lime Street for the first time stood, slack-jawed as they surveyed the scene before them. Hawkers, one eye on potential customers and the other looking out for coppers, stood with baskets full of goods or pushed barrows brimming with wares, animal, vegetable and mineral from every corner of the globe that had never been intended for sale in Liverpool, but were smuggled from the docks for that very purpose. Albert and Potter bypassed the raucousness until they reached and entered the relative tranquillity of The Vines public house.

Albert looked around and was impressed by the surroundings as well as the clientele. The long gilded bar was matched in length by huge ornamental mirrors that reflected the busy barmen and their prosperous patrons.

"Well, it's better than the pigpens you used to frequent," Albert said. Potter laughed and slapped him on the back. He pointed to a table. "Take a seat, I'll get the drinks." Albert sat at the round, marble topped table and watched Potter as he cut his way through the cigar smoke and revellers to the bar. The short walk to the Vines had been a relatively quiet one, littered with patchy small talk. Potter had sensed Albert's humour and was happy enough allowing him to mull, while Albert felt comfortable enough in Potter's company not to feel obliged to blather. He had continued to reflect on his earlier contradictions.

Potter returned with their drinks. He dragged over a stool, sat down and after taking a drink addressed Albert.

"I could see your mind was weighing heavy on the way here Albert, but you must have some questions for me." Albert took a hesitant sip of his drink, his face contorting.

"I see you've not lost your fondness for a drink," Potter laughed. Albert smiled. He was eager to put to one side his conflicting emotions and he did indeed have questions that needed answers.

"Where to begin? How are things on the sunny Wirral, and how is Mrs Potter?"

"Mrs Potter has the constitution of an ox and as long as she is in the service of your mother, is happy, thank you, Albert."

"And my mother, Potter, is she well?" he asked.

"She is well, Albert, she mourned your father for a long time, and even now she remains in black, but she prospers. In fact she is quite the philanthropist, very respected, and sits on a number of boards and committees." Potter reached for his drink as Albert digested the information.

"She's never instructed you to reach out to me?"

"I'm afraid not, Albert, forgive me, but you're well aware of her obstinacy." This time it was Albert who reached for his drink, taking a large gulp without sign of an adverse reaction.

"She knows you're in Liverpool?" he asked, as the burning liquid settled in his chest.

"I'm here at her request, she's quite taken with Pastor Wise and has become a staunch supporter. He delivered a sermon in Birkenhead last month, she met him afterwards and on hearing about some of the skirmishes his addresses have caused, on both sides of the water, grew concerned for his safety. She put me at his disposal. I spend a lot of my time in the town now, organising his security." Albert raised his eyebrows at the news, although it didn't at all surprise him that his mother was an admirer of the pastor and his incendiary views. The pastor's surveying of him entered his mind.

"Wise was aware of who I was." He said it more as a statement than as a question.

"I informed him of your parentage, yes. I apologise if you take offence," Potter spun his glass on the table in half revolutions. Albert looked at him; there was something different about him. He was more at ease, happier. Potter looked up.

"What did you make of the pastor, Albert?" Albert's response was delayed as a young girl approached the pair selling cockles and mussels from a basket she carried around her neck. Potter gestured towards the girl,

"Albert?" Albert used the interlude to take a drink.

"No, thank you, Potter," The girl looked dismayed that she had lost a potential sale. Potter looked at her.

"Ah come on, Albert, you were always fond of you're sea food, and your looking a little gaunt." He leaned to one side enabling him to fit a hand into his pocket while remaining seated.

"Two trays of mussels if you will, miss, both with a generous helping of vinegar," Potter took out a handful of coins and finding the one he wanted gave it to the girl as she lay the second tray in front of Albert. The girl took the coin and began counting out change. Potter dismissed her, a mussel already halfway to his mouth.

"No, no, for you, away you go now." The girl gave a little curtsey and continued on her round.

"So Albert, Pastor George Wise?"

"Watch out for him lads, the big bastard there."

"God almighty but he's big." Driscoll looked and saw that Malachi wasn't looking in the direction that he was discreetly pointing.

"No, not him, although look out for him as well, he's auld but all the same…No look the other big bastard there, he's the real enforcer, a dirty, mean bastard he is." Malachi followed the discreet nod and gave an audible gasp.

"That's the fella who turned Bernie Hopwood into a vegetable down Sebastopol, one punch is all it took him. He took Hopwood's lead pipe to the head and didn't blink! I was there, I saw it with me own eyes." Driscoll and the rest of the gang looked at Malachi and he nodded confirmation as he wrung his hands, still looking across the crowd at the big man who suddenly looked in their direction as if aware he was the object of their attention. Malachi quickly averted his eyes.

"Oh Jesus," he whimpered as he looked at the floor. Driscoll tutted at him. "Have a look at yourself Mal' will yer! Once the div'l begins with his sermon all hell will be let loose, just make sure you stay out of the big bastard's way, sure he's big enough not to miss."

Malachi wasn't convinced. He could have kicked himself for allowing Driscoll to twist his arm to join the gang who were going up to Everton to stop the O's and their new champion from desecrating St Francis Xavier's. He couldn't give a toss for St Francis's or any other church for that matter; he knew for a fact that the majority of the lads had pissed up against the wall of St Mary's more times than they had been to mass in it. He suspected it would be the same for the fellas from all the other parishes who would be making the crusade up to Everton. He had told Driscoll as much.

"Ach, I can't be arsed traipsing up that hill for no good reason, Driscoll, let the O's do what they want, sure it's their parish, worse goes on in ours."

"Sure c'mon Mal, it'll be a hoot and you'll never get a better chance to crack a few O's. We're all going up and when we get back we'll have a few jars to celebrate. I'll stand you a few if you haven't got the coppers." That had been the clincher for Malachi although Driscoll continued, "We'll be a regular army by the time we arrive, why they'll be walking down Scotland Road in droves as we speak, the meeting point'll be Scotland Place. What'll it look like if the parish of St Mary's, The Mother Church, the oldest Catholic church in the city, isn't represented? We'll collect the Holy Cross boys as we go through, not that they'll be much use! It's a parade, a regular carnival, and you should see the O's tremor as we go marching through their territory unopposed." Malachi licked his lips.

"I'll work up a raging thirst banging those Orange heads in. Are you sure you can stand me a few jars with which to slake it?" Driscoll smiled as he replied,

"We'll return conquering heroes. I'll be surprised if we don't drink the house dry!"

Malachi looked over at the big man again, his memory reverting back to the day outside the Nonpareil. He winced as the sound of Bernie Hopwood's jaw snapping in two reverberated around his head. He looked for an escape route, wondering who was friend and who was foe, there was no way of telling. Apart from the few well-dressed heavies creating a cordon in front of the chapel everybody looked as ill clad, ill shod and ill fed as the boys from St Mary's. The last thing he wanted was to wander into one of the many gangs of O's in the crowd. He continued to wring his hands as he turned full circle. A booming voice caused him to jump.

"Do priests drink Holy Water?" George Wise took to the soapbox placed outside the Chapel of St Francis Xavier, he ignored the cheers of the crowd as, fist clenched above his head, he repeated in his baritone.

"Do priests drink Holy Water?"

"No they drink whisky!" The well rehearsed reply, or lack of one, easily distinguished Catholic from Protestant. With one short sentence the simmering suspicion that pervaded the street was transformed into knowledge, and battle-lines were drawn as pockets of rival sects re-established their positions, ensuring that they were not left on the wrong side of the divide. Minor scuffles broke out and kicks and punches were thrown but the unannounced truce held and all eyes returned to the pastor who continued, after his deliberate and illuminating pause.

"Brethren, I see we again have guests among us. One wonders how the Right Honourable MP for Scotland Ward continues to afford to reward them all with a pot of ale on their return to the slums." This was greeted by exaggerated laughter from his supporters and a seething silence from his opponents.

"Well, maybe for once they can act in a civilised, decent manner and be rewarded with some schooling? What do you say boyos?" Pastor Wise turned his gaze to his supporters.

"Oh they look worried! Well, they don't need to fret so, there won't be a test!" Again his supporters replied with derisive, delirious laughter. A stone thumped against the wall, far enough away from George Wise to suspect one of his own followers had thrown it.

"Ah, they have reverted to stoning their own places of worship now I see, is nothing sacred to them? Maybe if I don the idolatry of their priests I can get away with any amount of sinning, just as they do!" With these words Pastor Wise took a set of rosary beads from his coat and put them around his neck. From his other pocket he pulled out a crucifix and held it aloft.

"Here now, do these idolatries allow me to say my piece, to fornicate with members of my congregation, to gamble in the courts, to drink and drink and drink?"

A single stone hit one of those in the protective cordon in front of Pastor Wise. It was the catalyst to mayhem. It was thrown from a group just to the left of the St Mary's gang; Malachi reckoned he recognised them from St Augustine's. A roar full of indecipherable insults and hatred followed an audible intake of collective breath. George Wise took his cue and, flanked by half a dozen thickset men, made his escape up Soho Street to the safety that the Presbyterian Chapel on Shaw Street would offer him. The air filled with flying debris as both sides threw whatever missiles they had collected en route. Pieces of slate, stone and rock rained down on unprotected heads and bodies. Bottles smashed, shards of glass splintering into legs and torsos. The injured staggered or were dragged to the rear of their respective mob.

The St Mary's contingent had escaped the airborne peril unscathed. Malachi had taken no part throughout, either offensively or defensively. Instead he had watched as, Albert, his nemesis had escorted the pastor up the hill toward Shaw Street and out of sight. He was still on his tiptoes looking up Langsdale Street when the crowd around him reacted to a surprising and unplanned enemy charge. An all-out charge was a rarity in these exchanges with those on both sides preferring to throw insults and missiles from afar and therefore enjoy a relatively safe, inexpensive evening of entertainment. Occasionally, if the odds were favourable, the opportunity arose to give a rival group a good kicking.

This particular charge was a consequence of the pastor's supporters, who having gathered toward the top of the hill enjoyed the advantage of the incline. To maintain balance as they bent to gather the slates, rocks and stones that had been launched at them they lay hands on the comrades directly in front of them, forcing them forward, causing a ripple effect that gave those in the vanguard no option but to stagger forward in a disharmonious straggle. Their opposition, sensing the impending attack, reacted by rushing headlong at their aggressors. Malachi almost lost his balance and risked being trampled in the ensuing stampede when Driscoll grabbed hold of him.

"C'mon Mal, snap out of it! Get stuck in, yer bastard, or there'll be no ale for you."

The two groups came together in a flurry of kicks and punches, those who carried weapons wielding them indiscriminately, as likely to bring their planks, sticks and pokers crashing down on the head of a friend as that of a foe. The attending police officers watched in mild astonishment as the situation suddenly intensified. Heavily outnumbered, they remained neutral, batons drawn, ready for anybody who strayed into their vicinity.

Malachi's reluctance and Driscoll's intervention cost the pair and they found themselves cut off from their group. The impetus of the initial charge had not abated and they could only flail at their opponents who flashed by, aiming their own strikes and blows which the pair were forced to dodge or parry. It was only when congestion ceased the charge that the fighting began in earnest with both mobs face to face with their antagonists. Malachi and Driscoll had been forced far through their enemies' front lines and such was the press that it was difficult to exact any telling blow and a meleé ensued. It suited Malachi and he whooped for delight as he found himself among those who habitually avoided any meaningful violence and injury by remaining at the rear of the crowd. They had inadvertently caused the impromptu charge and now floundered as they found themselves reaping the consequences in the midst of the retaliatory attack. Elbows, knees and short uppercuts cleared them from Malachi's path, while Driscoll remained in the safety of his friend's wake, gouging at eyes and fish-hooking those that his comrade had winded, wounded or debilitated in any way that left them defenceless to his malice.

The remaining lines turned and fled in any direction that offered sanctuary, and Malachi found himself towards the crest of the incline at the top end of Langsdale Street. He drew breath and looked down from his elevated position at the meleé, which was on the verge of petering out. The majority of those taking part had either fled or lay prone. Only a hard core remained and the fighting among them was intense.

"Jesus, but we gave them a pasting Mal," said Driscoll as he put a hand on his friend's heaving shoulder.

"We need to be getting back among our own though, it does us no good to be this far up the hill. C'mon, let's give them lot a wide berth and get home, the coppers'll be here in force soon enough," he continued. Malachi wasn't listening. His face, which had been flushed from his exertions, had drained of all colour. He had seen the giant in the middle of the fighting, swatting men aside as he prodigiously rained blows with his right hand and swung a gold-topped walking cane in the other. Without a word Malachi spun around and tore up what remained of the hill towards Shaw Street. Driscoll blanched, torn between being left alone or running further into Orange territory.

"Mal, come back! What about yer pints?" he screamed.

Albert drained his glass in one and slammed it back on to the bar.

"Another toast! Landlord, another round here," he shouted.

"Albert, we've toasted everything from potatoes to your walking cane, what can possibly be left?" asked Potter, exhaling a lungful of cigar smoke.

Albert picked up one of the glasses the landlord had just deposited on the bar and held it in the air.

"To Potter!" he exclaimed before draining it in one go. Clad in the attire of gentlemen, overcoats and bowler hats obtained from pawnshops with money given to them by their benefactor so that tattered clothing and matted hair could be hidden, the entourage cheered. The majority of them owed their turn in fortune to Potter.

"To Potter!" they toasted with genuine exuberance. Albert draped an arm over Potter's broad shoulder.

"There, hear how your army adores you," he slurred. Potter ignored the compliment and unwrapped Albert's arm from around him.

"It's you that's their hero! Although you're going to end up getting yourself on a murder charge the way you've been tearing into the Papists these past months," Potter semi-scolded. Albert laughed.

"Come now, Potter, do I detect a hint of jealousy? God knows you've no need to worry, there are enough of them to go round. Isn't that the real point of Pastor Wise's wrath?" Potter shook his head.

"It's no laughing matter, Albert. Granted the odd one needs a good seeing to, but a short, sharp smack is sufficient for the majority of them, they're either so malnourished, drunk or both. The way you go laying into them with that cane of yours, why it's only a matter of time before one of them ends up dead."

"Well, that'll please the pastor at least, one less Fenian to corrupt and threaten the good and pious of the town," laughed Albert as he raised his hand to attract the attention of the landlord.

"It'll be no joke when you're on the gallows, Albert," sighed Potter, knowing his advice was falling on deaf ears. Albert forced another drink on Potter.

"Come now, Potter, less of the old woman act. Another toast!" He roared.

★ ★ ★ ★ ★

Jobe tried in vain to find a position that didn't expose a jutting bone to the surface of the unforgiving pallet. His mother had covered it with old blankets and newspaper in an attempt to provide a modicum of comfort but Jobe imagined that even a half dozen of his old horse-hair mattresses wouldn't make any difference to the hard and unyielding pallets he now called bed. He lay awake, trying to make sense of the troubling events that had taken place around him. His main cause for concern wasn't the removal of his iron bedstead and mattress, which his father had manhandled down the stairs alone a few weeks after he had taken the box of toys, but the change in his parents' behaviour, especially that of his father who had now become a stranger to him. In his mind's eye he replayed his last excursion on his father's shoulders, enjoying the rocking motion his giant but seamless strides created. The incessant commentary his father provided regarding everything they witnessed or experienced on their travels.

"You see there, Jobe, the mighty Albert Dock. It shares its birthday with me, it's forty-two years old today but on the day I was born it was only ten and the greatest dock in the world. Prince Albert himself came to open it."

"That's who you're named after," cheered Jobe.

"You're right, well, I like to think I'm named after both."

That summer's day, his father's birthday, was the last time he could recall seeing him happy. The summer sun that had shone on the hills had been replaced by grey skies and icy winds. For a long time he had fretted that he was responsible for the change in his father but he observed that his mother had also fallen from favour. He took solace from the fact that he wasn't responsible for the decline in his father's temperament but that relief was diluted by sympathy for his distressed mother, who had endured the mutating humours stoically. The angry exchanges that now took place unsettled Jobe and although he wasn't frightened by the cross words and raised voices they weighed heavily upon him.

"Who is Pastor Wise, mother?" he had asked one day. His mother stood over the scullery sink scrubbing at one of his father's collars. She turned and looked at Jobe for a moment before answering, a malice to her voice that he hadn't heard before.

"Ooh he's St George to your father, Jobe, but really he's a demon, a horrible, nasty, devil of a creature intent on bringing misery to this town. D'you want to know what the good and God-fearing people chant to him as he's walking the street?" Jobe wasn't sure he wanted to know, his mother had never addressed him in such a manner and it was unnerving him.

His mother, abandoning his father's collar and letting it fall to the floor, had stooped and approached Jobe as she spat out a verse he hadn't heard before, "Minister, Minister, quack, quack, quack. O go to the div'l and don't come back."

Jobe had turned and fled from his mother's unrecognisable features as she repeated the verse, the words of the rhyme branding themselves into his brain.

A few days later, it not having been too cold, his mother had allowed him to sit outside and draw with a rogue piece of chalk he had found jammed between the skirting and floorboard in his bedroom. It was a picture of his mother and father hand in hand while he sat above them on his father's shoulders. His father had come up the street and stopped in the gateway observing him. Jobe, under the impression his father had stopped to admire his work, continued with his sketch, carefully adding three huge smiles to each of the off-scale faces while continuing to sing the rhyme he had heard from his mother. Jobe moved his hand quickly as his father's boot came crashing down and landed squarely on his mother's face, scuffing the chalk and ruining her smile. He was knocked off balance as his father brushed past him and into the house.

"Kathleen! Kathleen!" Jobe knew there was to be contention on hearing his mother's full name bawled around the house. He cringed in the doorway as his mother entered the room from the other side, wiping her hands on her pinafore.

"What is it, Albert?" she had asked as sanguinely as possible.

"What is the meaning of teaching my son those filthy Fenian lyrics?" Jobe wondered at the word Fenian but knew it couldn't be proper from the way the blood drained from his mother's face.

"Are you forgetting, Albert, that your son is one of those filthy Fenians?" she spat.

"I allowed you to christen my son a Catholic to assuage your irrationality, but we agreed that this was never to be a religious house." His father towered over his mother as he stood twisting his moustache.

"It is only you who has raised the issue of religion in this house, Albert. Do I not attend mass without making any fuss about it? Have I ever once attempted to force my beliefs on you, well, have I?"

"Yet I come home to find my son singing insults about Pastor Wise."

"Oh, Pastor Wise again is it? That great ambassador for religious tolerance! Wasn't it him who stirred up the trouble last week that ended up with Father Riley being hurt?"

"Hurt? Hurt? A mere trifle, why Pastor Wise was almost lynched by a rabble at the weekend,"

"Well, I'm sorry to hear it was only almost, he could do with been strung up, isn't it him reigniting all the old tensions?"

"Old! Old! Are you so naive? There is a fight for survival taking place this very moment, right now. It's impossible for a good man to find a job, walk the streets in safety or even go to church in peace thanks to the feckless imbeciles that continue to pile into this town by the day." Jobe returned to the front step, closing the front door behind him. He began to drag his foot across his drawing distorting the chalk lines until they were unrecognisable. All the time he was doing his best to ignore the raised voices coming from inside.

The reverberation of the front door slamming dragged Jobe from his daydream and back to the discomfort of his pallet. He turned on his back and looked at the ceiling. There was enough moonlight filtering through the uncovered windows to watch his breath as it evaporated into the cold still air. After a pause he heard the muffled voice of his mother.

Kitty blew out the solitary candle and sat alone in the enveloping darkness. The remnant of wax that remained would be saved to wake Jobe and see him off to school in the morning. She heard the front door closing and Albert entered the parlour. Kitty wrinkled her nose as the potent alcohol fumes pervaded the room superseding the remnants of candle smoke. The glare from the glow of the candle flame had long since diminished from behind her eyes but the darkness was so complete that she could only sense Albert floundering about in it.

"The candle's here. I'm sorry but there's only enough left to see Jobe off in the morning." Kitty took the box of matches from her lap and silently placed them under the wooden chair she sat on. Albert had assumed his wife would be upstairs asleep and that he was therefore alone. He felt exposed regardless of the total darkness. He was about to feel his way over to Kitty but dismissed the notion.

"Well, I hope it'll be enough to see us all off. I'm afraid we're due to be evicted next week and I for one will not be around to experience that particular pleasure." On standing Kitty experienced a sickening sensation that felt as if her insides remained where she had been sitting.

"But Albert, we've sold all we had in order to live… the money that I had saved, we agreed it would be used to pay the rent, there was enough. Surely we have a few months yet?" The couple looked towards each other but remained veiled from sight by the consuming darkness.

"Yes, well…I'm afraid that specific venture never came through, dearest." Albert rocked on his heels in order to keep his balance. Kitty scrabbled under the chair and grabbed at the box of matches. She stood and struck a match at the same time holding it out so she could see her husband's face. The phosphorous flash illuminated the short space between them and Kitty closed her eyes against the flare.

Albert gazed at the vision before him, the glow of the match lending his wife's beauty an ethereal quality that caused his breath to catch in his throat and almost choke him. His resolve wavered and he wanted nothing more than to reach out and caress her cheek, to reassure her that he would always be at her side and there was no existing entity that could separate them. The match spluttered out and Albert heard Kitty scraping another. Her eyes opened and his breathing was checked for a second time, so sharply that it caused him to take an involuntary step backwards. Her eyes emanated a hatred that he didn't believe she could possess. Framed within the beauty of her face it seemed to him she resembled a harpy from the childhood tales that Mrs Potter would regale and terrify him with. A surge of irrational fear tingled up his spine causing him to shiver.

"What's that Albert, someone trampled over your grave? Well I'll make you a vow right now Albert, if my Jobe...our Jobe! If he suffers from the ills of this world because of you I will put you in your grave myself and God forgive me I will dance, I will dance upon it, Albert Warburton!"

Chapter III

1889

The gentleman had been surreptitiously observing her for at least five minutes. He was stick-thin, dressed in black velvet, and Kitty could sense his vexation as he paced the road opposite. First up and then down, muttering to himself while stroking his chin. Without warning he strode out into the road, oblivious to the existence of an oncoming tram. Kitty felt her heart sink to her stomach. She lowered her eyes as he approached, praying that he would pass into the public house behind her. She wasn't surprised when he didn't, instead coming to a stop directly in front of her. Her eyes remained lowered, fixed on his shining laced-up boots. She had endured the leering looks and coarse, lewd remarks spat in her direction for the majority of the evening, but the finely attired gentleman was the first to actually stop and address her.

"May I enquire as to the services you are willing to participate in?" Kitty gasped and looked up. She found herself looking into a face that conveyed doom and malevolence. Strands of wispy white hair escaped from under the top hat that crowned a very long, very old and very thin face. She tried to take a step back but found that she had already pressed herself flat against the public house wall. She made the sign of the cross. A smirk started at the corner of the old man's mouth and his tongue flicked out, playing along his thin bloodless lips as he stroked his wrinkled cheek with a gloved hand.

"Hmm, very pretty, very interesting. Now what say we end this charade and you accompany me across the road there?" He broke off his conversation as the door to the Vines swung open and a small group of men decanted out into the street. One of them drew his company's attention to the incongruous spectacle before them and they continued down the street laughing loudly. The old gentlemen cast a disdainful glance in their direction before continuing.

"Before you reply, let me inform you that I will make it very much worth your while if you are willing to acquiesce to my small requests." Kitty froze and watched as the hand stroking his cheek moved towards her own.

"Kitty?" Kitty turned her head to see Albert standing resplendent, the silk top hat he wore causing him to tower over the scene. She remained against the wall, terrified that any movement would bring her into contact with the gloved hand that had become static, but remained hovering in front of her face.

"Oh, Albert," she beseeched. The old gentleman, his thin bloodless lips pursed, glared at Albert before silently withdrawing his hand and moving away. Kitty remained fast against the wall and watched as he made the short walk to the Adelphi Hotel and disappeared inside.

"Kitty?" repeated Albert. She looked at Albert, magnificent in his top hat and tightly tailored overcoat and peeled herself from the wall with as much composure as she could muster. She subconsciously patted down her dress. Even though she had put her hair up and was wearing her best she felt the weight of the disparity between them. Kitty became aware of the two men accompanying Albert. They too wore hats and overcoats but Kitty noticed patching to the bottom of one of the men's trousers and the worn docker's boots of the other. She found herself wishing that Potter were in attendance.

"I'm sorry Albert, I had to find you," she explained. Albert took out a gold pocket watch that Kitty had never seen; he looked at it before returning it to his breast pocket.

"We've received a telegram. Jobe has passed the scholarship test for the Collegiate, he's been accepted." Kitty became breathless giving Albert the good news.

"The Collegiate, a scholarship, well, well..." he replied as he passed his gold-topped cane from one hand to the other.

"That's right Albert, isn't it wonderful! His future will be assured, who knows he may end up at Oxford or..." Kitty was cut short as Albert suddenly interrupted.

"And why, may I ask, the haste to track me down?" He asked not looking at Kitty but monitoring the smooth momentum of his cane.

"Well, we've to send a telegram of acceptance before the week is out, Albert, time is of the essence." Albert suddenly took a grip of his cane and brought it down hard against the ground, startling Kitty. He looked her in the eye.

"Excuse my obtuseness, but what, may I enquire, do you mean when you say... we?" His question asked, Albert proceeded to afford his full attention to the cane as he continued to pass it from hand to hand. Kitty blanched, her worst fears being realised.

"But Albert...It was always your dream for him... we..." Albert again snapped his head up.

"There it is again, that word...we!" This time Albert took an intimidating step forward and stared into his wife's upturned face.

"Do I understand its implication correctly? That you are implying there exists a You and an I? A partnership? An association? An...Us!" Albert spat each term with such unadulterated revulsion and vehemence that Kitty, for the second time that evening, found herself shrinking against the wall of the Vines. Her tongue grew leaden in her mouth and she felt it would choke her; she was unable to check the apologies that tumbled from her lips.

"I'm sorry Albert, forgive me. It isn't about us, it's about Jobe, I could never afford his uniform, books…I haven't the money Albert," she stammered. Albert's face lit up in mock enlightenment.

"Ah so…there we have it…money!" he almost applauded.

Kitty felt her timidity fall away as her blood rose, flushing her cheeks. Responding to his intimidating step forward and the threatening tone of his voice she forced herself from the refuge of the wall until she was almost under the brim of his hat.

"It has been months since you forced your wife and son into the slums, with not a thought for their welfare. Have I come to you for a penny in that time? How dare you accuse me of begging!" Kitty stood her ground as she awaited his response.

"And how dare you accost me regarding the education and advancement of a Papist," he responded.

"He is your son, it's his only chance! It is your duty, Albert."

"My duty? To fund the intellect of another Fenian mouthpiece?"

"Ah, it's the religion, that's your excuse again, is it Albert? I wonder is it the Wise Pastor who pays for your finery or are you back suckling your mammy now that you have rid yourself of your Catholic family and the associated shame." Kitty roughly fingered his overcoat, looking him up and down as she spoke. Albert was taken aback at Kitty's touch and the mention of his mother, but quickly regained his composure.

"I say, if the desperation to educate your son is of such import, perhaps you should have paid more attention to the codger's proposition. If it was his age that caused your squeamishness I'm sure one of my men would cross your palm with a few shillings." He turned to his associates, and with a blitheness one would attach to remarking on the weather, offered them his wife.

"Lads? I have the means to provide a sub if needed." He nodded towards her.

"I can attest that it's nothing special, you know how Catholics are, but it would pass the time and I'm sure the landlord would allow you use of the barrel-keep for a copper." Kitty turned toward the two men as their vacuous faces lit up in understanding. She pushed herself past Albert and bolted along Lime Street without looking back.

As she turned off Marybone into Marlborough Street, Kitty saw that the short walk to her court was in darkness. She hoped the gas-light had broken again and that the High-Rips hadn't put it out so they could lurk in the shadows and use the cover to creep up on their victim.

She chided herself, only too aware that the newspapermen had helped to create the High-Rip myth by sensationalising the deeds of a few rag-tag delinquents. Every crime or act of violence was attributed to them and splashed across the front pages. As a consequence even the skinniest miscreant could strike fear into the most burly of men by hollering the battle cry 'Hiiiigggghhhhh Rrrriiiiiippppppp!'.

The sky was clear and the glow of the half moon shone off the cobbles enough for Kitty to find her way to the entrance to Number 4 Court. On clearing the narrow passage and entering the court the moonlight was cut off and a single gas-lamp feebly illuminated the gloom. She kept to the wall until she reached the steps of her cellar, her ears intent on picking out the slightest noise. The fear of a High-Rip attack had subsided now, replaced by the worry that someone would swing open the privy door located at the top of her steps, forcing her down them. She had already lost count of the times the men of the court, those that had the decency to use it, fresh from the pub, had misplaced a step on leaving the privy and arrived at her front door in a tangled heap.

Instinctively holding her breath, she reached the top of the steps unimpeded. The constant stench that permeated the area near the privy made it impossible to breathe freely without gagging. Kitty had done her best to rectify the issue but her efforts bore little fruit. The matriarchs of the court had poured scorn on her attempts to sanitise the privy.

"Suppose them from up the hills have shite that smells of roses don't they?"

She had tracked down the night-soil men and through charm alone persuaded them to attend to court 4's privy then, unable to afford the coal to boil the water, used buckets straight from the stand-pipe to sluice out the pit and scrub the bench, her hands blue and numb from the cold water. The children of the court, those that were allowed to approach the snob from Everton, revelled in refilling Kitty's bucket from the tap in the middle of the court. Each time they returned struggling with their load, Kitty would delight them with the mythical stories of her childhood or the verse of a song that kept them occupied throughout. Those children not allowed to help or even approach Kitty sat sullenly watching events from afar until, once their mother's backs were turned, they would join the other children in the fight for the privilege of fetching Kitty's water. The sanitation was now a weekly occurrence and although none of those who patronised the privy ever offered to help, their dexterity had greatly improved when depositing their night-soil and some of the children now brought buckets of hot water that their mothers had heated over the fire.

She tried to open the front door quietly but her lungs were bursting for air and she fell into the room gulping in a great lungful of the staleness within.

Jobe had heard her coming down the steps and from behind the curtain that partitioned the one small room into two tiny ones she heard him repeat the question he had asked the previous three nights.

"Did you find him, Mother?" Kitty silently scowled at herself, under the impression she had woken him. She popped her head around the thin sheet of material although the inky blackness obscured everything.

"Not tonight, but I'm sure I will tomorrow." Kitty was glad of the darkness that cloaked her lie and her tear stained face. Jobe was about to ask another question but Kitty interrupted him.

"Not now sweetheart, it's late, sleep now and we'll speak in the morning. Goodnight and God bless." She readjusted the sheet and, after feeling for it with her foot, sat down heavily on the crate she used for a chair. Although she knew there was a candle next to the remains of the loaf her Da had brought her, lying on the upturned bucket that served as a table, she remained in the dark. Jobe still struggled to eat the dry, stale bread, gagging as he attempted to swallow, but, if she could get a small fire going in the stove, she would be able to toast some of the staleness out of it and it would suffice for breakfast. Kitty sat in the impenetrable dark unable to see her hand in front of her face, or her tears falling silently on the cold flagged floor.

★ ★ ★ ★ ★

Jobe looked around the court, only his forehead and eyes visible above the top step, which in the strictest terms was breaking another of his mother's don'ts, but scarcely enough to be conscionable.

"Don't set foot upstairs into the court, Jobe," she had said. Again he had protested.

"But Mother, I'll be a prisoner in this cell," he said. His mother had tutted. He appealed to her anxious tendencies.

"I'd wonder if I didn't die from the lack of fresh air," he said dramatically.

"Ach Jobe, it's just for a while, and there's not much fresh air up there anyway! Remember it's like one of your adventure books, and look." She went and pulled the sheet of dirty fabric across its piece of wire.

"Didn't Mr Duncan tell us it was two rooms?"

The narrow slice of sky he could see above the court was just gaining some colour. It was difficult to measure time in the cell, such was the lack of natural light but it must have been hours now since he had heard the court noisily come to life as those with employment left on their long walks to reach it. His mother had left their cell early, creeping around so as not to wake him. Taking advantage of her absence he had opened the door and crept out on to the narrow, dank steps that led up into the court.

The court was a tiny cul-de-sac, not more than 15 feet across. The narrow passageway he had entered through on his first day in the court was the only access for both people and air and he imagined that neither of those that passed through could be very salubrious. He noted with a hint of satisfaction that the court was almost an exact parallel. Four dilapidated doors faced each other, one on each side of the court. These doors were seemingly the only entrance to the four floors above them, which he noted, neck craned back, by counting the cracked, grime-caked windows. Many of them were broken and had been stuffed with dirty rags in an attempt to keep the chill out. A thin layer of soot covered everything, including the steps that he now sat on. Even though the dampness of the court caused the dust to settle Jobe fancied he could feel the black matter entering his throat and nose as he drew breath. The privy was just to the right of his head and though his mother had enticed the muck-men to empty it with regularity and scrubbed it out herself each weekend, the smell was still enough to make his eyes sting. On each of the dozen or so occasions she had cleaned it he had begged to be allowed to join her up in the court, but to no avail.

"Remember I warned you about the dogs, Jobe? Well, these children can be just as vicious and then some. Let me get a feel for them, see who's who and perhaps next week I'll introduce you." Jobe hadn't been satisfied and it was torture to listen to the sloshing of water and the children shouting and shrieking as his mother regaled them with tales of Cliodhna, Queen of the Banshees or taught them the verses of the old songs.

He continued his reconnaissance of the decaying foundations that made up the court, following a scum-covered trickle of water back to a dripping, rusted standpipe that protruded at an angle from stained and cracked cobbles in the middle of the court. Then he saw the dog.

It must have been still for a very long time because he couldn't have failed to notice its movement in the tiny space; he wondered if it was asleep. Most of the dogs he had known of were small and although they sometimes yapped loudly their owners would easily control them with a reprimand if it were a man, or a comforting word if it were a lady. He tried to remember a time when he had seen a dog without its owner but couldn't. Dogs were one of the things his mother had warned him of on the day they had arrived in their new home.

"Look, Jobe," she had said as they were led down stairs that were covered on one side by raw sewage that had leaked from the privy that stood at the top of them. "It's just like one of the caves from your pirate stories. I wonder if there's any buried treasure in here?" Jobe thought it very unlikely. He held his nose and stepped over the amalgamation of faeces and urine that had found its way under the door. Mr Duncan, a small balding man whose face had been badly burnt failed to conceal his pretended ignorance of the filth by stating in his lisping guttural voice.

"Hmm, I'll have a word with schuperintendent of the night schoil-men. You will get usched to the schmell and I can asschure you that even during the heaviescht downpour the privy upschtairsh will not overflow, but you musht impressch on your neighboursch the need to be more shalubriousch with their schecretionsh." Duncan had shown his mother a small wood-burning stove and then pointed to a dirty sheet that was held up by a wire spanning and separating the room.

"You schee, it has a partition here, I really schould be charging you for two roomsh. I could eashily rent it to another family," he said as he pulled the sheet across, dividing the room in two. He spoke as though his nose was blocked and he dabbed at a trail of spittle that leaked continuously from the side of his mouth.

Jobe wondered if the man could smell anything through his melted, fused nostrils. Duncan left them alone in their new room and his mother beckoned her to him. She held him closely for a while and although she was silent he could feel her body shuddering and knew she was crying. When she released him her eyes and cheeks were glistening but she was smiling.

"Now look here you, although this is going to be a grand adventure, a holiday, there still have to be rules. You know most of them because they're the same as we've always had, but there are some more here because this is like one of your fantasy stories." She took pause and became very serious, holding Jobe by the shoulders.

"You know, Jobe, how sometimes there can be danger in your favourite stories and if the heroes aren't clever and careful they could be killed or taken prisoner or have their princess kidnapped..." Jobe nodded his understanding.

"This is just like that," his mother continued.

"You need to be clever and careful all the time, promise me you will, Jobe." On promising and ensuring he had understood her message his mother had proceeded to give him a list of do's and don'ts, mostly don'ts.

"Don't ever go out alone. Don't ever go off with anyone." Jobe had interrupted her.

"I'm sorry, Mother, these are all the rules from our old house," he said. His mother had agreed.

"Okay, remember all of them and don't ever go into the privy upstairs..." Eventually she had arrived at dogs.

"Beware of them, Jobe, they're not like the wee yapping fellows from the pleasure gardens. These are sneaky, intelligent creatures, like the hungry wolves from your old picture books, especially when they're in a pack. You make sure you give them a wide berth." Jobe didn't know how he was supposed to run into a pack of wolf-like dogs if he wasn't allowed out but he didn't interrupt his mother as she carried on with her list of don'ts.

This dog was big. It lay, taking up a ridiculously large space in the corner of the court. It still hadn't moved.

He was about to ascend to the top step and contravene a plethora of his mother's don'ts when two smartly dressed men entered from the passageway. Jobe wasn't quick enough to dodge out of sight and as they cast furtive glances around one of them noticed his head poking out from the cellar steps.

"You there, rouse your neighbours, tell them to congregate around the standpipe here," he called. Jobe looked mutely at them, not only for disobeying another of his mother's don'ts but also because he felt a rush of irrational guilt at being caught on the steps.

"Don't you ever talk to strangers, Jobe!" she had said, and he had protested. "But Mother, Father always told me to respond when spoken to, it is rude and ignorant to do otherwise," he had said.

"Not here it's not, you're not to speak to strangers Jobe, understand?" she had insisted, and Jobe had nodded his acquiescence.

"You, boy! Rouse your neighbours I say!" When the man still received no acknowledgement from Jobe he shook his head, taking him for a simpleton. Unbeknown to him every household that the court comprised was now aware of the two official men who had entered their domain. After a minute or two the men realised they were purposely being ignored. The man who had summoned Jobe called out;

"Ho there, we're from the corporation, we've come about your court being photographed."

No sooner had the words been spoken than doors opened and faces appeared at the filth-caked windows that overlooked the court. Jobe ducked out of sight, he crouched on the steps, his mouth perilously close to the black sludge. He wrestled with himself internally before reaching his decision and cautiously projecting his head back into the court. His view of the standpipe was now blocked and he marvelled at the number of people who had spilled out of the front doors into the court, packing it tight. He was even more surprised when, looking up, he saw those who found they couldn't push their way into the court or were too infirm to try, appeared at each of the cracked windows, competing with each other to obtain a view.

Although the court was packed tight the corporation men made no effort to make themselves heard and Jobe struggled to pick out a single word. Those who had been forced to the back of the court and found themselves next to the privy glanced curiously at him before diverting their attention back to the stand-pipe and those delivering the information. The only clear words that Jobe was able to discern came from the men as they were leaving the court.

"And for goodness' sake, can somebody get rid of that dead dog!"

The carnival-like atmosphere that pervaded the court was palpable.

"Ratbones, funny name for a family of toffs," cackled Marge O'Grady, mispronouncing the name to a neighbour as Kitty cleared the passageway into the court with a bag of fruit her Da had given her. Marge O'Grady stopped talking as she passed and Kitty continued to the cellar steps only stopping to give an orange each to a half dozen children who were sitting just inside the decrepit front door next to them. Kitty was exposed to an odour akin to that of the privy as she bent to deliver her gifts. On receiving their bounty the children retreated into the bleak interior ripping at the peel with their teeth.

"Rathbones," thought Kitty. She knew some of the family enough to say hello to, had attended their charity events with Albert.

Although happy that a glimmer of excitement had entered her neighbours' lugubrious lives, that they had something to look forward to and be proud of, Kitty herself couldn't care less about the news the men from the corporation had given to the residents of the court. That it was to be photographed for a study that was being carried out by some philanthropists, who she now knew were the Rathbones.

They were apparently planning to find solutions to the overcrowding, poverty and sanitisation of the slums. To allow the subjects of their study a modicum of dignity, and no doubt to avoid muddying their boots, they were not going to come prodding and prying into the slums and courts but would use photographic evidence to help compile their data.

Kitty knew that there were plenty of well-to-do people who weren't daunted by a visit to the slums: not just the zealots who doled out their bread for the price of attendance at a prayer meeting but those who fed their morbid fascination with poverty and degradation by observing it first hand; using those unfortunates who dwelt in the slums for cheap entertainment and even, in some cases, to slake their immoral tendencies. She had seen groups of slum-watchers who had congregated at the railings of the pleasure grounds awaiting their guide for the evening. Although they made efforts to dress down and become inconspicuous, they still resembled royalty rather than those they were hoping to infiltrate.

Court Number 4 Marlborough Street had for whatever reason been selected to be photographed and the news had spread like wildfire, not only along the other courts of the street but also through the parishes of St Mary's and Holy Cross that sandwiched the little thoroughfare. The court had already suffered scandal as news spread that a woman and her son from Everton had moved into the court. It was only the confirmation that it was Nelly and Fergus Flynn from Standish Street's daughter that had prevented the formation of an outraged mob.

The communal solidarity that existed within the slums and the courts was born from mutual experiences, the daily struggle for survival that resulted in the neglect of every other pursuit that was beyond the mere means of existence.

Now that it was perceived the court was being shown favour by philanthropic toffs, the solidarity had been suspended and both parishes and the remaining courts on the street had renewed their sniping with vigour, now accompanied by a healthy dose of jealousy. Any difference was magnified, any deviation from the economic condition or good fortune regardless of its guise, met with open hostility. Now that those in Court 4 would not only be recorded and framed for posterity, but would benefit from their court being made over, cleaned and whitewashed, set them apart from their neighbours and made them fair game. The slights would become topics of conversation wherever a resident of Court 4 ventured, in shops, pubs or when passing a janglers wall or corner, the favourite haunts of gossiping matriarchs.

"I wouldn't thank you for it, being gawped at by those do-gooder Bible bashers." "Aren't they all O's anyway, probably friends of them tangerines from Everton."

They had all too often been advocates of petty, seething envy themselves and to find themselves the target of it now presented those from Court 4 an opportunity to walk with their heads a little higher and their backs a little straighter than usual.

The only positive for Kitty had come when she learned that the walls were to be cleaned and prepared for the coat of whitewash they would be receiving.

"I've never understood it, Jobe, if they truly want to capture the filth and dirt people live in then why do they whitewash the walls?" Jobe had explained that the walls of the court were so soiled and soot-covered and the deficiency of natural light so stark that the flash of the camera had no chance of working in the usual dank gloom of the court. Kitty had nodded at her son in total ignorance but was happy at least that the court would be spruced up a little.

★ ★ ★ ★ ★

The three urchins stood in a circle on one of Great Crosshall Street's ollers, a patch of waste-ground adopted by children as their playgrounds, the last drops of urine they could muster splashing on the mud and over their bare feet. Michael began to fix his crusted cut-offs, pulling them up and wrapping the string around his waist for a second time before tying it tightly.

"Is that your contribution, Michael? Jesus, my baby sister pisses more," piped Timmy Malone in disgust. Michael wasn't fussed. He had purposely not pushed too hard. The last time they had played jelly and custard he had strained so much his head had spun and he had almost fainted. The other lads finished and pulled up their pants. Michael already had his piece of stick and had begun to stir the urine into the mud.

"Ere, wait for us Mick, most of it's our piss after all," stated Timmy. The three of them began to mix with their sticks.

"Jelly and custard, Jelly and custard," they repeated rhythmically. The boys didn't notice the old man come up behind them.

"What's all this now, have you boys no more imagination than to be stirring up piss and mud for your entertainment?" he asked. Michael looked up to see his grandfather.

"Hello Mr Flynn," chimed his two companions. Fergus shook his head sombrely at the three boys.

"I'm sorry for you boys," he gesticulated over to Holy Cross Church.

"Don't you know it's a mortal sin to urinate in the shadow of God's house?" he said. Timmy Malone looked worried.

"What's urinate?" he asked. Paddy Molloy elbowed him.

"It means to piss, idiot," he hissed. All three looked up at Fergus. It was Timmy Malone who spoke, looking at the other two accusingly.

"I told youse we should have went rabbiting down Leeds Street." He turned his attention to Fergus, fear etched on his face.

'Ah no Mr Flynn, is there anything we can do, there must be something? What if we go to the priests' house and ask can we scrub the step?" Fergus rubbed his chin.

"Well, I wouldn't go telling the priests what it is youse have been up to." Fergus made a point of examining the mush they had created.

"Well, that's something, it's not dried up yet. I'll tell youse what, if you can get home before this is dry, making the sign of the cross all the way, mind you, and then do your mother a great help, really help her I mean, with whatever chore she sets yer too, the harder the better, youse might, just might, be ok." Timmy Malone and Paddy Molloy were off down Great Crosshall Street; their right arms a blur as they hurriedly made as many signs of the cross as possible. Fergus held on to Michael's collar before he could race off.

"Haven't I told you about hanging around with those Fontenoy boys, look at them, thick as bricks." He let go of his grandson's collar. Michael looked at him.

"But the mud, granda, it's drying," he protested. Fergus shook his head.

"You see how stupidity is catching, c'mon with yer now, let's see if I've got some jam and bread for yer in the house." As they walked up toward Standish Street Fergus looked down at his grandson.

"Why is it that you never play with your cousin Jobe in the courts?"

"Me da says I'm not allowed to on account of him and his mammy being filthy O's'"

"Well the big lummox should know better than instilling disrespect for your aunt into you, besides when they were younger your da and Jobes mammy were inseparable!"

"I don't think it is because they're O's at all, I think he's scared that it'll upset Grammy," confided Michael bashfully. His face turned white.

"Aw no, she'll kill me, I've forgot her jug!" Michael desperately rifled through the pockets of his cut-offs, pulling out a sixpenny piece with obvious relief. He looked at his grandfather.

"She sent me ages ago, what'll I do?" His mortal sin against the church was forgotten in the face of raising the ire of his grandmother.

"Did she give you a jug to return?" asked Fergus. His grandson thought a second before shaking his head.

"No, I dropped the last empty she sent me with I'm to tell Ness she'll have me da return his empties." Fergus smiled conspiratorially and ruffled his grandson's coarse, dark locks.

"Here's what's to be done, give me the tanner." Michael obediently gave his grandfather the coin.

"Now you get yourself back to your gran'mammy and tell her that I took the tanner off you as you were about to go into the Powers. Tell her I was drunk and made you accompany me down to the Goat's Head on the Dock Road because I wanted your help carrying a package I was picking up from a Russian sailor." Fergus paused.

"Have you got that so far?" he watched as Michael relayed the information in his head, his lips moving silently before nodding. Fergus continued.

"Now tell her the Russian fella never turned up and I sent you away and went into the Goat, got it?" Michael went through the process of getting his story straight, his lips moving as he practised the conversation in his head.

"Got it!' he said, smiling. The story was a good one and as far as he could tell it would be his granda in all the trouble and not him, he might even get a bit of bread and some milk if he laid it on thick about the forced march to the Dock Road and back.

Nell's nose twitched as her husband entered the room. She ground her teeth for the bread and milk she had given young Michael and made a mental note to give him a good whack for his lying when she saw him next. Fergus ducked under the empty washing line pretending to falter.

'You can stop your charade Fergus Flynn, you've brought no more fumes into this room than was already here." Nell's rocking was frenetic, such was her choler, but given the lack of missiles Fergus felt it safe enough to drag an orange box nearer to her and sit down on it.

"I'll tell you once and never again Fergus Flynn, there'll be no more of my money squandered on that treacherous O' daughter of yours."

"Squander? Nell, have you heard yourself, you're sending out for a jug while our daughter is around the corner starving to death, her and your grandson." Fergus spoke the words softly as his wife continued her rocking.

"Your daughter Fergus Flynn, your grandson! What's the do now, has my prophecy come home to roost? Has her grand O' finally consigned her back to the slum she had no right in leaving?"

"No right? Is that it, is that your problem all these years Nell, are yer jealous? Would you resent your wee babby daughter doing her best to escape this shite that we've had to endure the last thirty odd years?" Nell stopped rocking and looked hard at her husband. Fergus put his head in his hands.

"I've allowed you to become this, Nell." He spread both of his hands to encompass his wife.

"To forsake everything, to sit in that chair and drink yourself into an early grave. I've done it because it was easier, Nell. Easier than watching you try to survive with dignity in this cesspit. Although you could have Nell, if anyone could, it'd be you. But I couldn't bear to watch that, I'd rather you sat and escaped this drudge by drinking yourself into oblivion. Don't you see it is me who failed us, it's me who dragged us to this godforsaken city. Jesus, I didn't even listen to the advice I received on the boat, didn't that widow tell me to beware of the Scotland and Vauxhall Road areas, don't you remember?" Fergus mimicked the hag, pointing his finger at Nell in a conspiratorial manner.

"Avoid them both like the plague! Avoid them like the plague or more than likely a plague'll be your fate."

"But I knew best, didn't I. We'll be better off with our own, I said. The city won't get its claws into us,

I said. Well it did, Nell! It got its claws, teeth and everything into us, ravaged us until we become the husks we are today, both of us staring at those empty jugs and knowing we'd give our right arm to have just one of them full." Fergus looked at the empty jugs on the table and unconsciously licked his lips.

"And it's not only the two of us but our children as well, the lot of them. Except her Nell, don't you see it?" Fergus's tone traversed from remorse to anger to beseeching. He took heart from his wife's lack of rocking and the faraway look in her eyes.

"We can't sit by and watch her struggle Nell, she's been out of the slums too long to come back and survive. If we don't give her whatever scant support we can, it'll do for her. And the boy Nell. He's just like her, he's a beautiful boy, too fair to be on the scrap heap at his age. Bright as a button he is, he could do something with his life if we'd just give him what help we can." Fergus leant forward and took his wife's hands in his. Physical contact of any kind was a rarity now, even on bitter nights during the winter they would lie apart, forsaking the other's body heat. Now, her hands clasped in his, he looked her in the eye.

"What d'yer say Nell, shall we do it, something of consequence, redeem ourselves through them?" His wife looked down at her husband's gnarled, scarred hands enveloping hers. Remembered the years he toiled on their rocky barren land, cultivating it inch by painful inch in order to provide for her. The sensation of his skin seemed alien to her. She returned his gaze and smiled at him.

"You do as your mind tells you Fergus Flynn, but you ever take so much as a ha'penny from this house in order to furnish those tangerines again and I'll flay the skin from your back and take yer kidneys for the dogs."

Kitty's mind convulsed at the words that little Sally McManus was screaming around the court.

"The Giant O' was here! The Giant O' was here!" Kitty's mind regressed back to a conversation she had had with her Da a fortnight before as he walked her to one of her charring jobs. She had bumped into him as he was returning from escorting Jobe on the long walk to the Collegiate.

Kitty stood stock still as the conversation played through her mind.

"It'll be more difficult for me to help you now, girl. Your mother isn't a bad woman, she's had it hard and it's turned her hard. I wish you could have known her in Ireland," Fergus' head hung, disconsolate. Kitty took his hand.

"I'll manage Da, I have my little bits, the slop-work, the charring, this one on Rodney Street is a good earner. They'll suffice as long as I can afford

Jobe's schooling, neither of us eat much and the hovel is almost free," she smiled at her Da. Fergus could see through her smile but was more concerned at her mention of slop-work.

He knew many of the unsavoury characters involved in the slop-trade. Employing women to transform rags into clothing with the skill of their needlework. Sailors fresh to shore after months at sea made excellent customers. Regardless of their creed, colour or culture they would arrive in Banastre Street, amazed that the world famous Paddy's Market could be contained in the grimy looking brick shed. Desperately seeking to rid themselves of their salt stiffened rags for functional clothing that they could wear while embarking on emptying their full purses in the pubs, taverns and gin palaces. The slop-traders who had their pitches on the earthen floor of Paddy's Market were perfectly placed to considerably lighten the sailors' purses, not only by providing them with cheap clothing but by offering another service that the seamen were desperate to partake in. The wages they paid their army of needlewomen were negligible and they preyed on the poverty of the women to cajole them into less skilled, less time-consuming but more profitable work.

"Who is it you're slopping for Kitty?" he asked, unable to keep a tone of trepidation out of his voice. Kitty was only too aware of his concerns.

"Don't worry Da, it's none of those pigs from Marybone, I know only to well what they're about. I'm working for a respectable Jew from up Pembroke Place way." Fergus nodded his head in silent relief.

"A respectable Jew eh? Well there's a first," he couldn't help adding before commencing with the conversation he had been delaying.

"Kitty, would you not look at selling your ring, consider pawning it maybe?" Kitty stopped and Fergus looked the other way, feigning that he was looking for traffic. She recommenced walking.

"I can't Da, what'll I say when he comes back?"

"Tell him you sold it in order to feed yourself and yer child, Kathleen," Fergus's frustration had shown in his tone and he looked sheepishly at the floor.

"D'you really believe he'll come back Kitty, it's been months now," he asked more softly.

"I do Da, and I want him to know that I trusted him, to be able to show him I never lost faith in him, never doubted him. He's going to need that, the guilt will eat him otherwise."

"Won't your waiting, your struggling show him that? Sure you could have your pick of every eligible man in every parish. There's a lot to be said for an economic marriage, Kitty, your worries would be over." Kitty swung her Da's arm as she had when she was younger.

"Ach, don't be silly Da, he's had it hard, his father dying has sent him to the drink and muddled his senses and the emergence of the Wise Pastor has turned his head, that's all." Fergus stopped walking and turned Kitty in his direction. Taking her other hand in his, he spoke into her face.

"It's done more than turn his head Kitty, it's turned him to breaking them! Catholic ones! And dozens of them, he's a regular bogeyman, the children talk of him, call him The Giant. A Giant O', they say, he has glowing green eyes, a silk top hat and a gold-topped walking cane that he'll put through your skull." Kitty shook her head at her Da's melodramatics.

"Oh Da, it's not like you to listen to children's prattle. He loves us Da, he left everything behind for me once and he will again, I just know it. Until that day I'll continue to raise Jobe and ensure he gets his education, and the ring will stay hidden away."

Sally's words broke into Kitty's reverie,

"The Giant O' was here! The Giant O' was here," she screeched. Sally was one of the children who always brought a bucket of hot water on what was now known as 'Sanitation Saturday'. No matter how tired Kitty felt after her hard week's work she always ensured that her half-day off was spent cleaning the privy with the children of the court. Kitty beckoned Sally over.

"Now then, what's all this chatter about a giant, eh?" Kitty was in a turmoil, her heart seemed to be beating in her throat but she managed to remain composed. Sally answered her excitedly.

"Oh Kitty, you should see the size of him, he truly is a giant! He has great green eyes and a shining silk top-hat and he had his walking cane with him, the one he uses to bash heads in." Kitty could hardly breathe.

"What was he doing Sally? Why was he here? Was he looking for someone? Did he mention my name? Did he mention Kitty Warburton?" Sally had gone quiet and Kitty realised that she was holding her by the shoulders and shaking her. Kitty immediately let go of her, instead hugging her to her breast.

"Oh, forgive me Sally, I'm sorry my love, I'm sorry, everything's going to be fine now, it'll be all right, d'you hear," she was blubbering now. The defences that Kitty had constructed and maintained for so long disintegrated with the news that Albert had finally come to reclaim his wife and son. Kitty fell to her knees, still holding the confused girl.

"It's over Jobe, we're safe now, everything is going to be all right." Sally broke free and looked at Kitty, wondering at her sobbing words and the tears streaming down her face.

"He wasn't looking for anyone Kitty, he came to see my Aunt Aggie."

Chapter IV

1890

The group of boys unenthusiastically kicked around a tightly bound ball of rags. Using the narrow passageway to Number 4 Court as a goal. Not one of them sported shoes and occasionally there would be a cry of pain as a toe stubbed against a jutting cobble or an opponents shin. Sporadically one of them would turn and look up the short distance to the junction with Marybone.

"He's late I reckon he's sneaked past us."

"Don't talk shite, how could he, we've been kicking our heels here for an age"

"Maybe he's played the wag today, stayed indoors."

"More shite, he'd have to be at death's door before his Ma'd let him off a day, d'you know how much money she wastes sending him to that shiteing school?"

"Why don't we give him a pass today, go down the docks, see if there's any untended carts about?"

"Ah you would say that, you're only scared of upsetting his shiteing Ma."

"Am not! She bandaged my leg the other day, she's nice, that's all."

"Well, he's not getting a shiteing pass, we'd be a laughing stock if we allowed a little shite from Everton amongst us without any molestation."

"But what about Michael Flynn, he's his cousin, isn't he one of us?"

"That shiteing traitor Flynny, isn't he always off down Fontenoy ways playing with our enemies, sure didn't he sneak some of our bonfire wood last Guy Fawkes night!"

"What if we've waited all this time and his granda is with him? There's no work down the docks, they're all on strike."

"He's right, me mam almost put my da's hook through his head last week when he told her he wouldn't be crossing no picket line."

"Aghh, what are we, a shiteing Janglers Wall? Let's get over to Great Crosshall Street, we'll cut him off there."

Jobe was unsure how to proceed. Running wasn't an option. The cap that had been wrenched from his head had been earned by his mother who charred and scrubbed so hard during the day that some evenings she was forced to abandon her needlework for fear that the material she worked with would be damaged by her raw and bleeding fingers. Her hand in a bowl of cold water, she would fret over the deductions to her pay the missed deadlines would elicit.

Even if he was willing to abandon the cap he doubted he would get very far; the majority of his tormentors were both bigger and stronger than him. The adults that meandered about seemed to have no inclination to help him, and judging by their look would have proved incapable anyway. His mother's words came flooding back to him.

"A group of wild and hungry wolves, Jobe." He had understood her characterisation from his first venture into the court. The children within had ceased their play, viewing him with ravenous eyes while they sniffed for any perceivable weakness. His mother had utilised the Saturday Sanitation to introduce him, remaining at the bottom of the steps wringing her already raw hands on the rusting handle of her bucket, ears pricked, before finally emerging.

"Everyone, say hello to my son Jobe, he's been suffering from a terrible chill this last few months and has had to remain indoors," she stated before inducing a mini-melée among those who didn't possess a bucket of hot water by placing her empty one on the ground. His novelty status and his peers' affection for his mother had carried him through his initial few outings. His manner, sense of humour and most importantly his ability to tell stories had cemented his place among the court's children.

The group now blithely tossing his cap from one to another were more reminiscent of a cauldron of raptors and he sensed their intent was real.

"Are yer lost, little toff?" asked a big rough-looking girl, her wiry red hair covering a face plastered with freckles to such an extent that Jobe wondered if they were one big unfortunate birthmark. He knew any attempt to retrieve his cap would be futile, only serving to provide the gang with further sport and to their irritation he made no attempt.

"No, I'm not lost, I'm on my way to Number 4 Court Marlborough Street,' he said matter of factly.

"Oh, so you've come to enjoy a bit of slum-seeing have yer? What was it, did you hear your rich mummy and daddy talking about us while you ate your steak last night?" "Well you might get away with trespassing on Marybone but us from Cockspur Street won't have any of it." The wind rushed from Jobe as, without warning, the girl swung her fist into his stomach. He doubled over in agony. A hand pulled him roughly up by his hair causing tears to pool in his eyes. He attempted to blink them away before they could spill out on to his cheeks.

"I don't know about steak, he looks like he hasn't eaten for a week," the owner of the hand commented, betraying a hint of concern. He released his hold on hearing an angry voice behind him and Jobe returned to his prone position.

"Ere, what's all this shite?"

Clutching his stomach Jobe fought to regain his breath and rid his eyes of tears. He recognised the deep, monotonous voice and groaned inwardly.

Could things get any worse? He looked up to see that half a dozen boys he recognised had turned on to Great Crosshall Street, joining his initial tormentors. The voice belonged to Tommy Molloy, self-appointed leader of the Marybone Boys who were all older than Jobe but not much bigger, stunted as they were by hunger and ill-health. Except for Molloy. He was a huge, hairy, beast of a boy and had led the gang's persecution of Jobe since he had emerged from the relative safety of the court in order to make the long walk to school, with his grandfather when possible, but alone if necessary. Forming a circle around Jobe they would push him from one to the other as they chanted.

"Ha Ha Ha, Ho Ho Ho, lookie here it's the shiteing O'!" or other lyrics of a similarly inane nature. The group would rifle through his bag, taking any remnants of food that they found and waving any books he was allowed to borrow in the air, but on his liberty and bag being returned to him he would always find that his books had been put back inside with a well-measured deftness. The pushing was as physical as things got and Jobe had stopped attempting to outwit the gang, finding it more tiresome than the actuality of being apprehended.

"I said what's all this shite," Tommy Molloy commanded instant respect and the majority of the initial group cast their eyes downwards. The freckled girl wasn't one of them.

"What's it to you Molly, we've caught ourselves a slum-seer and we're going to teach him a lesson," she sneered. Tommy Molloy looked at his companions and laughed.

"It's Molloy and you're on our side of the road, that's what it is to me," he snarled as he turned his attention back to the intruders.

"You know the law Molly, all boundaries are null and void when it comes to O's and slum-seers. He's ours and we're taking him back across to decide what's to be done with him."

"Is that so Freckles? Well the whole shiteing country knows what you get up to on that side of Vauxhall Road don't they?" "What'll you do, murder him for shiteing sixpence like you did poor Richard Morgan? They should have hung the whole cowardly shiteing lot of you, two was never enough!" The whole Cockspurs Gang bristled at mention of the 1874 murder that had outraged the whole of the country and remained a stain on the parish. Freckles struggled to compose herself.

"Everybody knows that the ghost of Thomas Cosgrove was to blame for that!" she spat through gritted teeth her face turning crimson. Molloy seized on her chagrin and sought to press home his advantage. He turned to his gang, pointing up the road.

"Ah another shiteing murderer from that side of Vauxhall! Not content with killing his wife, he done for himself with a draught of shiteing poison."

"That's right," confirmed Freckles. "And Richard Morgan died exactly where Cosgrove was buried," those behind her nodded solemnly at her words. Molloy wasn't satisfied.

"But what you're not making mention of is that Cosgrove was buried at shiteing midnight with a stake through his shiteing chest so he could never rise and make mischief again, you've no shiteing excuse for your backward, murdering ways."

Jobe looked up at the girl whose fingers were digging into him, noting that her skin, those patches that weren't covered by freckles, was steadily turning a deeper shade of crimson at each insult.

"So I hate to break it to yer but you shiteing Cockspurs'll be taking him nowhere, we'll be taking him back to his home." Freckles shook herself.

"And as if you would know where he lives yer, big pudding," she retorted.

"Oh I know all right yer see this little toff here is no shiteing slum-seer, he lives in Court 4 on Marlborough Street, same one as Joe here." He turned to a boy whose cut leg Jobe's mother had cleaned out and dressed the week before. The boy still had the rag tied around his knee, but now it was grey and looked greasy. The boy nodded his confirmation.

"Yeah that's right Tom, he lives in our court, in the cellar. His mam…" Joe trailed off as he noticed Tommy's frown.

"So you've got two choices, you can go back to your shiteing side of Vauxhall Road empty handed, or you can go back empty handed and bloody nosed!" Freckles wasn't appeased and attempted to grab at Jobe's blazer. Although Molloy had no qualms when it come to hitting girls, especially ones as big and ugly as Freckles, for once he engaged his brain rather than his fists.

"His Da is the Giant O'!" he said. Freckles let go of Jobe as if she had just heard that he was riddled with leprosy. She looked at him with awe and then turned to Molloy.

"The Giant O's son!" The legend that the Giant O's son lived among them had spread like wildfire around the surrounding parishes. It was the reason behind Freckles' and her gang's expedition from Cockspur Street across Vauxhall Road and into enemy territory. The excitement of encountering such easy prey as Jobe had caused all thoughts of the Giant O' and his son to evaporate. Tommy Molloy took the opportunity to pull Jobe back and deposit him behind his gang.

"So what's it to be, Ginger? Are yer leaving of your own shiteing choice or is it to be fisties?" he asked. Freckles bristled and Jobe watched as both gangs' postures subtly changed. He pushed through the protective line in front of him and calmly approached a boy with a slate-shaped head who flinched and blinked in surprise when he realised he was the objective of the Giant O's son. He clutched the cap more tightly, then, looking down, understood Jobe's intent and threw it to him. Jobe caught the cap and then slowly lifted his hand and pointed up Great Crosshall Street.

"Go," his voice was almost a whisper, but each of his tormentors heard it as if it had been a roar. As one they turned and fled, a shock of ginger hair bobbing at their front. Tommy Molloy looked at Jobe as if he were a Maxim machine gun. He grabbed Jobe and swung him on to his shoulders with ease. He had found a new weapon in his fight to protect the Marybone Boys' boundaries from the ever-encroaching shites of Vauxhall and Fontenoy.

"Three shiteing cheers for the Little O', Hip shiteing Pip…"

An avalanche of memories cascaded into Jobe's mind as he was hoisted onto Molloy's shoulders and he was powerless to quell the tears he had refused to release a minute before from flowing freely down his cheeks.

Kitty, although loath to do so, could see no alternative but to impart her findings about Albert to her son. Her conversation with Aggie Keogh had provided her with fresh optimism but she remained shaking and red-eyed following the tumultuous emotional torture she had endured. On returning to the cell she had beckoned Jobe to sit down, and though he was concerned by his mother's state, he tore into the thick slice of warm buttered bread, that she had given him as he sat cross-legged looking up at her.

"Your father was here in the court, Jobe." Sparing him the cruelty that she had suffered she didn't pause or draw breath but added quickly. "He wasn't here for us, son, I doubt he even knows where we are. He was here to see Mrs Keogh. He was on the Wise Pastor's business."

Kitty, still sobbing, had followed Sally into Mrs Keogh's room, plotting a course among the multitude of children who sat in the gloom of the hallway making oakum by picking at pieces of old rope. A roaring fire gave the room a snug feel but was already covering the freshly whitewashed walls, painted from tins that the photographer's engineer had lost, with a layer of soot. Mrs Keogh, her silver hair falling thick down her back, shooed another group of children into the already packed hallway with a stream of expletives. Seeing the state of the usually composed and confident Kitty she sat her down on a worn and frayed but comfortable Chesterfield chair, forcing a cup of hot tea into her shaking hand, flatly refusing to answer any questions or even discuss her exotic visitors unless she took it and sipped it down. Once Kitty had drunk some of the tea and re-mastered her breathing Aggie Keogh sat down and explained the origin of her bounteous visitors.

Her John had been imprisoned, falsely mind you, he was a drunk and of that there was no denying, but he was never violent, not like they had claimed. While awaiting trial he had been held in the Main Bridewell at Cheapside, where he was, she admitted crossing herself repeatedly, such a regular that he was usually allowed his own cell. Finding another soul already in there he had taken exception, but after the intruder had allowed him use of his newspaper and managed to acquire him some cigarettes from the guards, John and his new lodger had enjoyed some conversation. Her John had a wide breath of knowledge, he was an avid reader, and could hold a good conversation when sober. The two had formed an incongruous friendship and when her John, following his appearance in court, had informed the man of his three-month sentence, he had told her John not to fret about family, that he would see to it that his wife and children would not suffer in his absence. His newfound friend had been true to his word. Aggie had now received several visits from well-to-do gentlemen, all bearing the lodger's well wishes, and more importantly a quantity of cash. O's, every one of them, but courteous and well-mannered ones.

'This Albert, the Giant O', your husband, he's only been here the once and that was today. I've heard the stories that do the rounds about him and Pastor Wise, but I can't help feeling they must be greatly exaggerated, you know what the soft-shites around here are like!"

Kitty had waited patiently throughout the monologue, but now that Aggie Keogh had invited her into the conversation she asked the question that was singeing her tongue.

"Would you have noticed whether he wears a wedding ring, Mrs Keogh?" she had asked. Aggie Keogh had smiled at her slyly. They had never spoken before but Aggie treated her as though they were old collaborators.

"He does Kitty, he does." Kitty almost slumped off the chair in relief. Aggie took her show of relief for faintness and ordered Sally to cut a slice from the still-hot loaf and slather it with butter. As with the tea, Kitty had no choice but to accept. Mrs Keogh had promised Kitty that if the Giant O' appeared at her door again she would send the children to find her. Kitty supplied her with a current list of her workplaces; it was a long list and Aggie Keogh had chided her, but also promised that one of her large extended family would track her down. Aggie had given Kitty a hug and then forced the remainder of the still-warm loaf and a dish of butter on her before allowing her to leave and share the news with her son.

"Do you see, Jobe, if he still wears his wedding ring his vows must remain dear to him. He still considers himself married, me his wife and you his son." Jobe looked at his mother wide-eyed, the bread consumed, his tongue stretched out, searching for the spots of grease that glistened on his cheeks, chin and fingers.

"There's more Jobe, you know how you like a good story and how you enjoy it all the more if there's a real terrible baddy in it, one that has the ability to scare you before you go to sleep. Well the children around here have no less vivid imaginations. They've got their own bogeyman, the Giant O' they call him. They say he has glowing green eyes, wears a silk top-hat and carries a gold-topped walking cane which he uses to bash in the heads of Catholics…"

"I've heard of him," Jobe interrupted excitedly.

"I've heard of him!" He had become fascinated by tales of the Giant O', even beginning to concoct his own stories, regaling his friends with tales about the green-eyed demon's latest misdeeds. Sometimes they were entirely his own creation but on other occasions he replaced the Giant O' with the antagonist of the books he'd read or stories he'd memorised.

"I make my own tales up about him, I made Nancy Bennett cry with one of them last week," he finished proudly before his eyes widened and he let the fingers he had been sucking fall from his mouth.

He stared at his mother, unblinking. Kitty knelt and took Jobe's face in her hands.

"I want you not to believe a word, Jobe. Your father is the gentlest man alive. Sure he is helping to protect the Wise Pastor but the only reason he would ever strike anybody is if he was in mortal danger himself." Kitty gently shook Jobe's head and then lightly slapped his unflinching face to rouse him from the comatose state he had entered. Jobe's eyes rolled in their sockets and the bread and butter he had just eaten came back up, covering the front of his blazer.

"Why don't you piss off Bacon Face, we're not paying a ha'penny more!" Mr Duncan swivelled to his left, his colourful handkerchief swishing through the air lending his turn an extravagance. It was impossible to detect from which of the cracked windows the shout had emanated. The extent of the burns to his face made it incapable of expression and belied none of the hatred he felt for his tenants. He dabbed at the side of his perpetually dribbling mouth with the handkerchief before turning back to the despondent residents at the stand-pipe. They listened to his lisping voice in dejection.

'The schmall increasche in rent ish the direct reschult of the vascht improvementsch that thish court hash benefitted from." Mr Duncan illustrated the improvements by pointing as he spoke.

"It hash been whitewasched, the night-schoil men are collecting regularly and I'm reliably informed that the gash-lamp there ish bright enough to illuminate the whole parish." It was true the court, although still decrepit and barely fit for human habitation, had enjoyed a slight renaissance.

"And why it is that you should profit from any of these improvements, what is it that you have contributed to any of them?" came a voice. Duncan again swivelled on his heel, but couldn't see an adult among the emaciated children who squatted on a step behind him. He looked closely; although the voice had been childlike, he was sure it must have come from an adult. He returned the baleful stares of those children brave enough to look at him before turning again to face his grudging audience.

"I think you'll all agree that the very modescht increasche of…"

"I asked why it is that you should profit from any of these improvements?" Duncan spun around, intent on identifying his heckler. A boy had emerged from the group of children and now stood independent of them. Duncan still couldn't believe a child had posed the query. He scrutinised him through eyes bereft of lashes or brows. The boy spoke again.

"What is it that you have done to improve the quality of life for the tenants of this court?" A shout of encouragement came from one of the windows.

"You tell that greedy Ham-Faced bastard, Jobe!"

Duncan didn't deign to discover the destination of the insult; he looked at the boy, perplexed.

"And where in the court do you live?" he asked, as he again dabbed at his mouth. He hoped the impertinent boy had a large family and relished the moment he would inform each and every one of them that they were evicted with immediate effect.

"I live below the latrine, in the cellar there," Jobe pointed over the landlord's shoulder. Mr Duncan nodded, his melted face revealing no clue to his burning frustration. There would be no eviction. He had found the cellar unrentable since its last occupants, a family of eleven, had died of fever. It wasn't the revenue the single mother generated but his depravity that was the significant factor behind his decision. The beauty had never missed a payment but he had enjoyed fantasies since the day she had moved in of the kind of payment he would elicit when the eventuality arose. Existing in the slum had corroded her figure but it was now nine months she had occupied the cellar and there had never been so much as a late payment, a fact that left him ungratified and only served to enhance his base passion.

"Well then, you've benefited more than moscht from the improvementsh, wouldn't you agree?" His chuckle was a lisping wheeze and the dribble that escaped his mouth frothed up on to his cheek.

"Yes, as has the whole court, but only as a result of my mother's back-breaking and disease-risking efforts, because you proved incapable of ensuring the night-soil men carried out their duty with regularity." Jobe's words were met with sporadic exclamations of agreement from a few in the court.

"Hear hear!"

"Well said!" Duncan brought his handkerchief to his mouth and looked around the court. Before he had the opportunity to formulate a reply Jobe spoke again.

"The walls you mention have been left to decay. They crumble with rot as a result of the soot and damp that has permeated into them and which now leaks into the rooms and our lungs. The coat of whitewash that the Rathbone's financed in order to take their photographs has only served to cover the problem, not solve it." Jobe's words were met with universal appreciation. Duncan's eyes flicked around the court, giving him a reptilian air as the shouts of support became more malicious. Jobe continued.

"And what possible relation does the lamp-lighter carrying out his duties with a better degree of dedication have to you?" Duncan was confused by the laughter that rebounded from the tightly packed walls of the court, ignorant of the fact that the quality of lighting was a direct product of Jobe's ingenuity.

His mother had nervously watched as he climbed on to Molloy's shoulders, wet rag in hand. She had directed him to do nothing more than wipe some of the grime from the glass panels of the gas-lamp. But once on his friend's broad shoulders he had made use of his vantage point, taking the opportunity to examine the inner workings of the supply valve and the three mantles. A crowd had gathered around, not all of them happy with Jobe's meddling.

"What are they up to now? High Rip vandals, is nothing safe?"

"He's going to break it altogether, we'll be falling over ourselves in the dark."

"Leave it alone, will you!" came the calls. Molloy, unable to see the protesters, his face pressed against the wall as he easily shouldered Jobe's weight, took offence.

"Can't you see he's only cleaning the shiteing glass," he had roared in frustration.

Jobe examined the three mantles and the valve supplying the gas and discovered that if he unclogged and manipulated the mechanism of the supply valve he could considerably improve the volume of gas feeding the mantles. The onlookers and doubters had gasped and then applauded as Jobe, finished with his alterations, had touched a

smouldering piece of wood to the valve. The mantles
came on in quick succession. Flash. Flash. Flash. The
parchment-like glow illuminated Jobe's smiling face
and lit up corners of the court that had remained
in perpetual shadow since its construction. The
lifespan of the mantles was greatly reduced but
Molloy and his boys entered into their communal
service with aplomb. Spiriting Jobe across the
boundaries of Marybone and into enemy territory
they hoisted him up so he could reach and unclip
the mantles, returning them to the courts like spoils
of war. Their forays had grown in regularity. Jobe
had manipulated the gas-lamps of all the courts on
Marlborough Street and now had to supply fresh
mantles to them all.

The interference of the lamplighter was easily
eradicated. Already the subject of abuse and threats
in streets that had been in darkness for days, he was
only too happy to deviate from the dreaded battle
cry of the High Rip that he would hear roared the
length of Marlborough Street whenever he entered
the locality.

The laughter of the court unsettled Mr Duncan.
It was the first time he had ever seen his tenants so
animated, actually expressing emotion. They had
always presented as the walking dead, shuffling
aimlessly in their grey rags, their grey faces bowed,
in perpetual search of the grave they would discover
only too soon. To witness them jeering, catcalling
and now laughing, coupled with the absurdity

of the well-spoken, articulate but obvious slum-dweller who had the audacity to challenge him was unsettling and he struggled to maintain his grip on reality. He forced his misgivings to one side, refusing to be cowed in such company.

"How dare you queschtion my management! Hell will be a cold place indeed the day I have to juschtify myschelf to the likesh of you!" He turned on the rest of the court, spitting and spluttering in his indignation, his handkerchief forgotten.

"Or any of you! I will evict thish entire court, every man, woman and child within if thish schow of dischreschpect continuesh!" The tenants who had openly cheered Jobe attempted to shrink back into the shadows of the court in order to escape the landlord's ire. Jobe was nonplussed.

"It would be of interest to know what the Rathbones would make of your threats." Mr Duncan wavered, how could this boy be aware of the efforts he was making to gain access to the higher echelons of the town's society? He had already donated a considerable sum of money to the Rathbone Foundation that he was assured had not gone unnoticed.

"And how would a cellar-dweller like yourschelf impart that information! What likelihood is there of you ever seeing a Rathbone!" Duncan bit his tongue until he felt blood seep into his mouth. How ridiculous to enter into a sparring session with this louse-ridden slummy. Jobe did not miss the landlord's subtle anomaly. He allowed himself a smile.

"I'm sure a letter to the *Mercury* would suffice, I hear they're avid readers."

Kitty put down her sewing as she listened to her son's tale. She sucked the numb tips of her fingers until they began to tingle and blanched at the thought of being evicted. She hoped there was an element of exaggeration to the exchange, but dismissed it knowing that it wasn't in Jobe's nature to embroider the facts.

"I know he's detested throughout the court, Jobe, but Mr Duncan has only ever been courteous and considerate to me. You can't go speaking to the landlord in that way. What'll we do if he decides to evict us for your impertinence?" She rubbed her hands together before picking up the pair of trousers that she was half way through, conscious of her deadlines.

"But he has no right to tyrannise the unfortunate of the court, Mother," replied Jobe.

"We're very lucky to have such a landlord, Jobe! Mr Duncan has always impressed on me his understanding and acceptance of unforeseen situations that could result in a late payment, but that doesn't mean you can go pushing his amiability to the limit by objecting to his rent increases in front of the whole court," she tutted as she was forced to unpick some wayward stitching that even a customer at Paddy's Market would find questionable. She sensed that Jobe was ready to argue his case further but curtailed him before he could start.

"That's enough now, Jobe, the next time you see Mr Duncan you'll apologise for your temerity, now wash your hands and prepare for bed." Jobe knew from her tone that she would accept no dissent. He would wait until she wasn't so exhausted to inform her that he had no intention of apologising to the bullying landlord.

He understood his mother's concern. Cellars were always the cheapest possible source of accommodation in the slum, especially one that was situated more or less under the privy, and he knew that his mother was approaching total exhaustion and illness earning the money they needed to survive, let alone the expense associated with his education.

Kitty watched, Jobe dipping his hands into the cold pail of water and admonished herself as she continued with her sewing. It was her fault. She had agonised about allowing Jobe his newfound freedom, calculated each of the myriad of dangers and issues it presented. Now that she had allowed the genie out she was as powerless to return it to the bottle as she was to return Jobe to the confines of their cell, or the court for that matter. Not only would Jobe himself rebel against it, but also, she imagined all of the children, and most of the adults too, would be up in arms against her.

Fear and pride wrestled for the ascendancy whenever she thought of how Jobe had reacted to and overcome their change in circumstances. He was the only living creature she had ever known to blossom in the slums but she constantly worried about the multitude of risks and threats he was exposed to. She couldn't imagine what Albert would make of the changes in Jobe on his return. Her Albert, the one of old, she was sure, would feel a sense of pride, revel in the durability, innovation and leadership that his son had shown.

And what about Albert? John Keogh's three months were almost served and if the Wise Pastor was planning on sending his wife and children another allowance before he returned it must be any day now.

Kitty chided herself again. She tried to refrain from thinking of Albert's return, instead using him and it as an inspiration to continue striving for their son. It was a source of comfort to her now and then, when she was overtired, or in the extremities of hunger, to take the ring from its hiding place behind the stove and imagine Albert placing it back on her finger. It would not even fit on her thumb now and the only request that she would make of him was that he buy her a thin necklace on which she could wear the ring until it fitted her again. She fretted about how he would view her. The lack of food, her work and her constant worry, in essence life in the slums, had aged her twenty years. She could feel her individual ribs and bones poked through her flesh where she didn't know they had existed. But she would soon regain her health and in the meantime the jutting bones would serve as a testimony to the hardships she had borne through her love for him.

Jobe watched as his mother carefully unwrapped the leftover slices of meat she had been given for her lunch by the cook in Duke Street.

"Can you wrap them for me please, Cook?" she had asked. The cook, a large portly woman who had herself originated from the slums, wiped beads of sweat from her head with her forearm.

"Why not eat now?" she asked suspiciously, although she already knew the answer. "There's hardly a pick on you girl, you're wasting away," she said, as she looked Kitty up and down.

"I'm very grateful for the free dinner, and I know it's against house rules to take food from the premises but I'll be late for my job on Catherine Street if I don't leave now. I can eat on the way." The cook wrinkled her eyes and looked into Kitty's before smiling.

"House rules, pah, isn't it me who makes them! Here, I'll wrap these pieces, but you eat this as I do." She reached over and grabbed a still-warm piece of beef from the silver salver, handing it to Kitty.

"Don't ask, I squarely refuse to wrap it. You eat it there in front of me as I wrap this for you," she admonished, refusing to take her eyes from Kitty. Kitty smiled, tore off a small piece of meat and placed it in her mouth. The sensation was almost overwhelming. The hot meat caused her to salivate uncontrollably and she brought the remainder of the piece to her mouth and ripped at it with her teeth. She wondered at the energy she could feel seeping into her body. The cook looked at her.

"You ought to take better care of yourself, those depending on you'll be all the worse if you take ill. How many jobs have you worked today?"

"Four," signed Kitty with her left hand, while using the thumb of her right to catch the grease dribbling down her chin.

"Four, it's only just past midday!" screeched the cook in alarm.

"No wonder you're stick thin, running yourself ragged all over this town," she added shaking her head and passing Kitty the wrapped beef. Kitty smiled her thanks.

"Praise the Lord I never give her the real number," she thought to herself.

Jobe watched as Kitty put the meat on a plate and added a freshly cut slice of bread from the loaf.

"Where's yours, Mother?" Jobe enquired as she laid them before him on the upturned tea chest.

"Oh I've eaten Jobe, I eat mine with the other girls, it's the only chance we get to have a good old gab," she said as she gathered together the breadcrumbs with her hand. Kitty, her back to Jobe, felt his eyes boring into her. He hadn't yet started eating.

"What did you eat, Mother?" he asked. Kitty had been waiting for the question and grimaced. She paused from her task and then spun around.

"Oh Jobe, how could I forget to tell you? You'll never believe the story that Janey Hopkins told me, have I told you about her, she's nanny to the Forsyths that I char for. Well, she told me that there were sightings of Springheeled Jack the last two days up near Everton." she pulled a crate toward him and sat down as she spoke animatedly. Jobe's eyes were wide.

"Springheeled Jack!" he exclaimed. Kitty picked up the scrubbed tin plate and placed it in his lap.

"Here, eat your bread and meat while I tell you all about it."

The half-dozen or so men couldn't fail to catch the attention of everyone they passed. Those unfortunates who did fail and found themselves obstructing the progress of the squad were unceremoniously shouldered or barged aside to create a thoroughfare. Grocers arranging their wares in crates outside their wooden-fronted shops were shouldered aside, their goods spilling on to the road, children playing on the pavement were skittled in all directions and the cornermen standing outside pubs in an attempt to intimidate the price of a pint from passers-by found themselves knocked into the gutter on their behinds.

The men all sported bowler or top hats, each of which had seen better days, and the onlookers they passed recognised pawnshop attire when they saw it. One hat stood out, its silk sheen radiant. The rest of the men followed behind the wearer, astonished at his knowledge of the streets and alleys they dissected. On passing through Adlington Street those that had made the trip before recognised Standish Street and Marybone.

Kitty barely had the strength to lift her head as she turned from Vauxhall Road on to Pickop Street. The only part of her body she was conscious of was her burning chest. Her clothes were still damp from the rain that morning and they hung from her, their weight almost equalling that of her body. She was eager to get home in order to dry off and get a bit of life back into her limbs before Jobe returned from school and saw her in this state. She clutched the wrappings of scraps she had procured for his tea to her chest as she turned into Marlborough Place, a narrow entry linking Pickop Street to Marlborough. Chin on her breast, eyes vacantly fixed on the cobbles as she dragged her feet, she didn't notice the incongruous group blocking the narrow entrance to Number 4 Court.

On reaching the passageway Kitty looked up, her red-rimmed eyes finding the cluster of men blocking it. She stopped, staring at them before comprehension cut through her exhaustion. She felt her heart beating strong in her chest, the blood pulsed through her veins and she ran at the men, bumping into one and causing him to falter. She threw the precious scraps to one side and ran to the cellar. Once inside she felt around for her wedding ring her raw hands scrabbling at the black hearth. Then she was up rubbing the soot from the ring as she took the stairs two at a time and raced to Aggie Keogh's tenement.

Albert appeared at the doorway just as she reached it. She couldn't stop and the testosterone that coursed through her body suddenly shut off. Kitty fell to her knees and buckled forward into Albert's shins. She held on to them kissing and rubbing her face against them.

"Albert, oh Albert." Her renting gasps for air distorted her voice. Albert looked down in bewilderment. He looked behind to the Keogh woman who couldn't see past him as his frame filled the doorway. He turned his body to one side allowing her to manoeuvre past him.

"Kitty dear, Kitty my love, come on now, up yer get," she said as she attempted to lift Kitty to her feet.

"Kitty!" Albert recoiled as he realised what was wrapped around his legs. Aggie Keogh looked up at him from bended knee.

"C'mon yer great lummox, get the girl up!" she demanded. Albert acquiesced and hoisted Kitty up. He was forced to unwrap her from his midriff and hold her at arm's length. He looked into her face in total shock. The beauty that he remembered had gone, her skin was grey and hung loose as if decomposing; he could see her skeleton pushing through her features.

"Albert, oh Albert, you've come. I wouldn't sell it. Look I have it here, it's here, give me your hand." Albert started to put out his hand and then, seeing what Kitty held in hers, retracted it and took off his leather gloves. Kitty saw the ring.

She awoke and looked up into Albert's face. His green eyes gazed down at her and she thought she must be dreaming. She closed her eyes again terrified of waking herself. She attempted to snuggle further into Albert, but couldn't. Something was amiss. She was standing, and why was she so cold? She heard Aggie Keogh's voice but could not understand her words. She was still in the court? The ring! Her eyes flashed open and she pushed against Albert's embrace, attempting to escape it. He slowly released her, ensuring she didn't topple backwards.

"That ring, Albert?" She looked at him, eyes wide and glistening with tears. Albert returned her stare, transfixed by the beauty he now recognised in the gaunt and ravaged face. The obnoxiousness he had demonstrated all those months before outside the Vines pub was nowhere to be seen and he looked at Kitty in despair.

"We're divorced, Kitty. I've remarried." Kitty didn't speak. Albert's words reverberated around her head. Nothing else existed for her. She turned and stumbled back towards the cellar.

Aggie Keogh looked at Kitty disappearing down the cellar steps and then turned her gaze to Albert.

"She'll not last much longer here," she said. Albert opened his mouth but found he couldn't speak. He took out his wallet and took out two white five pound notes. He held out the money, still unable to find his tongue. Aggie Keogh took the money.

"On the Holy Gospels she'll receive this, but there's only skin and grief left of her, it'll take more than money to save her," she stated sagely. Albert tipped his hat to her before striding from the court.

The pace he set made it difficult for his men to keep up with him and they resembled overgrown children as they half trotted in his wake. Albert paid no heed to the urchins and young men who had congregated and now followed hurling insults and missiles.

"Shall we disperse them, Albert?" One of his men enquired from behind him. Albert replied with a curt shake of his head, oblivious to the agitators. Memories of Kitty filtered through his mind and he quickened his pace as he brought his handkerchief to his eyes.

The strap of the satchel cut painfully into Jobe's fleshless shoulder and he readjusted it for what seemed the hundredth time. He consciously ignored the many hawkers who inhabited the pavement. Fishwives, their baskets piled with winkles, cockles and mussels. Mary Ellens, baskets of apples and oranges spread in front of their dirty legs and bare feet. The shoeshines, chip-girls and newspaper boys, everyone with young figures but sporting old and wrinkled countenances, created a cacophony, all trying to bring attention to their myriad of wares and services. Instead he utilised the long walk down the steep descent to revise what he had learned in his lessons before his compartmentalisation of the classroom. Although he relished the discussions and debates he enjoyed with tutors and students, utilising them to stare down men like Mr Duncan, he had no choice but to relegate them to the recesses of his brain that didn't accompany him into the slum. They had no place in his reality and if he attempted to carry them into it he wouldn't last long. The majority of students and a fair number of his tutors were of the opinion that he had no place in theirs and barely acknowledged him. Those that were not offended by or made the effort to look beyond his threadbare and malnourished bearing were rewarded with a keen-minded, altruistic individual.

He regarded his academic experiences as a daily excursion into escapism, part of his distant past that he frequented, but no longer belonged to. A place that it was imperative to have fully departed by the time he arrived back in Number 4 Court.

Jobe no longer shared his mother's optimism that his father would return and pluck them from their existence in the court. If, as legend stated, he walked the streets in pristine silk top hats, perfectly tailored overcoats and carried a walking cane topped with a solid gold handle, then why was he allowing his wife and only son to subsist in the slums? Jobe had deliberated over the issue at the same time as witnessing his mother's deterioration. Although it weighed heavy on him he had decided that he would relinquish his scholarship and leave the Collegiate in order to lighten his mother's burden of acquiring his books, uniform and shoes. He had discussed the situation with his grandfather who was of a like mind.

"I've tried to make her see reason son, but I think the thought of your father returning is the only thing keeping her upright," his grandfather had told him. "Your attending the Collegiate is as much for him as it is for you," he added.

"I'm thinking of leaving, Granda, getting a job, removing some of the strain from her," he had said. His grandfather had laughed.

"Well, it'll be over her dead body, but maybe we can broach it with her together. I can certainly get you something down the docks, your cousin Michael will be starting there if the knobsticks haven't taken all our jobs at the end the strike."

The distant cries of a boisterous crowd seduced his eyes away from the cobbles. He had reached the bottom of the hill and looking up he could just make out a commotion on Great Crosshall Street. The stimulation the slum provided doused his despondency and in his eagerness to join the excitement he ran across Byrom Street eliciting angry shouts from carters and tram drivers. With his bag thudding against his legs he continued to the junction with Fontenoy Street before coming to a dead stop. Stalking towards him, shielded from his ever encroaching pursuers by a band of burly men was his father, dressed in all his Giant O' finery and clutching his gold-topped walking cane. Jobe remained in his father's path. He had played out this scene in his mind on numerous occasions and was formulating his opening salvo when a man with a bowler hat came from behind his father and swatted him out of the way. Jobe fell into the door of the Australian that had just been opened by a toothless hag, sent by those inside to see what all the noise was about. Regaining his feet and pushing past the hag he found the crowd had passed him by and his opportunity to accost his father had gone. He clutched his bag to his stomach and tore up the remainder of the street in the direction of the court and his mother.

Fergus mulled over the outcome of the union meeting in Bank Hall, if what could be called an outcome had been reached. The strike differed from those he had supported throughout the seventies and eighties. The newly formed National Union of Dock Labourers had provided a sense of cohesion to the struggle, to such an extent that all members working on the north-end docks had downed tools and were all out. The show of solidarity, supported as it was by the coal heavers and carters with talk that the firemen and seamen's union were in discussions about coming out in support, could actually force the ship-owners to listen to the timeless demands against exploitation, slave wages and the hated stand where they were forced to gather each morning in the hope of a days work.

Scabs, the strangers shipped in from other ports and sometimes the bosses themselves, were still unloading ships but it was slow work carried out by unfamiliar hands and the unchanging forest of masts and funnels along the waterfront told their own story.

There was as usual a contingent ready to return to work for the employers, using the caveat of only for those bosses willing to acquiesce to union demands. As far as Fergus could figure any return to work would only serve to fragment the solidarity of the men and weaken their collective bargaining power. Edward McHugh, leader of the NUDL, had posed the question.

"Are we willing to work for such gentlemen who have never been an enemy of the union?" The differences of opinion within the ranks were highlighted when a carter had responded, "Aye, if we get terms then let's go back to work lads!" He was immediately set upon by a huge unionist who ruined his nose with a haymaker of a right before bundling him to the edges of the crowd. Fergus could feel that something had to give, and soon. On leaving the meeting he had seen an unfortunately placed carter attempting to transport a wagonload of grain. A group of boys, ship-scalers, had stopped the horses and mounted the wagon, spilling the grain to the ground. Six mounted police had been on the scene in no time, quickly supported by one of the new meat wagons crammed with coppers. On surveying the scene and the size of the crowd it seemed the decision had been made to leave the carter and sacks of grain to fend for themselves. The coppers withdrew back along Stanley Road, the crowd's cheers and insults ringing in their ears. Fergus knew from old that the retreat was one that would not be repeated.

He had been on his feet for a long time and he held his breath as he shuffled past the Northern Dispensary on Vauxhall Road. A Mary Ellen sat contentedly outside, her wares almost sold. Fergus wondered why anybody would want to buy fruit or vegetables from such an insalubrious location. He had convinced himself a long time ago that the air surrounding the hospital was contaminated and always avoided it. Only his aching knees and feet had led him down that particular route, the quickest home. He reached the junction with Marlborough Street still attempting to regulate his breath and wondered at the lack of children or idlers outside the courts. Continuing on he turned down Pickop Street and on reaching Marybone realised he still hadn't seen a soul. He popped his head into Stewarts Butchers.

"Ho Sid, what's the do? The streets are deserted out here," he said. Sid, the personification of a big beefy butcher put down his cleaver and walked around his counter. He pointed across to Holy Cross Church.

"You've just missed the tail-end of them. The Giant O' was here with a group of heavies, the children, and some of the men, are tailing them, right noise they made as they passed here." He finished speaking and watched as Fergus, without another word, walked off in the opposite direction towards Marlborough Street. Shrugging his shoulders Sid returned to his shop and picked up his cleaver.

Fergus limped through the court and was about to start down the cellar steps. He came to an abrupt halt when he noticed that the front door was wide open. Kitty was pugnacious in her efforts to prevent the noxious air from seeping into the tiny cell, only ever opening the door a crack, barely allowing enough room for admittance.

"Jesus Christ," he would protest.

"Can yer not open the door girl, I know I'm stick thin but…" he would add melodramatically. She would respond by pulling him through the narrow opening by his arm.

"Will you stop yer whingeing and just get in so as I can close the door Da."

Seeing it open was both alien and alarming. Fergus set off down the stairs, with each step descended he heard more keenly a low animalistic mewing noise that was wrought with agony. He shuffled through the open door. The curtain that offered a modicum of privacy to Kitty and Jobe's pallet was closed. The noise was coming from behind it. Fergus pulled back the curtain, his heart thumping in his temple.

Jobe lay face down, his back heaving with silent sobs. Every few seconds he would emit the unearthly sound that Fergus had heard on the steps. He breathed a sigh of relief. The lad must have crossed his father's path, had the fears that they both shared confirmed to him by the big bastard. Fergus wished he were twenty years younger.

He would wait with his grandson; comfort him, until Kitty returned. It might be no bad thing that the truth was out, although it would be raw, they could now hold a proper conversation on what the future held. He approached Jobe.

"There there, son, come now…" His eyes adjusted to the gloom and the words on his tongue turned to ash as he recognised Kitty's dark hair trailing out from under her son's heaving body.

Chapter V

1890

Fergus cradled his daughter's lifeless head in his lap alongside that of his grandson. The cell was in complete darkness now and he had no idea of the time that had passed since he had found his daughter and grandson. His legs had given way and he had silently slumped to the cold floor, his back against the damp wall. He pulled them both into his lap. Although one of them was breathing both were dead weights. Jobe had become quiet now, only the sound of his breath and rise of his chest separated his countenance from that of his mother. Fergus caressed both of their heads. His tears had long since stopped and he stared unseeing into the dark.

The flicker of candlelight caused him to blink and his dry eyes stung as their lids flicked across them. He became conscious of a voice that he didn't recognise.

"Oh Mary Mother of God no! Oh Jesus, Mary and Joseph please no!" The candle came closer as the owner of the voice knelt down.

"Fergus it's me, John Keogh's wife, Aggie. Fergus can you hear me, Fergus can you hear me, it's Aggie Keogh. Ah please God no," she cried as she knelt before them.

"She's dead Aggie, my beautiful baby girl is dead."

★ ★ ★ ★ ★

Fergus put up no resistance as Jobe was gently eased from the crook of his arm but when he felt hands pulling at Kitty he came to life. He had lain for so long with the weight of his daughter and grandson in his arms that both were numb, and although he managed to lift his cramp-ridden arms, his fingers could make no purchase and Kitty's lifeless body was taken from his grasp. He was then pulled up from the cold, hard floor. They had been brought across to Aggie Keogh's room, where Kitty would spend the night. She had been laid out on the bed, a thin sheet covering her.

"She had this clutched to her breast," said Aggie as she put Kitty's wedding ring on the table. Fergus took the ring and turned it in his hand. The warmth of Aggie's fire had revitalised his limbs and he stood, walking over to the bed. Pulling the sheet back from his daughter he stared into her face before lifting her arm. He attempted to place the ring on her woefully thin finger and cried out as he realised the ring wouldn't even stay on her thumb. Aggie had come and taken the ring from him.

"I'll keep it safe, Fergus. I have something else in my possession, we'll discuss it tomorrow." She had brought him back to his seat at the table.

"You're welcome to stay the night with her, you and Jobe."

Jobe had slept on the bed next to his mother, just as he had whenever he had suffered night terrors. Now he stirred from unremembered dreams, waking to face the nightmare of reality. His mother lay lifeless next to him and his granda sat wide awake at the table where he had left him. Aggie had tried to get them to take some breakfast but neither had accepted.

"Well, it's for the women now Fergus, we need to prepare and dress her. It's time." Fergus knew there was no interfering with women and their duties. He took Jobe by the hand.

"Come now lad, let the women see to your mother," he said as he took Jobe's hand. Jobe broke free from his grasp but only in order to place a kiss on his mother's forehead.

"I'll send one of the girls for you when we're ready Fergus. Don't forget I have something here to give you," said Aggie as she saw them out.

Although lost in grief Jobe still felt a foreboding about entering his grandmother's rooms. He was under no illusion how she felt about him or his mother. Fergus read his thoughts.

"Don't you be worrying now Jobe, you've enough to be contending with. This is your home now," he said.

Jobe looked around as they entered the barracks. Each room he passed through was much larger than the cell he had shared with his mother and there was a glut of furniture in every one.

"Go on son, have a seat, I'll get a fire going and put the tea on." As his granda finished speaking Jobe heard a woman's voice.

"Is that you Fergus Flynn, where in God's name have you been all night? I hope you've been down to them bleeding docks and found out if all that nonsense is over." The owner of the voice entered the room. She looked at Jobe as she stomped over to a rocking chair near the fireplace. Jobe watched her as she began to rock. The chair became organic as her heavy frame sank into it and the two became one living entity. Her wrinkled face set, the bottom lip curling into her mouth where teeth had once been. What remained of her hair flounced with the swell of her chair.

"What is this, Fergus Flynn?" she said as she built up a rocking motion. Fergus said nothing until, satisfied that the fire would take hold he stood up on creaking knees. He pulled a crate to the table and wearily sat down.

"I've some terrible news Nelly. It's Kathleen. She's gone. She died last night," he said without looking at his wife. Nelly said nothing as she rocked back and forth. After a minute Fergus looked up at her.

"Have yer nothing to say Nell?" he asked. Nell looked at him, keeping her eyes fixed on his face as she rocked. She inclined her head towards where Jobe sat.

"And I suppose we'll be stuck with her tangerine now, will we!" As she finished speaking she realised that she had somehow fallen out of her chair and was now lying in a heap against the wall. Her brain was unable to process what had happened and although her instinct was to right herself, stand up and get back in her chair, she found she couldn't move or breathe.

Jobe had watched in horror as his grandfather, moving with a speed and agility he didn't associate with him, grabbed a heavy clay jug from the table and in one motion brought it crashing against his grandmother's head as she reached the forward zenith of her accelerated rocking, magnifying the impact so she came out of her chair with such force that they flew in opposite directions, their organic connection severed. His grandmother came to a stop in a bundle against the wall.

No sooner had she landed in a crumpled heap than Fergus was on her, hands clasped tightly around her throat. His cries and shouts were incomprehensible but within seconds people were running into the room from all over the barracks.

"Someone fetch a copper quickly, he's killing her," came the shouts. A heavy man that Jobe knew as Bog entered the room and took in the situation instantly. Unlike those covering their mouths with their hands or shouting for the intervention of a constable he rushed over and pulled his father away from his mother, holding him in his arms.

"Da, Da calm down, what're you thinking of?" he shouted. Jobe realised that his grandfather, although breathless, was calling his name, trying to reach out to him. He stood from the seat he had taken only minutes before and approached his grandfather. Before he could reach him a huge shape created a barrier. A burly constable had pushed his way into the room and assessing the scene in seconds, grabbed Fergus. Without speaking, he manhandled him from the room.

Fergus was powerless in the grip of the burly copper but tried to reach out to his grandson. His breath had deserted him and he could only mouth his name silently.

Jobe recognised his name on his grandfather's lips and latched on to him in a futile, one-sided tug of war that was over in a second.

Pins broke from the gloom of the barracks and into the early morning sun. He couldn't envisage the short walk to the Main Bridewell posing any significant problems. The family inside had been more concerned with ministering to the woman, his prisoner's wife he assumed, and her not insignificant injuries. Only the scrawny boy who had attempted to hold on to the old man had followed him out of the tenement and still lagged behind. He decided there would be no need for a wagon. He would deposit the prisoner at the Main Bridewell before returning to the scene and carrying out his investigations. It would probably be a good idea to bring along an inspector as, from what he'd been able to take in, it seemed likely the investigation would turn into that of a murder. Those meandering the streets barely registered the unremarkable sight of a drunk being escorted to the cells to sleep it off. Pins was aware that the culprit serenely accompanying him to Cheapside didn't smell of alcohol and although distant was walking steadily enough. They were making good progress and he wondered if he could get any sense out of him that he could impart to the desk sergeant. He loosened the heavy armlock he had initially applied.

"What's it all about then, eh?" he asked with as much good nature as he could muster. The prisoner remained detached and Pins decided to try another avenue. He manhandled the prisoner so that he looked back on the road they had taken and the boy who remained on their trail.

"Who's the lad?" he asked. He was unprepared for the sudden paroxysm that shook the perpetrator's body as he made a bid to break free of the loose hold. Pins reapplied his initial armlock with even more pressure.

"Woah, woah calm yourself or I'll hurt yer! What is it, you looking at bashing his head in as well?" His prisoner slumped at the words and he was forced again to loosen his restraint to prevent snapping the prisoner's arm as he collapsed to the ground. Pins could have kicked himself for initialising the investigation rather than just getting his compliant prisoner, who was shouting now in a hoarse voice, to the clink.

"Jobe, Jobe come here son." Pins sensed the old man he held up was unravelling. His legs had completely given out and his eyes and facial expression implied that his mental state was becoming detached from reality. Pins knew it was only the boy he could entreat. He looked up at him.

"You! Away now!" He scolded belligerently. The tone he used was usually enough to disperse an aggressive group of cornermen but had no effect on the boy.

"Away with you I say, go on, beat it," he said again as he drew his truncheon in mock threat.

"Is it a lick of this you're wanting, because it's what's in store for you." Pins ground his teeth. The spectacle was attracting a crowd and he despaired at his decision to initiate his cack-handed inquiries. He turned his frustration on the spectators that had gathered on the crossroads that linked Vauxhall Road, Hatton Garden, Tithebarn and Great Crosshall Streets.

"Beat it the lot of you, now," he snarled. Those not used to dealing with officers of the law meekly continued on their way but those who had a regular brush with Pins and his colleagues remained unfazed and with no other pressing business to attend to were becoming an obstruction. The reputation of the bear of a copper ensured that nobody intervened physically or even verbally but he couldn't be sure how long that would remain the case. He had dealt with a similar sized crowd a few months back in Sawney Pope Street. Breaking up a game of pitch and toss he had suddenly found himself surrounded by a pack of belligerent youths intent on recouping the handful of coins he had scooped up off the ground. He was relatively new to the Holy Cross beat and knew it was imperative to show these kids, who were only ragamuffins after all, that he couldn't be cowed. A few insults, quickly followed by missiles, had been launched in his direction. He responded to neither, but on seeing a number of newcomers removing heavy buckled belts he knew the time for self-preservation had arrived. He toppled the nearest agitator and picking him up by the ankles spun him like a dervish. Those that were not skittled on to their backsides fled from the possessed copper, their pennies a distant memory.

He chided himself. He didn't have a prisoner, possibly a murderer, in custody at the time, one he was still supporting from slumping to the ground.

The man's head had dropped to his chest and Pins wondered if he were drunk after all, his mind telling him one thing, his nose another. Many were the times he had physically dragged a prisoner to the Bridewell by a foot, but it didn't seem proper with this one. He looked the suspect over, checking for lice before, decision made, he hoisted him over his shoulder and continued on his way to Cheapside. The spectacle over, the crowd dispersed of its own accord; only Jobe was left to follow. The weight of the prisoner was negligible and Pins' long strides had him approaching the nick in no time. As he inwardly chastised himself he paid no heed to the boy trailing in his wake.

Jobe tore down the remainder of Cheapside and along the intimidating wall of the Bridewell, reaching the only entrance just in time for the heavy, almost medieval, wooden door to slam in his face. Jobe sank to his knees, forlornly banging his fists against the door.

The women of the court had shown their disdain for the new cellar-dwellers by withholding from them the habitual warm welcome reserved for newcomers. No well-wishers had appeared at the door before his mother had a chance to unpack or sweep the miserable room, as was customary, neither was there anybody looking to borrow a pan or a penny or those looking to sign her up to the many subscriptions that ran continuously in the courts. The collectors of the funds to bury a child who had just died in one of the top rooms, the raffle to win a pig which was at that very moment being fattened in one of the tenements and the collectors of the penny funeral fund were all conspicuous by their absence. Even those in perpetual search for a new pot-pal, someone who would be able to chip in and make up the price of a jug of ale to share, remained aloof.

His mother had taken the ostracism well, expected it and explained to Jobe that the slums had their own systems and hierarchies every bit as complicated and convoluted as those of the Houses of Parliament. "They hated me for having the affront to escape the drudgery of the slums, Jobe," she had said. "The fact that your father is a Protestant only fuelled their resentment, but they'll soon come around," she added. The priest had mirrored his flock's lack of Christian charity; there would be no example of turning the other cheek or celebrating the return of the prodigal daughter from his pulpit.

"The shame of the returning, would-be mobily upward pervert is a lesson to us all" he had preached on hearing of her return to the parish. His mother had found it difficult to swallow.

"Father Connor baptised me, gave me my first communion and confirmed me. Have I ever forgotten my orders? Did I ever miss a single mass in

St Francis'! A mobily upward pervert? For Heaven's sake!"

The lack of opportunity to contribute to the penny fund had also incensed her.

"The penny fund'll be of no use to us Jobe, praise the Good Lord, but the biggest fear of those around here is not for that of themselves or one of their own dying, but that they'll find nowhere to spend eternity but in a pauper's grave." She made the sign of the cross before continuing.

"If they won't take my money now then I'll ensure they can't ignore my contribution when your father comes for us, it'll be enough to pay for the next half dozen funerals."

Jobe placed the bread back on the table without taking a bite from it. His mother now lay in the shell of a temporary coffin that Aggie Keogh had presumably sent for. The women had dressed his mother and said that now, in peace, she had something of her former beauty. Jobe couldn't see it. It was his mother's vitality and spirit that had made her beautiful; what he saw now was nothing more than the coffin she lay in, a shell.

"Your mother wasn't in the penny club Jobe, but I can arrange for Father Connor to contact the parish." Jobe looked at the two white fivers that Aggie had lay on the table as she gave him the piece of bread.

"Will that be enough?" he asked.

"Jobe, that is all you have in the world, that and her ring, you're going to need it. I could try and see what a collection would fetch if you don't want a pauper's…a parish funeral. Your mother was very well thought of…" Jobe looked Aggie Keogh in the eye.

"…in the end," she tailed off under his scrutiny.

"I want the money used to provide the best funeral it can and I want you to see to it that the ring is buried with her," he said. Aggie Keogh looked at the boy who had taken on the countenance of a man and although she knew the ring must be worth five times the amount of money on the table, she didn't argue. News of Fergus' arrest and Nell's demise had spread like wildfire.

"What will you do now son?" she asked. He looked at Aggie and softened, she owed him nothing and yet here he was sitting in her room.

"Can you see what price my school things'll fetch Mrs Keogh."

Jobe's neck involuntarily concertinaed in a futile attempt to burrow further into the muffler that protected his neck and face from the sub-zero conditions. The stand for the Waterloo Dock was positioned outside the dock wall, next to the majestic turrets that held the gates in place.

The March winds had blown into April and the protection the wall offered from the biting, incoming gusts from Liverpool Bay was diluted by the gale it channelled the length of the dock road. The stand had no covering and the dockers who converged on it, like those at every other stand, were exposed to whatever the elements threw at them.

Old hands burrowed themselves into the throng of humanity, shielding themselves from the worst of the gale. The two distinct class of dock labourer stood together under the leaden sky. Lumpers and stevedores, responsible for unloading incoming ships or loading outgoing ones respectively, mingled with the porters whose responsibilities included weighing, marking and stowing the incoming goods. Indiscriminate from each other as they stood stamping feet and rubbing hands, swapping gossip, tobacco and snippets of information regarding incoming vessels, what loads they carried and where they would be berthing. As newcomers Jobe and his cousin Michael found themselves squeezed out to the fringes, adrift from the collective warmth and the invaluable intelligence.

Although the still dark sky showed no hint of colour the stand was already crammed with between one hundred and fifty and two hundred men. The relative calm and goodwill of the men gathered would degenerate into a haphazard melée when the first of the foremen appeared at the gates. Conversations would be ended mid-sentence as the stevedores, lumpers and porters separated into their specific groups. Mufflers would be pulled down and cap peaks raised as men stretched up on their tiptoes, grabbing their neighbours' shoulders for added leverage in an attempt to make themselves visible. The foreman's beady stare raked over the mob as he feigned ignorance of the shouts of the men. He would settle his gaze, lock eyes with individual dockers, inspiring a split-second of euphoria, before moving on without acknowledgement, revelling in the part he played in the pantomime that played out before him. The calls for his attention became more frantic and friend elbowed friend in a desperate attempt to gain an advantage. Growing bored, the foreman would give those he had recognised and selected from the outset a curt nod. Transgressions would be forgotten as those selected readjusted their scarves and made their way to the gate. Those who were unknown would only be acknowledged if there was a ship with a quick turnaround, or one full of perishables that had arrived to the dock late, generating a pressing need for men.

The arrest of their grandfather had resulted in the easy employment he had promised the two boys failing to materialise and they trudged the length of the North Docks in an attempt to find work. Only on occasions when considerable numbers of men were summoned inside the gates would the cousins, along with the still drunk, simple, old and infirm who haunted the fringes of the stand with them, get the opportunity to advance close enough to the gates to see a foreman up close. Even then, among the dregs, Jobe, given his age and diminutive stature, would remain unseen. Michael, unlike his cousin, took after his father Bog for size, and looking like the best choice of a bad lot would sometimes be taken on. He would wink at Jobe and strut through the gate, entering into the clandestine world of the docks in the wake of the old hands.

The Waterloo Dock foremen hired men notoriously early. Scallywags quipped this was to ensure the foremen could afford the time for the spectacle of a fist-fight or two to break out before taking on. The positive of the early draft was that the men who found themselves on the wrong side of the creaking dock gates as they were pulled shut still had a glimmer of hope that they could make one of the neighbouring stands before the foremen had recruited for the day. Those with an abundance of optimism would race off, dodging through the traffic, oblivious to the fact that their last-minute appearance would severely hamper their chances. Men that didn't share their optimism or have the energy or compunction to go haring along the Dock Road would laugh as they watched them while contemplating what their next move would be.

There was always the chance of being taken on at an afternoon stand. This offered a second chance at selection but for those not local entailed traversing the Dock Road for the entirety of the morning in freezing conditions in a usually forlorn attempt at earning a half-day's pay. Those with a few coppers burning a hole in their pocket found the lure of a blazing coal fire and a pint or two was too much to ignore and sloped off into one of the multitude of taverns that littered the Dock Road. Once the escapism of a few pints was tempered by the reality of empty pockets they would stagger back into the cold armed with a drunken optimism that the second stand would replenish their misspent coppers. Those physically exhausted from middle of the night rousings and multiple-mile walks, mentally exhausted by the constant rejections, would stride off without looking back, beginning the long journey home, each step heightening the dread of their children's disappointed, hungry eyes and the resentful, baleful looks from their wives that would be enough to make them repeat the cycle the next morning. Jobe, with nowhere else to go, would bury his face further into his muffler and head down, shoulders hunched, roam the Dock Road in the hope of gleaning some positive news regarding the second stands.

The striking men, on their return to the stands, had initially struggled to get taken on by the resentful, spiteful ship-owners and their foremen. The knobsticks, outsiders shipped in from other ports, and scabs that broke the strike had learned their roles well during the five weeks of industrial action. On occasions those who had blacklegged during the strike found themselves working next to the unionists who had threatened and abused them as they crossed the picket lines. The number of accidents and injuries suffered by the scabs rocketed. As the wounded were led off with a bleeding head or stretchered away with a crushed leg there would invariably be a docker with outstretched arms pleading his innocence.

"The rope just snapped." "My hook slipped." "That rigging must be faulty."

The scabs and knobsticks held an impromptu meeting, the result of which was categorical. They must protect themselves. Wasn't it them who ensured the docks continued to operate during the union strikes? The ship owners would realise their predicament and show empathy. They would strike. The unionised men had been re-employed en masse. Hearing that the scabs had the temerity to go out on strike and seeing their scantily manned picket lines had caused the first glimmer of a smile to cross Jobe's face since his mother's death and grandfather's subsequent incarceration.

"Jesus, Jobe, that's the first time I've ever seen you smile,' his cousin Michael had exclaimed while they waited under a sky that was just beginning to show a hint of colour. That had been almost a month ago and Jobe had still not managed a single shift.

The winter assizes were held in St George's Hall. Jobe had never been inside the grand building. He sat alone in the gallery, the demise of his grandmother doing little to end the ostracism she had imposed upon him. His extended family, taking up the majority of the public benches, behaved as if he didn't exist. Even Michael, in the presence of his parents, had ignored him. The rest of the benches were filled with familiar faces from the parish, a number of them rustling bags of toffee they had purchased from McGhee's Confectioners on Great Crosshall Street on their way to the court.

The prosecutor for the Crown had urged the jury to reach a verdict of murder, as in the eyes of the law, a mother and grandmother had been killed by an unlawful act of violence.

"It remains murder," he concluded. "Regardless of the human emotion surrounding events. For this reason the prisoners life must be forfeit."

Jobe had watched his grandfather throughout. He seemed tiny in the large semi-circle dock were up to twenty or more defendants could be tried at once. Nothing that was said, either in accusation against him or in defence of him seemed to register.

Dr Commins, acting for his grandfather, had summed up by imploring the jury to be mindful of the fact that Fergus was an upstanding, hardworking member of the community.

"This was not a wife who was repeatedly stretchered to the infirmary, forced to call on the local constable for protection or reduced to a drudge by a brutal and tyrannical husband. This was a wife who felt the love of a good man, good husband and good father. As the prosecutor himself has stated, there was no premeditation involved here, no drink-fuelled spite, no murderous intention, just a freak blow, doled out spontaneously, while in the very deepest pit of despair. A despair brought about by the loss of a cherished only daughter."

Judge Justice Day sitting straight as a board throughout, ensconced in polished oak and every bit as intimidating as the Aberdeen Granite pillars that dominated the court looked down at the shadow of the man in the dock and informed him that although there was no excuse or justification for murder the immense emotional components of the case that had made the accused indifferent to all consequences bound him to accept the lesser charge of manslaughter the jury had arrived at.

He left Fergus and those observing under no illusion that, if it was not for the deluge of tragedy and raw human emotion that engulfed events pertaining to the case he would have had no qualms or doubts about donning his black cap before passing sentence. Jobe got the impression that the judge was disappointed there would be no opportunity to theatrically pull on his black cap and condemn his grandfather. He couldn't help feeling that the gallows would have been quicker and more humane than the three years hard labour his grandfather had been sentenced to.

He looked back at the picket line again, unconsciously shaking his head. The crowd began to swell as men shifted their positions and Jobe didn't need to stand on his tiptoes to know that a group of men had appeared at the gate, clipboards in hand.

Molloy looked down the road. He was beginning to think that maybe Jobe had finally been taken on when he saw his slight frame turn into the street. He shook his head and readjusted his new boots before setting off to meet his friend.

"I don't know why you bother Jobe, if your shiteing face doesn't fit there's nothing down for yer. Especially if you look as if you weigh no more than a shiteing docker's hook." Jobe shook his head; half of it remained buried in his muffler. He was frozen through. He had watched as Michael had, once again, sauntered through the Waterloo Dock gates, this time without looking back at him. Jobe, as usual, had walked the length of the docks and then tried again at the afternoon stand. All to no avail.

"Look at yer, shivering, you'll freeze to death before you get a shiteing start, and I suppose that shiteing cousin of yours got took on," Molloy cursed.

Jobe began to reply and realised his muffler was distorting his words. He pulled it down, his face raw where it had been rubbing.

"It's a good thing that Michael's getting work, he says he'll let the foreman know that we're both Fergus Flynn's grandsons," he explained. Molloy spat into the gutter.

"Pah, you can't be trusting that shiteing little shite Jobe, he'd sell you out for a ha'penny." Jobe couldn't help smiling at Molloy's ire. He continued. "When're yer going to see shiteing sense and follow me into the gang?" He took a step back so that Jobe could appraise him fully.

"Look at me, new hat, new boots, new strides, why me belt alone is worth a day down the shiteing docks. You'd be a dead cert Jobe, yer brains are worth more than all of our brawn put together." Jobe shook his head.

"It's not for me Molloy. Taking from folk who've less than us doesn't appeal to me."

"Are you shiteing blind Jobe, there's nobody with less than you," Molloy pulled a bundle of tickets from his pocket.

"Where would you be without these?" He peeled a ticket from the stack and held it out for Jobe. Jobe took the ticket and read it. It was a carbon copy of those Molloy had already given him but it gave Jobe an escape from his friend's accusing eyes.

'LEE JONES' FOOD AND BETTERMENT SOCIETY'

One Night's Admittance to the

Marybone Homeless Shelter

"I've enough of these to keep a roof over your head for the next twelve months," continued Molloy as he flicked the tickets with his thumb. "But is that what you want for yourself Jobe, to be sleeping among the shiteing penny hangovers?"

Jobe folded the ticket into his pocket. Before Molloy had, by whatever means, acquired the bundle of priceless admittance chits that ensured he would have a roof over his head each night, Jobe had, on more than one occasion, spent the night strung up against one of the penny hangovers. Those unfortunates who were not deemed deserving or desperate enough by the army of volunteers who scoured the slums handing out chits entitling the bearer to a bowl of soup, a pallet and a coarse blanket on the packed floors of the Marybone shelter were not entirely ignored by Lee Jones's charity. The opportunity to purchase a penny hangover was always on offer.

On the first of these occasions, following a bowl of hot soup, Jobe was intrigued to be led down a dank set of narrow stairs into the bowels of the shelter to the entrance of a damp, low-ceilinged room that was perfectly square and had what appeared to be high backed church pews against each of the walls. On arriving at the entrance to the cellar the men, and surprisingly more than a few girls, were informed that it was imperative to retain an orderly line. Despite this the line disintegrated before long as men and women jockeyed for position. It reminded Jobe of the melée on the stand and he was bemused by the obvious determination and desperation to be first into the room. A minor scuffle broke out, more verbal than physical, and a voice that startled Jobe boomed out.

"Anybody judged to be cajoling or causing consternation will be escorted from the premises. Pennies will not be refunded!" Following this directive the dishevelled queue regained a semblance of order. On being allowed into the room and finding a seat on one of the unforgiving benches Jobe instantly understood the clamour to be among the first to reach the pews. The lucky few were already rolling up rags they had secreted somewhere on their person to use as pillows on the overhanging ends of the benches whereas Jobe and his peers who found themselves with a neighbour on each side had no option but to remain stiffly facing forwards.

When everybody was in place, crammed shoulder to shoulder, a dwarf entered the room. His large head seemed to heavy for his body and swayed precariously from side to side with each step. Four pieces of rope trailed behind him, each one as thick as his forearm. One after the other the ropes were stretched across the benches at a height so arms could be draped over them and the ropes secured from one end to the other. After completing his task with well-worn practice the bulbous-headed dwarf surveyed those seated with a scowl, as if daring someone to raise a complaint. Content that his captives were secure he stomped out of the room. The sound of his heavy footsteps ascending the staircase dissipated and men and women began to writhe and wriggle, to the chagrin of their neighbours, in a futile attempt to gain an inch more space, which might afford them even a modicum of comfort.

Jobe could never have envisaged such a reality. He was amazed to find that as well as the usual suspects, the drunkards, vagabonds and beggars who he was expecting, there were working men, their clothes betraying their profession. Painters' overalls, porters' coats and even a postman in full uniform were draped over the ropes. The women scattered about the benches offered no outrage to the fact that they were sandwiched between two men and focused only on finding the comfort that would prepare them for sleep. Jobe knew with certainty that his penny would only serve to keep him warm and dry, there was no chance he would be visited by the luxury and escape of sleep in such circumstances. The man immediately next to him had already slumped forward and only his rhythmic breathing indicated that he was still alive. Jobe woke with a start the next morning among a writhing and wriggling mass of humanity who, like him, had pitched forward on to the cold floor when the rope supporting them had been cut without warning.

"It is five o clock in the morning," the dwarf called in his booming voice as he stomped from the room, a huge pair of scissors in one hand and the trailing ropes in the other. Jobe looked up at Molloy. "It's only until I get myself fixed down the docks Mol," he said. Molloy softened his tone.

"I look up this street at the same time day after day, hoping that I won't see you coming down it. That you'll have been took on for the day and my waiting'll be in vain and I'll only be ordering one plate of bacon and eggs from Ma Boyle. I'm sure that if you got a day you'd be running the whole of the docks by the end of it but it's never happened Jobe, not once, and it's not going to," he said with finality. Jobe looked up at his only friend in the world, he never ceased to surprise him.

"You're still standing the shiteing bacon and eggs though;" he grinned.

★ ★ ★ ★ ★

Jobe looked round, estimating his odds against the bedraggled crowd standing around the Stanley

Dock gate. He actually fancied his chances of getting a day's work. The stand was heavily populated as usual, but the main body of fit and able men was missing. In all likelihood they where at another stand were it was known the need for hands was high. Jobe, although hopeful of being selected in their absence, cursed that he wasn't privy to the information that rippled between those in the know. Union buttons and badges were slowly superseding the secret handshakes and passwords that had been prevalent throughout the century but the priceless information was no more forthcoming because of it.

The opportunity to push through a mass of elderly, infirm and still drunk men was one that had never presented itself before. Jobe slunk his way through what would usually be an invisible barrier jealously guarded by elbows, cursed warnings and on occasion fists, until only a couple of rows of men stood between him and the dock gate which was creaking open. The foreman weighed up the rabble with undisguised disappointment. He visualised his cut-off line markedly and Jobe reckoned, with rising excitement, that he was easily within it. The foreman's right hand blurred like that of an orchestra conductor and within seconds a dozen men had been selected from the ranks Jobe stood in. The foreman's hand came to a pause and he surveyed those in front of him. He dipped an index finger at Jobe but before he could act on the command a group of thirty-odd men burst from

Lightbody Street and sprinted towards the stand. The foreman, his index finger still lingering over Jobe, raised his left hand to counter the decree.

Jobe ignored the obvious excitement of those who pushed past him and on through the dock gate at the behest of the visibly relieved foreman. Their hysterical babble made no mark on his conscience.

"Did you see the little bastard I clobbered, he'll not remember his name for a week."

"The little shite won't be lurking in the shadows for a while, that's for sure." Jobe wheeled away from the gate before it could come to a shuddering halt in his face. It was time to submit to his friend's constant badgering.

Molloy led him through an abandoned, ramshackle house, the smell of frying sausages wafting from somewhere within.

"They're a shiteing hard bunch mind Jobe, so don't get nervous or worried, you're with me and that's enough," he said as he removed a tar-stained board and ducked through a hole in the middle of what would have been the parlour wall. The hole led them into a room that was warm and well furnished. A huge pan of sausages sat precariously on a bent and rusting stove sizzling and spitting away. Jobe didn't notice any of it. Lounging around the room was a group of boys, a good number of who were nursing injuries of varying degrees. Molloy stood gaping, for once lost for words. Jobe wasted no time in assessing the situation, and having made a visual scan of the bloodied noses, blackening eyes and possible broken bones approached a boy who had a lump that was almost an exact replica of his bulbous nose, protruding from the dead centre of his forehead. He appeared to be drifting off to sleep.

"Ho! Ho! C'mon now, wake up, that's it, look at me! How many fingers am I holding up?" he shouted into the boy's face as he knelt in front of him. Jobe's words shook Molloy from his trance.

"What in the name of Mary and shiteing Joseph has happened here?" he asked in a whisper.

"I'll tell you what's happened," said a young man sitting in a high-backed Chesterfield chair. He held a blood-soaked rag to a cut on the side of his face but still managed to look composed and authoritative.

"Check the sausages Rodger," he motioned to a boy before continuing.

"We were ambushed by the Logwood Gang, that's what happened, sneaky bunch of motherless bastards that they are. We gave a good account of ourselves though, isn't that right boys!" The proclamation was met with muted groans of pain and sniffling. He rose from his chair.

"The fight'll go down in history," he roared as he shadow-boxed in a neat circle, his dirty rag flapping about.

"The Battle of Silvester Street they'll call it, like something from the Crimea it was." He looked around, noticing the lack of enthusiasm for his words and feints and sat down again clutching the rag to his open cheek. He gestured to the boy poking at the sausages to dole them out. Jobe, having ensured that a relatively unharmed boy sitting next to his patient understood his orders not to let him drift off to sleep, stood and looked at the boy in the chair who had just taken first pick of the sausages. He was among the smallest in the room and although his face was pinched and wizened, it projected a jocular, mischievous quality while his penetrating eyes brimmed with intelligence.

"The Logwood Gang? Isn't that just a name for a group of working men, dockers in the main, who refuse to allow the High Rip to take their hard-won wages without a fight?" he asked blithely. Molloy shook his head and put it in his hands, looking at his cousin in the Chesterfield chewing on a sausage and looking at his accuser philosophically. He took another bite of his sausage and having chewed and swallowed it slowly, dabbed at his lips with an imaginary handkerchief.

"And who, may I ask, are you?"

"My name is Jobe, pleased to make your acquaintance," replied Jobe, holding out his hand with a smile. After a second the young man stood, and took the proffered hand with a smile of his own.

"I'm Silky, honoured I'm sure."

Molloy blinked unbelievingly on hearing his cousin, Silky's, response.

"At last I can get rid of these shiteing Lee Jones chits, Joe Kilbane has been pestering me for them for an age. He can have the shiteing lot for tuppence a go!" he pronounced gleefully to nobody in particular. Silky looked at his foul-mouthed cousin quizzically before returning his attention to Jobe.

"And the High Rip as you call them don't exist, there's no such gang. They're a figment of a newsman's imagination, something to strike ghoulish fear into their readership. Of course I won't deny using the call from time to time. It's been a useful concoction to me and my boys."

The dilapidated house served as home to the majority of the Blackstock Street Boys. Even those who had somewhere to call home would, more often than not, spend their nights in The Den. In the weeks that followed Jobe became accustomed to their habits of sitting late into the night and sleeping late into the day although he didn't partake in their heavy consumption of alcohol or their equally extensive tobacco smoking. Their late nights were often dictated by the kind of crimes, what Silky would allude to as 'jobs', they were undertaking at any given time, although a good proportion of the jobs were carried out in broad daylight. All the while Jobe was appraising every facet of the gang's operations.

Silky listened to his proposals, even evolving some of them, with good grace, but remained sceptical of the new direction Jobe advocated for the gang.

"What's the boys' biggest fear?" he asked the three lads who sat around the unsteady table. Silky had decided that Jobe's ideas needed further discussion. Understanding that The Den was refuge to the majority of his boys he never ordered anybody out so that he could think or speak, instead preferring to go on walks, or as on this occasion, retreat to one of the snugs in Ma Shanks. His trusted lieutenants Molloy and Face were invited along to discuss Jobe's ideas.

"Coppers," they all replied at once.

"Not the ones who're content to give you a lick of their truncheon and send you on your way, no it's the jobsworths who'll drag you to the Bridewell and see you before the Madge," Face elaborated. Jobe still couldn't help staring at Face whenever the opportunity arose. Molloy had informed him that nobody, not even Face himself, could remember his real name. Some buck had christened him Face at the Window from an early age and he now went by the simple abbreviation of Face. So unfortunate were his squashed and upturned features, the tip of his nose pointing towards his right ear so that the left side of his face appeared flat, his left nostril became an enormous black hole in the middle of his face, as large as one of his eyes, that he constantly resembled a hungry boy pressed up against a baker's window as if attempting to smell and taste the wares on offer through the glass itself.

"And who is it that supplies the police, the Madges and the courts with the information and evidence that condemns us?" Jobe didn't wait for a reply.

"The people, that's who, despite your best efforts to cow and intimidate them, there's always one morally upstanding citizen, and there always will be!" The three boys around the table looked at each other nodding. There was no disputing Jobe's logic.

"So don't you see the answer? he asked. His three companions looked at him, blankly, inviting one.

"Rather than take what little those around us have, we give! Rather than bully and harass, we support and we help! We look after the people, which in turn gives them a reason to look after us." Face was mortified, unable to stop his mouthful of beer from spraying out of his lopsided mouth, which contorted to such an angle that the spray shot vertically, straight into his own eye, almost blinding him. He wiped and blinked away the beer as he roared his umbrage at Jobe's plan.

"So you're saying that not only should we stop taking what we want, from who we want, but what we do take we give away?" He asked incredulously. Silky took a deft swig of his pint, smacking his lips loudly as he swallowed. He held up a hand to his friend.

"Just a mo' now Face, I sense your ire, but indulge me if you will," Face brought his hands to his eyes. He knew Silky had heard something of influence.

"Say it was to transpire that you found yourself in front of the Beak with a charge sheet as long as this arm, your name dotted all over it," Silky held out his silk-clad arm and began tapping his finger at certain points, as if to illustrate Face's name on the imaginary charge sheet.

"Oh he's just itching to sentence you to twelve of the best and a good spell in the Kirkdale, but, shock horror," Silky camply brought his index knuckle to his mouth and bit on it.

"There's nobody on the witness stand to describe or testify to your villainous acts! Oh my, the Madge is in a right pickle now isn't he? You're on the stand smiling and waving to your friends and family, readying yourself to be reacquainted with their joyfully accepting bosoms. The Madge is beginning to feel a prickly heat, he's almost passing out with rage, but hang on a mo', he's gone and forgot all about his loyal boys in blue, his good old friends from the constabulary, who now, together and

181

in unison, concoct a way of snapping you away from the warm bosom of your friends and family, dragging you back, kicking and screaming from the sunny jaws of freedom and locking you away in Kirkdale with a back that's been striped by a dozen!" Silky had brought both Face and Molloy to the edge of their seats with his imagery, before sending them slumping back to their seats as if they themselves were waiting for a meat wagon to transport them along Stanley Road to the gaol. He let the pain of the imagined defeat sink in before continuing.

"Now let's imagine the scene again, our friend the Madge has got a witness on the stand, but rather than each nod of their head condemning you to another lash they're telling his honour how you couldn't have been involved in the frightful acts the constable has described because all the time you'd been unblocking their stove pipe or manfully struggling along with a peck of potatoes on your back, reducing the suffering of the chronic rheumatism that haunts their nights and blights their days, why he deserves a medal, not a whipping Your Honour!" He finished his dramatics and addressed Face directly.

"Can't you see it Face, if there's anything in what Little Jobe here says we can turn the snitching slobs into alibis! They'll become an insulating layer between the coppers and us. It won't just be The Den that'll be our lair, it'll be every street in the Parish," he beseeched.

Face could see the logic behind the argument but was afraid of ceding ground to the little snot-rag who had only just come among them.

"Pah, it's all a load of my arse, there'd be no end to what the mugs around here would want from us, all they'd do is take and take and take! Well, they'll be getting none of my share, that's for sure," he vented. Molloy, who had been an observer throughout, became suddenly animated. Silky jumped back in mock fright.

"It'll shiteing work, it has shiteing worked…he's done it before," he stammered, before launching into an account of how Jobe had become a hero of the courts by doing nothing more than making a few gas-lamps glow a little brighter.

For Jobe's hopes to become reality it was imperative there was a peace with the Logwood Gang. He was well versed in the injustices faced by those who earned their living on the docks. His grandfather's stories and opinions had been the beginning of his education but his own time spent on the stand had left him only too aware of the unrest and chagrin of the long abused workers. The Logwood Gang were primarily organised for defence but were not averse to carrying out reprisals against any youngsters they thought may be affiliated to or part of the High Rip, and although they made efforts to retain an element of anonymity Jobe was aware of more than a few who participated in the loose vigilantism.

The industrial discontent that had threatened to blossom for so many years eventually bloomed and took root in its spiritual home on the docks. Issues of pay and conditions temporarily diluted the sectarian troubles that plagued the city. Hundreds attended the meetings organised by union firebrands such as James Sexton, returning to the courts and pubs with details of strikes that were taking place in Southampton, Bristol and London. The general consensus was that another strike would soon be called in Liverpool.

The National Union of Dockers League was predominantly made up of unskilled Catholics. Members of the Logwood Gang would inevitably be among the numbers. They had been formed by groups of dockers and other workers for their own protection. For years gangs of youths had found sailors and dockers, foreign and domestic, easy pickings and plagued them. The shriek of 'Highhhhh Riiiippppp' became synonymous with having up to a dozen miniature raptors emerging from the shadows swinging pipes, knives and belts. Even the most hardened of dockers was vulnerable to having their hard-earned wages, and anything else of value, stolen while leaving them in such a state that there would be no chance of earning for a long time to come. Just another injustice to be borne by the honest and hardworking.

He utilised the solidarity of the meetings to approach various individuals, brokering a parley and informing the sceptical dockers that his gang were not only exploring differing ventures but were also eager to atone for mistakes of their past, namely, the mistreatment of their hardworking neighbours and comrades. The meeting took place on the outskirts of a dockers' meeting. There had been a pause in the discussions in order to listen to an address from James Sexton. On applauding Sexton as he stepped off the gantry Jobe added the caveat that the truce didn't hold for child and wife beaters. The dockers were incensed.

"Who d'you think you are to instruct a man on how to treat his wife, it's nothing more than a ploy that'd leave most men open to your filching, filthy little fists," came the retorts. Jobe was adamant. The majority of boys who sought the safety and security of The Den had fled from beatings doled out by violent fathers, uncles, lovers or customers of their mothers. They revelled in the opportunity of returning the savage beatings to men who wore the same filthy moleskin trousers and dirty jackets as their own assailants. The sour smell of stale ale was so redolent that they could close their eyes and imagine they were returning the spite in full.

"Then they'll mend their ways! Any wives or mothers who're carted off to the Northern in the middle of the night will wake the next morning to find their husband is in the next bed to them, with injuries thrice as grievous." Jobe's demeanour, added to the fact that he had sought the men out alone, lent gravity to his words. The men looked among themselves.

The gang were unhappy with the development, not only at seeing one of their most lucrative and relatively risk-free lines of operation closed off but also because there would be no more of the punishment beatings that offered them, unaware of it as they were, a cathartic release from past violence.

Silky sat in his high-backed Chesterfield attempting to fix a gold-rimmed monocle into his right eye as he addressed the gang.

"The Logwood Gang are becoming more of a threat to us every-day, they're showing people round here that we're not infallible. The scream of High Rip won't cut it any more."

"Look what happened on Silvester Street a few months back! Why, it's only a matter of time before they come charging in here with their four-be-twos! There'll be new jobs that won't just yield enough for the odd pint and pan of sausages, times are changing and it's us that are changing them." He finally mastered the monocle and, theatrically screwing his left eye shut, surveyed his compatriots through it as if inviting their defiance.

The new peace with the Logwood Gang paid dividends from the off. Their inside knowledge of what was transpiring on each dock provided the gang with unprecedented yields while at the same time reducing the risks involved. The initial discomfort that the gang felt about the truce with their enemies was soon appeased.

Docks could be targeted with a precision that negated the randomness, risk and waste of effort associated with pilfering from a random cart, or dockside. The certainty of yields gave fresh impetus to the effort put into the planning of jobs. It had always been a loose railing, crumbling wall or laxly guarded dock that dictated their targets, but furnished with knowledge Jobe and Silky were able to formulate plans on how to access specific wharfs.

Never one to overlook ability it was Silky who had hit on the idea of hiring boats and utilising the sailing skills a number of the gang had accrued while serving time aboard the Catholic Floating Reformatory Ship *Clarence*. Under cover of darkness, and using stealth, a tiny fleet of rowboats could cruise straight into the mouth of a dock before leaving in the same way laden with ill-gotten and lucrative spoils. The ease of their piracy resulted in an over- exuberance that became their only adversary. Soaking feet quickly becoming wet calves, signalled that a boat's weight capacity had been overloaded and precious cargo had to be thrown overboard before they were scuppered and sunk by their own greed.

The education 'the sailors' had received on the *Clarence* was not infallible either, a fact that those charged with steering their mates to the plunder illustrated with a certain panache. It was such an occasion that sealed Jobe's fate.

All lamps had been covered as they approached the dock. River and sky merged into one, veiling the boat in complete darkness. The small boat suddenly shuddered, sending all hands pitching forward. It took a second for the initial furore on-board to subside; hissed insults informed them that they had collided with another vessel, bringing both boats to a grinding halt. The muted tirade aroused Jobe's suspicions. His mind spun, who else could be inching their way along the granite harbour wall in complete darkness? Another gang was imitating their unique ruse and he lifted his oil-lamp, illuminating the faces on the other boat. He would find out which of the Logwood Gang had betrayed their trust and there would be a heavy price to pay. His mind stumbled into incomprehension when he saw his cousin Michael staring back at him. It was only when he discerned the panic and the accents of those telling him to dim his light that he realised they had rammed a boat full of scabs bypassing a dock-gate picket and he dropped his lamp overboard with shock.

Jobe cancelled the planned job and judging by the direction the scab boat took he imagined their day's work had also been scuppered. The scabs on board probably thought they were union men intent on capsizing them. Jobe was totally estranged from his family and his move further along Vauxhall Road away from Marybone to The Den on Blackstock Street meant he didn't even see Michael in passing. To think that he had become a scab illustrated the complete breakdown which must have occurred within the family following the departure of his grandparents. Jobe mulled over the chance encounter but on deciding there was nothing he could do about it forced it from his mind, giving no further thought to his cousin's disposition.

Pins didn't resent having a larger than usual beat. As far as he was concerned it was a direct consequence of his ability to do his job, and anyway it wasn't as if he were forced to plod the whole lot of it. His patch overlapped that of other bobbies, his remit being to ensure his presence was felt in the largest possible locale. He was good at his job and everybody knew it, colleagues and crooks alike. He wasn't a notebook copper, not by any stretch. He understood that his job didn't just involve nabbing crooks to hand over to the Justices and Magistrates who sat in the their chambers oblivious to the trials and tribulations of real life. They couldn't remove the shadow of crime or fear of violence that hung over people's everyday lives like a heavy shawl. Just as they couldn't alleviate the poverty that it was born from. Sure he served up his fair share of scum to be sent down. The murderers, pimps and con artists were better behind bars than lurking on the streets. But why take the breadwinner from a family? He knew when his own rough justice was more conducive. The opportunistic thief. The drunk. The cornerman. The young hooligan. They just weren't worth the paper. A few cuffs around the head sufficed as a punishment and it had a less detrimental effect on the family. He'd seen too many wives and children who, innocent of any crime save being a dependant, were sentenced to a prolonged period of starvation before the Workhouse or death became the only choices.

He liked to think he made a small change to people's days, if not their lives, whether they knew it or not. Appreciated his efforts or hated him for them. He limited at least some of the negatives of people's lives, as only he could. But that was only part of his role. He put as much effort into getting to know which of the snot-nosed, scabby-kneed kids rolling in the gutters were particularly destitute as he put into catching criminals. Nobody in the force appropriated more chits from the Policemen's Benevolent Fund than he did. Every one of them would be distributed justly. He knew coppers who used the chits to curry favour in the community, not particularly bothered if they were going to those most in need or not. His were in no way intended as sweeteners to the desperate, but at times relationships made through them invariably did lead to information that he could use while doing his proper job.

One area that had transformed itself into a relative area of peace and tranquility was the usually notorious area within the triangle of Vauxhall Road, Marybone and Blackstock Street. There had been times he couldn't get out of the area, such was the deluge of incidents. But as if by a miracle reports of muggings, burglaries and violent crime had all but diminished overnight until they had become virtually non-existent. It had been an age since he had heard the slip-slap of bare feet on cobbles only to turn and be greeted by a wide-eyed child who, too breathless to speak, dragged at his sleeve in their desperation to get him to the room where their father was bashing in their mother's brain.

Dilapidated doors, behind which he knew anything but the cheapest bread was a luxury, were replaced with new ones and his nose twitched at the rich aroma of roasting joints of meat that wafted through them. The Benevolent Fund chits he collected in advance remained in his pocket for longer periods of time. Children who usually sat on sooty steps, too exhausted to play, so emaciated that he genuinely worried whether they'd still be alive on his next beat, frolicked in the gutter, the slight hint of colour in their cheeks lending them an almost healthy glow.

The St Patrick's Day festivities had been something to behold. The main roads remained untouched but it seemed that every street and court was decked out in green and white, each one having at least one trestle table that was laden with bread and butter and cakes. There was an air of true celebration and cheer rather than the usual simmering antagonism and encouraged hostility.

He was aware he had the natural and accepted arrogance of one who was head and shoulders above his peers professionally, but he wasn't so arrogant as to think he was behind the comparatively seismic changes, and he had no desire to begin enquiring or investigating what was behind the changes in fortune, happy that at least a small portion of his beat was prospering. Even the local hooligans were keeping themselves quiet and out of his way.

His shroud of self-imposed ignorance was ripped away by a snivelling wretch from Holy Cross.

"I recognise you, didn't I arrest your grandfather for the murder of your grandmother?" he'd asked.

"It was manslaughter," came the haughty reply. "I've got information that is watertight, it'll give you two gang leaders Jobe Warburton and Tommy Molloy."

He ended his shift early that day and made his way straight to the Steam Engine in Edge Hill, not far from where he lived. He drank so much that night he had to be carried home by the landlord and his son. But all to no avail. He woke the next morning having retained every particle of the information he had been fed. Regardless of the seemingly boundless benefits it was sowing for the downtrodden and desperate of his beat his professional conscience couldn't ignore direct evidence, especially regarding organised crime. He was amazed that kids, hooligans, could pull off anything so sophisticated.

Chapter VI

1891

The cutter pulled its way clear of the heavy river traffic, its single mast bereft of sails. The screeching gulls, intuiting that the small boat's wake would provide them with little opportunity of feeding, had long since circled away to follow the steamers that churned up the waters exposing a variety of marine life that were defenceless against their insatiable beaks. The tidal pull existing within the murky depths remained unrepresented on the placid surface and the boat cut serenely through the gentle surge.

Jobe felt his stomach rise and fall with each gentle ripple that slapped against the hull. Experiencing the individuality of each tiny swell he gritted his teeth against the urge to throw up. He imagined his internal organs tumbling about like apples and oranges in a Mary Ellen's basket. Six boys, no older than himself, battled manfully against the current. They seemed unperturbed by the surges and lifted the thick glistening oars with ease. The thick woollen guernseys they wore made them impervious to the freezing cold that numbed his exposed face and neck. The hems of their immaculate blue trousers somehow escaping the lagoon that sloshed about their ankles, soaking him to his calves. Their jauntily positioned glazed hats lent credence to their unruffled demeanour, remaining perfectly in place even though *his* head lolled about like a drunk sitting on the Sailors' Home steps.

He looked over to Molloy who he knew would be sat bent forward, head buried between his knees in an attempt to avoid the gut-wrenching effects the boat's movements were having on his stomach. Before their escapades with the gang Molloy had never so much as set foot on board a ferry to New Brighton for a Bank Holiday picnic. He was always ribbed mercilessly by the lads aboard the rowboat who revelled equally in another profitable raid and the lack of retribution his passive state afforded them.

"Ha, is that Tommy Molloy with his head bowed and his hands and eyes clasped tight?"

"Well, it's a bit late to be praying for your sins to be forgiven now, isn't it Molloy."

Jobe leant forward, his intention to mimic Molloy. As he placed his head between his knees he found his inner balance was so badly impaired that the small readjustment caused him to momentarily lose all kinetic cohesion and he pitched forward, sprawling uncontrollably into the midriff of one of the officers who traversed the boat as if on a Sunday stroll. The officer caught Jobe, cuffing him in the face before pushing him back to his bench. The blow contained enough strength to send his head reeling back but his face, numb from the cold, registered no pain. The slight tingling sensation that buzzed along his jaw-line as it began to swell was a source of distraction from the churning in his guts and he tried to focus his attention on it as he gripped his head with his knees.

Four officers moved about the cutter, each dressed in similar attire to the boys, although they wore blue jackets over their guernseys, each of the gilt buttons polished to such a shine that they managed to dazzle in the murky gloom of the Mersey. He felt the blood throbbing in his temples and although his new position didn't assuage his tumultuous stomach it at least reduced the chances of meeting one of the officers' eyes and receiving another thump for impertinence.

"Aye-aye what's all this shite? Are you taking us for shiteing O's now, is that it?" Jobe lifted his head on hearing Molloy's raised voice. He took an intake of breath. The cutter had come alongside an enormous square-rigger, its hull ascending into the sky. He'd seen hundreds if not thousands of ships, both at the docks and out on the Mersey, but being so close to the hulking entirety of a full rigged ship took his breath away. His awe was broken by Molloy's voice; a hint of anxiety had entered into it, causing it to break, transforming the shout to a shriek.

"Ho! You louse-ridden shiteing maggots we're not dirty O's I tell you! Why're we aside the *Akbar*? What's all this about, eh?" The four officers weighed

Molloy up. He was as big as any of them and Jobe could see they were loath to initiate a wrestling bout on board the cutter. A heavy rope ladder, thrown from the deck of the *Akbar*, crashed in to midships with a wet thump. One of the officers immediately reached for Jobe, grabbing him by the armpits and hoisting him into the air in one fluent movement. Jobe had a sickening sensation as he hung in mid-air. Time seemed to freeze as he looked down at the oarsmen back-rowing to maintain their position as the ravenous Mersey foamed between the two hulls. He flailed for the slick rope ladder which he caught hold of, immediately freezing into the foetal position. Molloy's inertia snapped on seeing Jobe thrown on to the ladder and he lurched up from the bench. His lack of sea legs was instantly apparent and he pitched forward. His panic to compensate caused him to topple backwards and he tottered, arms flailing, before landing in a heap.

The officers were quick to take advantage and as one, three of them sprang forward, landing on him in a flurry of knees and elbows. The fourth, after ensuring Molloy was sufficiently restrained, began to buffet Jobe around his haunches and backside forcing him to forgo the safety of his entwinement and climb the stinking, slippery rope. The battering to his legs continued until he reached a height that allowed the officer to begin his ascent behind him. The cessation of the beating to his legs and the added weight of the officer pulling the glistening rope ladder taut made it easier for Jobe to climb the thick but fraying rungs. He allowed a modicum of his concentration to wander and worry about the fate of his friend. He knew the cutter was moving away from the *Akbar* from Molloy's shouts which were growing fainter with distance, although still distinguishable over the creaking of the hull and his own and the officer's grunts of effort.

"No, you've made a mistake! It's me who's the shiteing O'! I'm the O' I tell you! Turn this boat around you shiteing Nancies or I'll choke the lot of yer!" Jobe, almost at the summit of his climb reached for the handrail of the *Akbar*, eager to see Molloy. He was dragged over the side and dropped to the deck like a fish released from the nets. Heaving himself up to the handrail he looked overboard to see the cutter moving away. He couldn't see Molloy but was aware of the space his friend must occupy within the boat. He watched in dismay as the three remaining officers continued to rain blows down upon it.

The sherry was warm but nevertheless caused her to shiver inwardly as she drained the remnants of the glass. It was imperceptible to the man standing in front of her save for a slight trembling of her hand as she leant to place the glass gently on the side table. Simmons took it as his cue to speak.

"He is aboard, ma'am," he stated stiffly. He wasn't immediately graced with an answer and remained standing to attention, a line of sweat beginning to form on his top lip. His mistress surveyed the shelves of books that lined the wall directly ahead of her as if searching for a specific title.

"Everything is in order?" she asked, her gaze still fixed on the far wall.

"Yes ma'am, he is to remain isolated until he accepts the change."

"And if he opposes?"

"There are provisions in place to deal with that eventuality."

"And our man can be trusted?"

"Irrefutably, ma'am," answered Simmons. His top lip was beginning to itch but he kept his hands clasped tightly behind his back. His mistress mulled over the information she had been furnished with as she again scanned the rows of books. She created a steeple with her hands and, lightly resting her chin on it, dismissed her servant.

"Thank you, Simmons. That will be all," she drawled. The man didn't relax a single muscle as he turned and made the long walk to the imposing French doors through which he could exit the library. She leant over and refilled her sherry glass from the crystal decanter; as the dark liquid neared the brim she spoke.

"Unless he refuses to accept the surname I never want to hear mention of him again." Before the first syllable had been formed on her lips Simmons had already come to an abrupt stop. He turned his head to look back at her.

"No ma'am," he said before turning and striding towards the doors.

Always an indefatigable volunteer for charitable organisations the inception of the Liverpool Juvenile Reformatory Association had caught the imagination of Rebecca Warburton. The Association had been formed in 1854 following the Government's Youthful Offenders Act which, for the first time, recognised law-breakers under the age of sixteen as a different group from their grown-up counterparts, providing the opportunity to separate them from criminally-minded adults. The chance to reclaim at least a proportion of the juvenile delinquents who infested the streets and swarmed around the docks had been championed by the town's philanthropists for years, and Liverpool was a city that put its theories into practice with gusto. Rebecca, with a verve and zeal for fundraising, had been welcomed into the group of progressives with open arms. Her efforts had been instrumental in bringing the first reform ship to the Mersey. The teak-built Indiaman, purchased from the Admiralty, had had an illustrious past, serving on the Indian, Pacific and Atlantic oceans. Her hard life was illuminated by the costs incurred to repair her rotting hull and fit her out in order for the first fifty boys to be brought on board with the remit of being morally reformed, educated and furnished with an industrial training to provide them the opportunity of becoming useful members of society.

Such was the ineptitude of those charged with purchasing and making the ship fit for purpose that the *Akbar* had lasted a mere six years before her rotting, worm-infested timbers were judged to be a hazard to life and limb and she was towed to the breakers' yard. Rebecca Warburton was adamant that such effort and expenditure would not be so frivolously squandered again. With the whole project in the balance she had canvassed hard to be appointed to the committee responsible for acquiring a new ship, utilising her influence, money and contacts in order to gain a seat.

Having illustrated her prowess for efficiency from the inception of the venture it was with her blessing that Captain Sualez took fifty boys overland to Plymouth and sailed the new *Akbar* around the coast to its berth on the Mersey, a third of a mile off the Rock Ferry shore. The risk-laden journey had proved fruitful. The ship had enjoyed a less illustrious past than its predecessor, spending forty-one of her forty-five year Royal Navy career safely docked in reserve. Rebecca had procured the society a ship that, although nearing its half-century, appeared as new as if she had just been launched.

The costs incurred to billet the boys were astronomical and were a constant threat to the project. Like a thrifty housewife Rebecca discovered that it was in the minutiae that the most effective cuts in expenditure could be made. Not content in shaving pennies from the cost of bushels of potatoes or replacing expensive beef shin with bullocks' head meat she never tired of finding other cost-cutting methods. Boys re-soled their own boots and sewed their own clothes, the ship's barber was given notice, his duties passed to the cook and drives were organised to urge the well-to-do from both sides of the river to transform a portion of their botanic-like gardens to the production of seasonal vegetables to sustain the insatiable appetites on board. By the time the Catholic dignitaries of the town, having witnessed the success of the floating reformatory, began to instigate the commissioning of their own vessel she had gained such a reputation for proficiency in the art of penny-pinching that the famous Father Nugent civilly sought her advice. A fierce proponent of the old adage "keep your friends close and your enemies closer" she facilitated all requests, answered all queries and offered innumerable and immeasurably valuable suggestions of her own, all the time gaining influence for herself, through contacts, associates and agents within every level of administration and personnel, both on deck and on shore. It was in this way that she became aware of a Catholic boy

with the unusual surname of Warburton who had
been sentenced to three years' service aboard the
Reformatory Ship *Clarence*.

★ ★ ★ ★ ★

Jobe sat on a narrow crossbeam, which was
hard and unforgiving but kept him out of the lake
of brine that covered the bottom of the hold he
had been locked in. He wondered what had been
stored in the hold before him. Another paroxysm
of shivering racked his body as he listened to the
constant creaking of the timbers, trying to ascertain
if it was growing louder or nearer, heightening his
fear, and sometimes hope, that the hull was about to
be gouged open by the frothing Mersey, which would
crash in and drag him to his death, but at the same
instant release him from his misery.

The officer who had harassed him up the rope
ladder, once having gained his footing on deck, had
dragged him down into the bowels of the ship and
thrown him into the dark hold without uttering a
word. There was no way of telling how long he had
sat in the dark dampness but during that time he
had been given, and eaten, three meals of dry ships'
biscuits which had been served with a watery gruel.

As well as convincing himself that the hold would
be reduced to kindling at any second he passed his
time worrying about Molloy and hoping he was
faring better than him. What was behind their

separation? Whatever it was didn't bode well for him, that was for sure. Molloy had told him all about the prison ships that anchored over the other side of the river. They were cold, bleak, dismal places. Those on board suffered such hunger that they fought over the old coconut husks which they used to scrub the decks.

Molloy had described to him the keen air of sectarianism that was festered on the Protestant *Akbar* and Catholic *Clarence*, which often spilled into violence whenever hands from either boat came together on dry land. The bi-annual sports day was a favourite. The athletics and football trophies that created so much pride for the governors of the respective ships paled into insignificance next to the unauthorised, undetected events of gouging, fish-hooking and kidney blows that the boys contested among themselves and which were the real victories of the day. What Molloy had said about boys who had been placed on the wrong ship caused him the most consternation.

"The very worst thing that can happen to a lad Jobe, is him being placed on the wrong shiteing ship and his fellows finding out that he's of the opposite colour. He's liable to find himself floating face down on the river before long."

Jobe comforted himself that his very Anglo-Saxon surname would offer him a veil with which to hide his Catholicism and he tried to recall every snippet of information Molloy had taught him about the ships. He reflected that his time spent locked in the hold was the longest he had spent apart from Molloy since he had been lauded as a hero for seeing off the Cockspur Street Gang singlehandedly.

His ears didn't discern the noise of the key scraping in the lock and he sat up in surprise as the door swung open and lamplight illuminated the damp hold.

"Jobe Flynn?" Jobe couldn't see who addressed him from the doorway, hidden as he was behind the flickering glare of the oil lantern. It was the first time since coming aboard that anybody had addressed him directly and he hesitated before answering, his throat feeling and his voice sounding alien.

"My name is Warburton sir, Flynn was my mother's name." The heavy door slammed shut without another word being said. Unnerved, Jobe remained in the darkness wondering at what had just passed, a feeling of dread emanating from the pit of his stomach. The exchange was repeated, over and over. The same sharp spoken question, delivered in a west country twang, followed by the door slamming shut on Jobe's response until he feared he would never see the light of day again.

"Yes sir, Jobe Flynn, that's me."

"You? But you're Jobe Warburton, if you've told me once you've told me a dozen times."

"No sir, there's no Jobe Warburton in here. I'm Jobe Flynn. I'm sorry if I've led you to believe anything aside from that."

"Is it stupid you're taking me for, boy?"

"No sir, excuse me sir, it's just that my name is Jobe Flynn."

"There's no Jobe Warburton in here then?"

"No sir."

"And there never was?"

"No sir. Never sir."

"You ever heard tell of a boy by the name of Jobe Warburton?"

"No sir. Never sir."

"Well then Flynn, my lad, what is it you're doing all alone in the dark and the damp? Let's get you fed, warmed and dried, shall we?" Jobe straightened up and moved towards the door, his knees and back cracking in protest. As he approached the lamp, near enough to be bathed in its light and feel a flicker of its warmth, a hand clamped around the back of his neck. He couldn't see the face but could smell the rum-soured breath and feel the flecks of spittle that showered his ear and neck.

"Now if a boy should all of a sudden become confused about his name again, he may find himself overboard, alone in the freezing water. What a pointless attempt at escape they'll say, why choose such a cold night, one with no moon they'll say."

"I can't see any chance of confusion sir, I've only ever been called Flynn."

Jobe was taken down a set of steps to what he was informed was the lower deck.

"Pick up 076, in there is your uniform and that next to it is your hammock." Jobe looked to where his gaze was being directed. Stored neatly in the middle of the floor was a pile of hammocks. Next to them were bags stamped with numbers. He found 076 and hefted it up. The bag, although seemingly empty, was heavy and cumbersome and looked as if it had been sewn together from scraps of old sail.

The wind whistled across the deck. Jobe stood naked, his duffel bag at his feet, shivering in front of those who had been assembled on deck. He imagined it must be the ship's full complement. Officers stood on the quarterdeck while boys watched from various vantage points, some even swinging from the rigging like bald monkeys. He had initially tried to stop his teeth from chattering but was afraid that his jaw would shatter with the effort and so stood under everyone's gaze while his teeth rattled away. A hogshead barrel had been filled with river water and placed on the deck; a plank leant against it served as a bridge to its lip.

"Officers...Gentlemen...This here is Flynn, our new shipmate on the glorious *Akbar*!" The west country twang reverberated around the ship and Jobe saw boys look at each other, eyebrows raised.

"Like all new mates, Flynn here has been blessed with the gift of a clean, warm uniform, but just like you afore him, before he can don it and come among us he first needs to clean the filth of his landlubber past that clings to his every pore!" The announcement was greeted with lusty hurrahs.

"C'mon then young Flynn. Let's get you used to the water shall we!"

Jobe saw no point in prolonging the spectacle and so stepped onto the plank which was upset by his weight and he flailed his arms in order to maintain his balance. The screams of pleasure and derision were instant. Jobe continued carefully up the plank, refusing to hesitate or wait for an order before plunging straight in. The water was almost at freezing point and his spine constricted as he submerged his whole body into it. The river water filled his ears, suppressing the caterwauling from the deck, and Jobe was happy in the knowledge that he had curtailed their entertainment. He remained under the water for as long as possible before exploding out, replenishing his lungs with fresh air and immersing himself again. The shrieks and howls had ceased a long time before it was suggested that the landlubber filth of his past had been sluiced from him and he was allowed to climb from the hogshead and stand on the deck to dry.

"It's a good thing there's a strong north westerly. With any luck you'll be dried and dressed before one of these here seagulls swoops down and attempts to peck away your maggot." The well-used jest was greeted with mirth. Jobe, intent on playing no part in the show, stood unabashed, his hands at his sides.

The entertainment was the last in a long list of chores that the boys had endured before it was time for their hammocks. Jobe found it easy enough to sling the hammock but his attempts to climb into, and remain within it, were another matter. The exaggerated whoops and cries of glee echoed around the lower decks and after enduring the ice-cold immersions with a stolidness that had diminished their enjoyment on deck Jobe now found himself voluntarily providing the end-of-evening cabaret. His eagerness to end the spectacle turned to fervour and only prolonged his torment. Jumping from a standing start, taking a run, diving head first from an angle, all ended with the same result. He would grab the hammock before his weight spun him over and he crashed to the floor. On the rare occasion he accomplished his task and found himself actually inside the canvas hammock, his negligible weight would again betray him and he would be flipped over, finding himself flat on the floor again. The boys screeched until the exhaustion of another long day overwhelmed them and they were lost to sleep, leaving him to his fruitless attempts. When the majority were breathing rhythmically a short, fat boy approached him. Jobe had never seen anybody with such a perfectly round face.

"Here," he said smiling and manoeuvring Jobe to one side. When he smiled his eyes creased until they seemed closed, and his face took on such benevolence that Jobe had visions of the saints his mother used to tell him about. The boy was only a head taller than the hammock but flopped into it before rolling out and standing aside. Jobe mimicked his actions until on the third attempt he was lying snugly in the hammock, marvelling at the comfort it afforded. He meant to turn and thank the boy who had saved him from another night on an unforgiving wooden floor but before he knew it a loud shouting was rousing him.

"Lash and stow, you lazy lubbers, lash and stow!"

Jobe's fingers struggled to interpret the messages being sent from his brain. The pre-dawn wake-up call that roused him from his first sound sleep in days had engaged his body but not his brain. By the time he unslung his hammock the other boys had already lashed and stowed theirs. Regardless of the barked orders and cajoling he was powerless to rid his eyes of their heaviness or shake off the lethargy that made his movements slow and ponderous. Exhaustion coupled with humiliation stirred memories of his daily eviction from the Marybone shelter, and his mind wandered back to being ousted on to the cold street and beginning the fruitless journey to the dock stands.

His sluggishness cost him his morning meal. As the other boys were savouring their hot porridge and pint of black coffee he was forced to sling, unsling and stow his hammock over and over until morning mess concluded and, along with the other boys, he filed into an airless room for three hours of schooling. The droning schoolmaster seemed intent on sending Jobe back to sleep and his eyelids fluttered closed on several occasions. Only repeated pokes in his side snapped his head back up from his chest and stopped him dropping off completely. The fingers that dug into his ribs belonged to the fat boy who had helped him master the hammock the previous evening. Each time Jobe tried to whisper his thanks the boy remained impassive and paid even closer attention to the monotonous tutor at the front of the class.

Following the torturous three hours of education the boys were set to work. Jobe and a number of others were provided with old coconut husks and designated an area of deck to scrub. Jobe scrubbed at the deck with the husk bemused by the hairy fruit he held in his hand and wondering why they weren't using sandstone for the task. Seeing the bulk of the boy who had helped him the previous night and during education he sidled over to him. He received some kicks on his way but none of the boys who delivered them were ever looking at him and he wondered if they were accidental or dealt on purpose.

"I'm sorry I didn't thank you last night, I was so exhausted I must have fallen straight asleep. But thank you." The boy continued scrubbing the deck, paying him no heed. Although it was a cold day sweat glistened on his round face with the exertion of his scrubbing but his expression was so vacant that Jobe wondered if he could be the same boy whose features had transmitted such warmth and personality the previous evening.

"I'm sorry..."

"No talking! If you're caught talking they'll find something worse for you to do and I'll be for it too. We'll speak at mess."

Mess consisted of the captains, boys who were deemed to be adhering well to the rules and principles of the ship or who granted certain favours to those officers with a penchant for them, overseeing the lowering of tables which had been lashed to the ceiling and ensuring each boy received his portion of salted bullocks' head meat, thin soup and ships' biscuits. A pint of black, unsugared, tea was also served to each of the hundred or so boys who gathered around the dozen tables.

Jobe found himself sitting next to the boy who had schooled him in the art of the hammock. His tin plate was already empty and he was busy crumbling the dry biscuits into his thin gruel. He spoke to Jobe while he ground. There was no trace of the vacant expression he had sported earlier as he focused all of his attention on ensuring every crumb entered his bowl.

"I'm Horatio, eat your meat. It's easier to chew when it's warm," he smiled as he lifted the bowl to his mouth and began to suck down the mush he had created.

"Horatio eh, that's a name apt for the environment."

"My real name is Horace, the others nicknamed me Horatio on account of me being such a bad sailor." His smile temporarily disappeared as he looked down hungrily at his empty bowl. Seeing it was completely empty he shrugged his shoulders and looked at Jobe, his smile returning, as one of the captains, the only boys allowed to walk around freely at mess time, leaned between the two, forcing Horatio to shift to one side. Jobe could see the definition of his well-built upper arm muscles and smell the rank sweat that leeched through his thin undershirt. He looked up at him as he spoke to the other boy.

"Well, well, Horatio, finally found a friend, have we?" he asked as he took hold of the boy's fleshy jowls. He let go, watching as his white finger marks were erased by the blood rushing back to the fat cheeks before turning to Jobe.

"We don't get many Flynns around here. Catholic name, isn't it?" The question was asked with the utmost geniality but Jobe recognised the malice in the captain's clear blue eyes. The boys who made up the mess, having satisfied their immediate hunger, were now looking up from their plates as they swigged their tea. Jobe saw no advantage in attempting to deny what could only be taken as an accusation.

"I'm Jobe Flynn, and yes I suppose I am a Catholic, although I've always been too busy surviving to take lessons from men in cassocks on what's right and wrong," Jobe looked away from the captain, pulling his plate of bullock cheek towards him and picking up his utensils. The captain, unable to compute the response, was stunned into indecision. He watched as Jobe wrestled with the tough meat, finally managing to cut a bite-size piece from it, and recovering from his stupor, but still at a loss for words, leant over and allowed a gob of spit to escape from his lips, letting it slowly dangle over Jobe's plate. The weight of the globule finally became too much and the sputum snapped, dropping on to the plate.

"We don't like papists eating meat on this vessel. I'll be seeing you later!" Jobe looked up at him as he left and saw the officer with the west country accent had witnessed the episode. Horatio interrupted his train of thought.

"If you were to just slice that piece," he hovered an index finger over Jobe's plate to illustrate his meaning.

"That piece just there, see, the rest of the meat is untouched," he advised. Jobe looked at the plate and after a second slid it across to Horatio who, nodding his thanks, immediately set to work with his spoon. Jobe watched as the captain approached the serving hatch to claim his own meal. The officer with the west country twang had followed him and was now whispering in his ear as he received his victuals. Horatio looked up from his plate following Jobe's gaze.

"Don't concern yourself too much with Cameron," he said, his mandibles working overtime to chew the tough meat that had gone cold.

"He's nothing but a bully, I used to get it something terrible but now that he's been made a captain he's got a full mess to persecute," he said, his face creasing into yet another smile.

Jobe's arms trembled uncontrollably as he lay in his hammock. The ceaseless scrubbing of the decks meant he was barely able to lift his victuals to his mouth by the time evening mess arrived. He had taken to slurping at his pints of stewed tea like a dog until he could risk lifting the mug without the contents slopping over the sides in his shaking grasp. Reducing the chance of the steaming black liquid spilling down his front, giving Cameron yet another opportunity to vilify him, not that he needed an excuse. Cameron had remained at his side since the day he had spat on his dinner, a malevolent spirit that haunted his every move. The attention the captain of the mess paid him eclipsed the petty menacing that those with position coupled with inclination revelled in meting out to the unfortunates in their thrall. It was specific enough to leave Jobe in no doubt that he was receiving orders from Mr Wilkes, the officer with the west country twang, who no doubt, Jobe reasoned, had somebody on shore whispering in his ear while at the same time lining his pockets.

In his discomfort sleep evaded him and although exhausted it at least presented the opportunity to exercise his brain and again contemplate his position on the *Akbar*. The conclusions he reached never offered any comfort. Did his father really view him as some sort of risk to his new life? So much so that he felt it necessary to strip him of his name and condemn him to a reform ship? He had kept a close ear out for tales of the Giant O' during his time in the gang. The streets were always awash with news of his deeds. His father, along with his pawnshop henchmen, had taken to frequenting Union meetings, his sole purpose to interrupt and intimidate those who supported calls to strike. Following the diplomatic sorties to members of the Logwood Gang Jobe had endeavoured to keep abreast of all news and developments, and continued to attend meetings. Listening to speeches while constantly hoping, and fearing, to catch sight of his father. The nature of his father's appearances led him to thoughts of his extended paternal family. His mother had informed him that they came from old money but wasn't sure where their interests lay. Did they extend to shipping and the warehouses or did his father pimp himself out to the ship-owners as he did to the Wise Pastor? Jobe wondered if his father's cameos were nothing more than an opportunity to assuage his basest tendencies, namely cracking the skulls of Catholics.

He contemplated his own Catholic skull which had been in danger since Mr Wilkes, content that Jobe had neither the stomach for, nor the audience with which to share his true identity, had ended his sentinel-like observations, happy to allow the dark lugubriousness of life aboard and the spite of Cameron and the rest of his shipmates to grind Jobe down.

His initial anticipation of mastering the sails, masts and wheel had dissipated. It had quickly became apparent to him that Wilkes would not allow him to learn so much as the most basic of knots. He was classified as one of those boys who showed no compulsion or understanding of sailing and were kept well away from the rigging, masts and the ship's wheel; instead they were enlisted to the purgatory of picking apart old ropes for use in caulking the ship or as in Jobe's case scrubbing and swabbing the decks.

The only light that Wilkes, he himself or Cameron and the rest of his peers couldn't extinguish was that which was emitted from his friendship with Horatio, who had become his constant companion. Jobe had attempted to avert the first hints of friendship after witnessing the toll that Horatio was paying.

His excess weight and lack of dexterity regarding anything nautical had led to his ostracism long before Jobe arrived aboard but his acceptance and befriending of the Catholic was beyond the pale, and Cameron punished him unmercifully on every occasion that allowed for it. His lack of nautical ability was surpassed only by his inability to defend himself and where those attacking Jobe knew they were in a fight Horatio proved to be nothing more than a punch-bag which did little to dampen the efforts of his tormentors.

"I think it'd go easier for you if you looked on your own tasks and left me to mine from now on, H," he said as he dabbed at a cut over Horatio's right eye. It was unusual that Cameron and his cronies would aim blows to the head or face, preferring to leave no visual evidence of their assault. Horatio pulled his head away, a hurt expression on his face that bore no relation to his injuries.

"Why would you suggest such a course?" he asked.

"The beatings you receive are because of me, H, it would be better if you publicly fell out with me, began to shun me, accost me at mess, something like that," Jobe explained.

"Nonsense Jobe, these bashings are nothing compared to the whippings I used to take from my father. Why, they'd have to throw me overboard to keep me from the side of the only true friend I've ever had."

"That could well be on the agenda, H, I know they'd do for me if it wasn't for Wilkes." Jobe had tested his theory that the officer was in the pay of somebody on shore by feigning to throw himself overboard. Mr Wilkes was still keeping him under close scrutiny at the time. Jobe had worked his way over to the rail, husk in hand. Ensuring Wilkes was in attendance, he stood and climbed on to the rail blithely looking down into the river. Within seconds he found himself in the arms of Wilkes who maintained his crushing bear hug until he had Jobe below decks.

"What is it that goes through a boy's mind to have him acting in such a foolhardy manner?" Jobe didn't reply, waiting for the officer to do the talking.

"Notions of escape is that it? Well, only an escape from life itself lies down that path, there'll be no more of it, why I'll ensure that your back is ribboned if there is any repeat of such behaviour!" Jobe sensed the concern emanating from the officer and he knew it had nothing to do with his welfare.

★ ★ ★ ★ ★

Jobe threw the last of the husks into the pail. The initial conundrum of why the usual sandstone used for scrubbing decks had been replaced by the alien shells of the exotic fruit were now well apparent. His raw hands were testament to the amount of scrubbing the deck received, his efforts alone were enough to reduce the hulking square-rigger to nothing more than a raft, and he detested the sensation of the hairy husks against his cracked palms. The creaking of a deck-board interrupted his thoughts and he tensed before spinning around with the heavy pail fully extended. It smashed into the midriff of a boy who was only a few paces behind him. Quickly taking a step back he saw that he was surrounded by boys from his mess who stood in a semi-circle, not quite numbering half a dozen.

Jobe, having nothing but the pail with which to defend himself, took another careful step backwards thus cancelling out the risk of any of his tormentors coming at him from behind. The boys waited, unsure how to advance. Jobe took advantage of their hesitancy and swung the heavy pail in a wide-reaching arc as if to illustrate its range. The pail was heavy and the boy who had been hit hung back on the fringes nursing an arm that could well be broken. The boys were used to Jobe utilising whatever was at hand as a weapon and although the pail looked incongruous in his hands it was heavy and nobody seemed willing to be the first to step into the wild arcs that were Jobe's defence.

"Cameron told us to make sure we do for him good," one of them said without taking his eyes from the pail. The boys looked at each other, particularly their wounded comrade, and with a shrug of their shoulders began to step backwards.

"Nothing urgent, Irish, we'll be seeing you later," said the last of them to file through the doorway. Jobe slumped in relief. His rubbed his tanned arms. His biceps, as with the rest of him, had shown small bursts of growth but he knew he couldn't have swung the pail for much longer.

The twelve-hour working day that dominated the boys' waking hours was enough to exhaust even the most zealous of attackers and Jobe was safe in the knowledge that the next time he spied his would-be assailants they would barely have the strength to sling their hammocks. He just hoped that Horatio would fare as well.

Horatio remained true to his word, refusing to forsake his friend regardless of the beatings, which neither concerned nor cowed him. Jobe took heart from the example set by his effervescent friend. Nothing about the hardships of life aboard the *Akbar* affected H, except for the hunger that gnawed at him constantly. Even this he would attempt to escape through daydreams.

"Oh it was a sight to behold Jobe, my father was like Rumplestiltskin and the bakery would be full of whatever you fancied! Pies! Pastries! Sweet or savoury! You could eat and eat to your heart's content and it would never empty," he would sigh as he scrubbed at the deck his eyes wistful and faraway. His features would temporarily darken.

"But if he caught you…" The darkness never lasted long and he would lick his lips, his smile returning.

"It was always worth it, no matter what form of torture he could dream up." Jobe would allow him his mental excursions, never interrupting, allowing him his escape from the despair and drudgery of his existence.

He resolved to repay the steadfast friendship H had given him. He was powerless to offer protection from the spite and malice of Cameron and other boys and so he set his mind to solving H's biggest torment, his own stomach. He was determined to find a way of assuaging his friend's constant hunger, although he did have grave doubts about whether H's appetite could ever be sated.

"What if I could offer you something as big as your father's bakery?" he asked one evening as H finished verbalising his favourite daydream. Darkness had stolen over the ship. A tall unctuous boy named Scully who had recently been promoted from a mess-captain to a petty officer was busy lighting oil lamps that hung from the three masts and were dotted at intervals along the rail. Jobe and Horatio were pulling up their final pail of water with which to swab the foredeck, their hands raw and numb. Horatio looked at him uncomprehendingly.

"There's no pies or pastries, well, not to my knowledge anyway, but there's plenty of other victuals." Horatio let go of the rope as he contemplated Jobe's meaning. Jobe was almost pulled against the rail by the unexpected weight. Scully spun from his oil-lamp and eyed the pair suspiciously. Horatio took up the rope again and began pulling in earnest.

"I haven't the foggiest what you're getting at, is it a ribbing you're giving me?" he asked.

"I've got a key to the stores," whispered Jobe. The bucket again clattered down the side of the ship as Horatio released his hold for a second time.

"The stores!" he said, his voice breaking with excitement so that he only emitted a barely audible squeal, which was just as well as they now had the full attention of the petty officer.

"Ho, what's all the commotion over there?" shouted Scully.

"Stop with your japes and get that deck swabbed or it'll be a report for the both of you!" Horatio concealed his excitement and pulled up the bucket with uncommon gusto.

The problem of how to access extra rations for H consumed Jobe, offering him a mental diversion from the crushing banality of his daily chores, and with his mind reactivated he found that he began to flourish mentally as well as physically. Ideas presented themselves which, after careful consideration, he was forced to discard. He watched, coconut husk in hand, as the fresh goods were delivered from the Liverpool docks by barge, but the milk, butter and specific fancies of the officers were closely monitored, checked once as they were taken on board and again as they were stored in the hold. Even if he could concoct a way of extracting a portion of the goods, he would then have to repeat the same feat the following week, and any discrepancies would result in a search, placing H in the line of fire.

With every ounce of his intellect concentrated on solving the problem only one solution presented itself and refused to be dismissed regardless of it being fraught with jeopardy. Access to the stores themselves would provide a route to the dried goods, fruits and vegetables that were plentiful and so accounted for in a more haphazard fashion. Any discrepancy, if noticed at all, would be minimal and probably put down to spillage or some other cause. But there was only one way in and he had never attempted to pickpocket anybody before, although he'd received schooling from a master.

Silky had refused to abandon his favourite and most lucrative earner. He had evolved his practice to an art, which he loved to use in around the business district of Dale, Water, and Castle Streets disguised as a sweep, porter or butcher's boy.

"The most important part of the whole play is not to allow the mark to see you as a threat and by virtue of their pompousness you'll remain invisible to them, even when you're right under their nose," Silky had informed Jobe as he tiptoed around The Den squinting through his gold-rimmed monocle which he held between his thumb and forefinger as if it were evidence of his hypothesis.

Even taking the arrogance and lackadaisical nature of the officers into account he was aware that his dipping skills were not even as good as second-rate and he was sure any attempt would be folly. He would need to prosper from some sort of diversion before he could even risk an attempt. A melée or a crush would have to occur where he would have the time not only to dip the heavy bunch of keys, but also remove the stores key, before replacing them. He would have discounted the idea if he had not already exhausted every other possibility. He couldn't risk confiding in anyone else in order to manufacture a distraction and his refusal to place Horatio in any danger meant that he would just have to be patient and wait until an opportunity presented itself, meaning he would have to act without notice or planning. Or so he thought.

"It's bloody freezing, it's too late in the year," protested the squeaky voice.

"What d'you mean freezing, summer's only just ending. Besides, I'll be in there as well, won't I?"

"What'll you be doing in there?"

"Well, ready to save you of course!"

"You needn't bother. I'll die from the chill in any case."

"Listen, it's the last chance for a slap-up meal at one of the governor's houses isn't it? Did you see the way Swigger and Higson were treated the last time they pulled it? Why that compass they were given will be worth a pretty penny when they're back on shore, engraved or not!"

"Yes, but they pulled it when the sun still had some warmth in it didn't they? We'd be offering up a lot more than they did."

"Yes, but old Braddock said we'd be on the foremast tomorrow, all we have to do is ensure we're on the fore course and it'll just be a small drop into the river, we'll be pulled out in no time at all." He noted the look of doubt on his co-conspirator's face.

"Look here, we've a long miserable winter stretching ahead of us. Don't you want a day on shore being treated like a lord? I'll easily find someone else if you don't."

"I still don't know…"

"You said yourself, the time is now, it'll be getting colder by the day and you're right about that, of course you are! We'll go tomorrow."

"I didn't say that, did I?"

"Think of all the lauding, we'll be heroes, well-fed and well-rewarded heroes!"

"Ok, tomorrow it is!"

Jobe listened from inside an old cargo hold that was now used for the storing of swabbing mops, pails and bolts of canvas that looked Jurassic. He had heard tell of the old ruse of falling overboard. Shouts of man overboard would reverberate around the deck and echo from any ships that happened to be passing. Before the warning bell could be rung one of his shipmates, always a strong, capable swimmer, would be overboard himself without any thought for his own life or limb and bravely keep afloat his spluttering, thrashing colleague until a buoy could be thrown out to them and they would be dragged up to the deck as heroes. The boys would be the toast of the ship. This was proof that the floating reformatory was indeed influencing the morality of boys who before their berthing on board would rifle the pockets of a drowning man before watching him go under. The Committee were only too ready to spread the word and lavish rewards and gifts on the said heroes. Jobe knew it would present his best opportunity and hoped that neither they, nor he, would get cold feet.

Following noon mess Jobe ensured he remained as close to the rail as was possible without raising any suspicion. He felt sure that the planned 'rescue' would go ahead. Both boys had landed themselves jobs on the lowest spar of the foremost mast, thus providing them an easy drop into the river below. Jobe felt his stomach tighten; he had high hopes his, albeit ignorant, partners in crime were committed to their part but wondered if he could fulfil his own. The omens were positive, old Braddock was the officer on watch, a dithering old sailor who had served as long as the inaugural *Akbar* and one of the officers onboard who extracted certain favours from certain boys.

As he was weighing up the possible outcomes an image blurred within his peripheral vision followed by a splash and a cry of 'man overboard'. The ship's warning bell hadn't reached its third peal before another boy had splashed into the water. The warning bell being rung was an open invitation for all hands to rush to the starboard rail. Jobe timed his movement, waiting for Braddock to limp to the rail. There was already a throng leaning over it shouting encouragement to the two boys. Braddock was forced to use both hands to part the crowd of cheering boys who had gathered to watch the two boys splashing in the river, trusting the the denseness of the crowd to bear his weight and keep him upright until he reached the rail and could see what was going on in the river.

Jobe saw his chance and, pressing his body against that of the old sailor, snaked his hand into his pocket. He retrieved the bunch of keys with ease. He kept his hands low, his fingers reading the shape of the keys like a blind man. He had only seen the stores key once, but had committed its shape to memory. A lifebuoy had been thrown overboard and by the changing dynamic of the crowd he knew that the heroes were being hauled back aboard. Time was waning. He recognised the key and manipulated it from the chain, sliding it into his waistband. The initial excitement of the rescue was subsiding by the second. Other officers had arrived and were busy marshalling the boys away from the rail and back to their places of work. Jobe had kept himself pressed against Braddock whose attention was focused on what was happening in front of him. Jobe lurched forward as if being pushed from behind, feeling the officer take a step forward against the added weight. He forced his hand and the keys back into the baggy pocket.

Braddock spun around and looked directly down at Jobe, a look of admonishment on his face, just as he removed his hand from the damp pocket. Jobe smiled and raised his eyebrows suggestively before taking a step backwards and out of the startled officer's personal space. Braddock's features remained creased with censure before they softened and he rewarded Jobe with a smile and a lecherous wink. Jobe moved away from the rail and returned to his dried coconut husk as a blanket was thrown over the two boys who remained huddled together in the buoy, teeth chattering. He didn't look up as the ship's Captain made a rare appearance on deck. He cleared his throat as he buttoned his long, thick overcoat.

"I was of the impression that these charades had concluded with the summer, but I see they have not! Very well, the next boy who *falls* into the river will receive a dozen lashes on being brought back on deck. The boy who rescues him will receive double! Do I make myself clear?" The boys chattering and shivering could not hide their dismay at the words; there would be no celebration or lauding of their shifting moral compass. The key dug into Jobe's stomach. He grinned down at the piece of deck he scrubbed.

The constant cold, the continued enmity of his crew-mates, the continual berating of the officers, and the mundanity of *Akbar* life; Horatio was immune to them all. Even on the nights that he and Jobe couldn't find an opportunity of sneaking into the stores and he fell asleep hungry, it contented him to know all of the foodstuffs on board were at his disposal. In his view Jobe was a little too cautious about visiting the stores but he had to admit his friend did have an eerie knowledge of the movements and habits of everybody on the ship which made it easy to trust his judgement. Besides, he had no choice.

"I'd put my life in your hands without blinking, H, but I wouldn't trust that stomach of yours with so much as a crumb. The temptation would eat you up until you had no choice. Besides, if it's me who is found with the key, you're away, scot-free." H understood the logic behind Jobe's words; he wouldn't trust himself with the key either.

He knew it was his ability to consume huge quantities of food that had booked his berth on the *Akbar*. His father had deliberately left the unsealed letter addressed to the Committee of the Floating Reformatory *Akbar* next to a tray of freshly baked hot-cross buns. The scent of cinnamon had drawn him in from the entry where he had been skulking, awaiting the opportunity to pilfer something hot, savoury or sweet, it made no difference. The letter beseeched the Committee to take his Godless, villainous and feckless son aboard in a bid to transform him into a worthwhile addition to society; it offered to pay the costs of his son's board plus a monthly contribution towards the upkeep of the ship. Although the letter terrified Horatio it didn't sate his appetite and he polished off the full tray of hot-cross buns two at a time right there in the kitchen, grunting and beating the table as he struggled for breath through the mush of warm pastry. The obligatory beating for consuming the pastries failed to materialise, illustrating his father's contentment with the fear and anxiety he had created with the letter. His father was at constant pains to introduce new methods of punishing him and H hoped that the letter was just another ploy to torment him psychologically in another bid to curtail his appetite.

Horace Brent had moved his expectant wife from the coarseness of Kirkdale across the boundary to Bootle for a better life. Although the burgeoning town was becoming ever more intertwined with the metropolis to its south the former village still retained a modicum of its rural origins, a direct contrast to the smoke-filled filth of the city Horace had left behind. The town officials were eager not to replicate the mistakes of their encroaching neighbour and the aspirations of the town were reflected in the naming of the rapidly expanding streets. Those that were not named after the grand colleges of Oxford were given the names of Shakespearean characters in an attempt to imbue pride and ambition in its residents. It was on the corner of Balliol and Stanley Road that Horace proudly created his new bakery. He watched over the sign-writer like a hawk as he added the legend '& Son' to the priceless sign he had brought with him from his old premises.

"What if it's not a son I'm carrying?" his wife chided, receiving nothing but a knowing smile as a response. The birth proved his intuition to be sound and he named the boy Horace, in his own honour. Following the birth of his son, Horace could do nothing but watch in despair as his wife began to waste away. She tried valiantly to appease the babe who continuously worried at her teat, but it was never satisfied and seemed to be suckling at her life energy. After her death Horace ceased to notice the child, blinded by his grief. When he finally ventured from the comforting cloak of grief that had shielded him from the world the boy had abandoned liquid and noisily sucked on sweetmeats. He didn't seem to be troubled by the void his mother's death had created, only becoming agitated if there was nothing at hand to stuff into his mouth. Horace wondered what crime he had committed to be tainted by such a curse.

H was sure he couldn't have been born greedy. His mother had died when he was still a baby and he often wondered whether the lack of mother's milk had created an insatiable appetite within him, but thought it more likely that the constant ire of his father was responsible for his love of food. He grew up surrounded by the perpetual waft of temptation, a by-product of the pies and pastries that his father produced for his shop. It became a constant itch that he couldn't help but scratch. The incessant harassing, chastising and bullying of his father completed the vicious circle and food became his only solace, his only comfort, the only warmth he could find in a cold world.

H's stomach rumbled loud enough to disturb his immediate neighbours. He added to their consternation by calling to his friend.

"Jobe," he whispered. There was no reply but he was unsure whether Jobe was testing him. His knowledge regarding the movements and habits of every soul on board, although benefiting H frequently also unsettled him, it just wasn't natural.

"Jobe," he whispered again, stuck in the limbo of wanting to be sure his friend was asleep but at the same time scared of waking him. His stomach rumbled again. It had been days since they had made a midnight sortie to the stores.

"So tell me again Jobe, does Braddock know you have the key?"

"Well, he wouldn't mention the key outright H, that'd be admitting that he's culpable for losing it," sighed Jobe in reply. He hadn't relished telling his friend that there would be no visit to the stores for a while.

"He'll have given the keys to the next officer on watch. They never bother with the formalities involved with the handover. They're supposed to sign for the keys, sign that all boys are accounted for, sign that everything is ship-shape on board, but they never do. Who knows if Braddock is even aware it was him who lost the key?"

Braddock had impeded Jobe as he was about to swap his coconut husk.

"What's the problem, Flynn?" he croaked.

"Nothing sir, this husk has had it, that's all. I'm just replacing it," Jobe held up the balding, split husk. Braddock took the husk from him, turning it over in his hand as he inspected it.

"Yes, you're right, this one's had it. Before you get another I've got a job for you below decks." Braddock led Jobe to the brine-soaked hold he had been locked in on first being brought aboard. As the ageing officer advanced towards him Jobe hurriedly informed him that he was Wilkes's boy.

"Someone informed him of my advances towards you on deck the day of the man overboard sir, maybe one of your own boys, insecure and jealous of the development." Braddock halted his advance.

"In turn Mr Wilkes has warned me to stay away from any other officers and demanded that I inform him of anyone making advances towards me." Braddock squinted at Jobe as if trying to penetrate his mind. He recalled Wilkes had covered the boy like a rash when he had been brought aboard. He chuckled squalidly to himself as he licked the tip of his filthy index finger.

"I knew that so-and-so was no paragon," he said, as if thinking aloud. He looked at Jobe as if only just realising he was still there.

"Oh well, shame, real shame," he muttered as he looked Jobe up and down before turning and shuffling away.

Jobe continued to explain his reasoning to the forever-hungry boy who was twisting his earlobe in concentration.

"Cook is responsible for accessing stores to fulfil the needs of all messes. It was only when the fresh goods were delivered today that it was discovered the key was missing. I was scrubbing the deck when Cook realised he'd left his key locked in the galley. Mister Stones attempted to open the stores for him, he looked a little perplexed but then he simply went and replaced the missing key from the bunch of spares that are locked away in the Captain's quarters. A hundred handovers have taken place since I took the key so no-one will be sure who lost it or how, but the officers must have caught it from the Captain, they've completed the handover impeccably all day."

"So nobody knows you've got it for sure," repeated H hopefully.

"The likelihood is that they're not even aware that anybody has the key H, but we can't be too careful, just a few days that's all, a few days."

During those long days it had seemed to Horatio that the portions on his tin plate had shrunk, leaving more and more of the chipped plate exposed.

"Jobe," he whispered for the third time. He got a response but not from Jobe.

"Shut your fat pie hole Horatio or I'll come over there and shut it for you!" He waited for a challenge from Jobe and when it was not forthcoming decided that he was asleep. He allowed the time to crawl by before eventually rolling from his bunk.

He unlocked the heavy door as if in a trance, pausing before pushing it open. He didn't like to betray Jobe and understood the danger in the course he was set on. He briefly debated returning the key to its hiding place and tiptoeing back to his hammock but after a second dismissed the thought and in the blink of an eye was inside the stores, locking the door behind him.

Jobe woke with a feeling of dread in the pit of his stomach. Something wasn't right and he knew without looking that H wasn't in his bunk. The absence of H's light snoring had troubled his sleep and a glance to his right confirmed his fears. H's hammock was empty. Jobe immediately rolled out of his hammock but no sooner had his feet touched the floor than the light of an oil-lamp appeared and the familiar cry of "Lash and stow, you lazy lubbers! Lash and stow!" rang out. Jobe didn't know what to do. There was no chance of sneaking off to the stores without being seen and he only hoped that H was aware of the time and making his way back to the lower deck.

The hammocks were lashed almost as one and H's became incongruously blatant. It soon became apparent to the petty officer that H's bunk was empty.

"Well, well, Horatio already up and at his duties, is he? Forever the diligent sailor that one," he quipped, smiling.

"Where is the barrel of lard?" he asked Jobe, his smile becoming a grimace. Jobe was quietly queuing to stow his hammock, doing his utmost to remain inconspicuous. He was powerless to assist H in any way except for keeping his mouth shut. Cook would be discovering the sleeping, possibly still gorging H, at any second and the game would be up. He remained mute, his hammock played across his hands. The officer stalked over to him. Pulling the hammock from his grasp he threw it to the floor before grabbing Jobe by the ear lobe. Just then the deck-bell began ringing indiscriminately. Jobe shouldered the officer aside and raced for the lower-deck steps.

The dead weight was transferred between the two officers and they continuously paused, hefted and readjusted their grip with each laboured step across the deck. Their quest to find better purchase resulted in the tightly wrapped canvas coming loose and the hands that had been gathered on deck gasped as a naked arm fell free. Cameron elbowed Jobe and nodded towards the dangling arm.

"Is it my imagination or has your chum lost a bit of weight?" He grinned at the lads in his immediate vicinity, glaring until they acknowledged his quip with embarrassed laughs and nods. All hands watched as H's body was unceremoniously bundled into a cargo net and hoisted on to a waiting cutter below. Jobe responded to the petty officers whistle's and trudged over to where he had left his swabbing mop, wondering all the time how the baker from Bootle would react to receiving the shrouded body of his greedy son.

Chapter VII

1892

The candelabra hanging from the low ceiling trembled with each heavy step, causing shadows to stretch and shrink as they danced around the small room.

"The damned impertinence of the man. He has no doubt organised this whole shenanigan to his own end. A martyr they're calling him! Martyr indeed! Am I not a martyr? Have I not martyred myself? Ministering in this city for over a decade, protecting good God-fearing Christians from the ritualism of Rome!"

Potter watched the Pastor's fleshy jowls quiver with rage and fought hard to suppress the smile that seemed determined to break out on his face. The only way he could contain his amusement was to refrain from looking up at him as he paced the floor of his rooms. He had been bristling for just over a month, since John Kensit Jr had appeared in the town, but on hearing the news of his jailing Pastor Wise had become apoplectic.

Kensit Jr had arrived in the height of summer and along with his Wycliffe Preachers had been espousing the dangers of ritualism in Church of England services at open-air rallies. A territory the Pastor felt was his own. Potter fancied the two were pages from the same book, attracted to Liverpool for the same reason, more concerned by the number of Irish Roman Catholics, the highest in any city of Great Britain, than the number of High Anglican churches employing idolatry and altar boys.

The younger Kensit had been welcomed into the city. The Protestant Truth Society that his father, John Kensit Sr, had established was viewed as a credible organisation formed to preach biblical truth and awaken people to the spiritual dangers of the day. He was even scheduled to speak in St George's Hall, another reason for Pastor George Wise to feel aggrieved, before the authorities became aware of the consternation his meetings were causing. The meetings gave Potter an understanding of how Kensit Jr could afford to graciously decline the offer of protection from Potter and his men that had been so kindly offered by his mistress.

The Wycliffe Preachers, bibles forever in hand, were such biblical zealots that they acted like warrior monks of old rather than the unassuming church curators they resembled. The disturbances they caused were so raucous that young Kensit had been summoned before the magistrates. He was offered the choice of being bound over for twelve months or jailed for three. Quoting the virtues of free speech Kensit Jr. had elected to serve three months. Pastor Wise had been offered the same choice the previous summer and chose to retain his liberty.

"Yes, he has created this farce to make me look the Iscariot! Well aware the public outcry will negate the need for him to serve his time. Kensit the Elder himself has already made plans to descend on us! Mrs Warburton was only too happy to inform me, almost swooning with the news. Is it seemly, I ask myself!"

Although Potter was the only other person in the room the Pastor was not addressing him. He aimed his outrage at inanimate objects in the room. The mantelpiece, fireplace and bookcase became his audience. Potter interjected regardless.

"Excuse me Pastor, but is this not an opportunity to show that you are the bigger man?" The Pastor stopped his pacing and looked at Potter.

"It is no secret that you have not seen eye to eye with Kensit and his preachers. Why not organise a protest meeting against his jailing, a rallying cry against the gagging of free speech? Strike back at the Irish sympathisers! By the time old Kensit arrives you'll be integral to any campaign calling for his son's release." Potter watched with relief as the Pastor rubbed his chin, the only part of his lower face not covered with bristling hair, a visible sign that he was deep in thought. He aimed his response at the thickly draped bay window.

"The Widow Warburton has organised an event to welcome Kensit Sr for the 25th. Over the water in Birkenhead, strictly invitation only. I'll orchestrate a nationwide outcry demanding his son's freedom before then. I'll concentrate the nation's ire to a meeting in St Domingo Pit."

The Indian summer continued and the sun retained enough warmth for those gathered on the front lawn of the Claughton Music Hall to continue to enjoy the drink that had been the fashion of that summer. Potter stood discreetly aside from the group, smiling as he watched Albert sip at his Pimm's, the elegant glass tiny in his hand. He wished the men he had brought over on the ferry and who had been consigned to wait in the stables at the back could catch a glimpse of their hero now. He knew Albert was extremely uncomfortable attending any events that the men would be called upon to secure. He didn't like them to be reminded how far removed from them he was, failing to understand that the men idolised him even more because of the gulf in class.

His mistress had forbidden his men, the very men she financed through him, to attend, only acquiescing to their presence on hearing of the furore at a meeting four days earlier which, according to reports, had been stormed by in excess of three thousand Catholics who had caused serious harm to those present. Potter had given strict instructions that there was to be no animosity shown to the Wycliffe Preachers regardless of provocation but had nevertheless felt the urge to make frequent visits to the stables where both groups had been billeted in order to repeat his orders.

Albert was linked on both sides. His mother on his right, the new wife she had foisted upon him on his left. It was the left link he frequently broke to sip his drink. Rebecca Warburton once again possessed the control over her son that she had been helpless in relinquishing but had never given up hope of retaining. Her preening showed no sign of abating. The wife she inflicted on her son, pretty enough by the day's fashion, provided him with the means to re-establish his standing and reputation within society but offered neither the love nor light with which to lead him from the darkness that enveloped him like a dense river mist. Potter read the discomfort etched on to his features and knew that he would give anything to be ensconced in the stables with the rest of the rabble. It was just as well he wasn't. The tensions between the two groups would have erupted into violence within minutes. Potter would have been powerless to stop it.

Since learning of the death of his first wife, Kitty, whom since her demise Potter himself had come to view as something of a paragon, Albert's craving for carnage knew no bounds. Not content with partaking in the pitched sectarian battles that had rattled through Everton all summer he had taken to quenching his insatiable appetite for violence by infiltrating the burgeoning union meetings that were endemic in the dockland. His interference left a sour taste in Potter's mouth. He hadn't forgotten his humble beginnings in Ormskirk and he more than empathised with those who fought for the right not to be violated or abused at the whim of their employers. The plight and problems that faced the working classes had been obscured by the sectarian strife and struggle that burnt through the city, the flames of which were assiduously fanned by those they served most.

Potter's whole family, along with the majority of his village, had earned the wages that barely kept them from the workhouse gates down the pit. He had itched to be one of the boys who lugged the coal up in tubs, only their eyes visible through faces covered in black dust; never noticing that they grimaced instead of smiling, coughed instead of laughing.

His mother had first led him by the hand into the pitch-black, half-flooded tunnel that crept down to the face. She had tears in her eyes as she warned him to stay by her side.

"Don't do anything unless I tell you! Keep your eyes closed and your mouth shut, and don't go breathing too much." As they descended to the coalface they passed boys, to small too be hurriers, sitting, their backs against doors that served as ventilation shafts. He would never forget the growing tap-tap of handpicks clinking against the seam or the coughs of the men who wielded them. His father and the rest of the men had gone down at first light, the women and children waiting for as long as they could before penetrating the depths to collect the black fruit of their men's labour.

She had shown him how to fill the tubs with the jagged rocks as quickly as humanly possible but without cutting his hands to ribbons, and then scuttle back to the surface dragging the heavy tub behind, crouching all the time.

"Ignore your knees, they'll last longer than your back will."

She had to push him the last few yards to the surface, dragging her tub behind her with her other hand. As he broke from the entrance to the pit she slapped him repeatedly on the back.

"Don't breathe in, cough, lad, cough." He had leant forward, hands on aching knees, and retched, black sputum flying from his mouth, black dust from his nose.

"Every time you come up from the pit blow that out, cough it up and spit, and look, do this," she said as she twisted her back from side to side and rolled her hips.

"Every time!" she repeated, before beckoning him towards the tunnel mouth. Only the seam being exhausted had saved him from the physical deformities and mental degeneration that had blighted her and his father.

The gurgling screams of his peers, boys no older than six, and the shouts of those trying to save them still woke him in the dead of night. The sounds continuing to echo in his ears while images of the desperate men attempting to squeeze through impossibly narrow passages played behind his eyes long after he had shaken off sleep and was sitting bolt upright in bed. The only grace the lack of light in the dark tunnel offered was that it masked the contorted expressions of those attempting to rescue the boy whose leg a cart or ventilation door had crushed before he became too exhausted to maintain his own weight and he sank below water level. He unconsciously rubbed his rough, lined hands that hadn't engaged in manual labour for decades but served as a constant reminder of his past.

"What's this Potter, not too cold for you is it?" asked Pastor Wise, shaking Potter from his reverie. The Pastor looked at him quizzically as the big man seemed to emerge from a trance.

"Mr Kensit is enquiring as to some of the landmarks that are visible across the water. I was wondering if you could come and assist?"

Potter invited Mr Kensit to follow his index finger and broadly encompassed the eight miles of docks facing them. He moved on to the Sailors' Home before bringing his audience of one's attention to the civic gems of St George's Hall, and next to it the Walker Art Gallery. Before he could continue the presence of Kensit's wife, a mole of a woman, interrupted him.

"Ah Mr Potter, if you don't mind could we postpone the tour for a second. My wife has been so eager to be introduced to the good Pastor."

Potter responded with a nod of his head and stepped back. Mrs Kensit shook Pastor Wise by the hand.

"Such an honour, Pastor Wise. We are eternally grateful for your ongoing efforts. We heard twenty thousand turned up at your meeting in support of John's liberty, such a number." Pastor Wise accepted the praise.

"To quote your heroic son on accepting his sentence, 'As long as I have breath, I shall continue to oppose error," he raised his glass.

"To John Alfred, a true Crusader!" A chorus of 'John Alfred' rumbled across the lawn. Old Kensit caught Potter's eye,

"Thank you for the tour Mr Potter, I'd be grateful if we could conclude it following the meeting."

Potter found himself looking forward to it, having decided that John Kensit Sr was as genial a man as you could wish to meet, every ounce the bookseller he was by trade.

★ ★ ★ ★ ★

Kensit Sr hadn't raised his voice once during the meeting, which went off without a hitch. He uttered every word as if he were in the reading room of a library but forced nobody to strain to hear him. He was certainly a man of books and letters, a true wordsmith. Potter's only concern throughout was how things were proceeding in the stables.

"Are you sure you won't stay with us the night, Mr Kensit?" his mistress asked back out on the steps of the music hall.

"You have done more than enough Mrs Warburton and I thank you from the bottom of my heart. We must decline your kind offer. I hope to lead a procession to the prison at first light to demand the release of John Alfred, to build on the sterling efforts of Pastor Wise here," he replied, as he half bowed to Pastor Wise.

"In that case we'll see you to the ferry, won't we Albert, it's a beautiful evening after all." She turned to Simmons who hovered in the wings.

"Please have the motorcar rendezvous with us at the pier, Simmons," Albert responded to his mother giving her all his attention, his wife a mere spectator.

"I was planning on staying in the city Mother. I have business to attend to this evening and was hoping to be part of Mr Kensit's procession in the morning." His mother bristled at the information; only those who knew her noticed the almost imperceptible signs, knowledge of which would have had her aghast.

"Of course my dear, attend to your business and accompany Mr Kensit on his procession." She turned to Albert's wife. "Anna can travel home with me, I'll expect a detailed report of the procession at dinner tomorrow," she finished by way of exerting her influence.

The walk down to the pier was a pleasant one. Potter's men filed discreetly on one side of the group, the Wycliffe Preachers on the other, both near enough to offer their protection but far enough away not to be in earshot of the conversation, which centred around the effort to have John Alfred released.

Approaching the waterfront they became aware of a group of youths. They were vociferous but presented only a minimal risk, which was reduced to less than negligible by the separate groups of bodyguards who converged upon them. As a distraction from any possible unpleasantness Rebecca brought the attention of the small band to the incoming ferry.

"Did you know there has been a ferry service from Birkenhead since 1150. It was known as the Monksferry," she stated proudly. "And oh, look, you can see the floating reformatory perfectly; you must come for a visit Mr Kensit." Kensit Sr never got the chance to decline or accept. A metal file came spinning from within the group of youngsters, striking the older Kensit above the left eye. Potter pushed past the screaming women - his mistress wasn't one of them - and knelt at the side of Mr Kensit. He passed Albert the metal file, which must have weighed all of two pounds, a concerned look on his face. It was his mistress who took control.

"On to the ferry with him Potter, the infirmary in town will be better suited to treat his injury."

It had been a long summer. The tragedy involving Kensit Sr produced a natural lull in his duties to Pastor Wise. Mr Kensit had seemed to be recovering from his injuries but the onset of pneumonia coupled with blood poisoning finally proved fatal and he died on October 6th. The respite from his duties presented Potter with the opportunity of keeping the company that he had been craving for what seemed like an age, namely his own. His mistress was content to accept the pretence of his presence being needed in the town. She had a trusted company of retainers carrying out her every whim and was quite happy to permit her husband's man to meander in the town while retaining the companionship of his wife, who was now a servant in name only.

Potter did have duties to perform in her name, mainly maintaining the core group of trusted bodyguards he had spent time financing and establishing. But he was happy to leave them to their own devices for a short time.

He drained his shot glass quickly followed by his jar and waited to catch the landlord's attention. The pub was packed to the rafters with seamen, dockers and, judging by the number of untended wagons obstructing the entrance, carters. The very men who Albert was helping to keep under the heel of their paymasters. He looked around, used to being head and shoulders above the crowd but surprised to find that a good number of the men equalled him in size, especially those of a dark complexion. He scanned the room, lost in his bleak thoughts and in no particular hurry to have his glass replenished when he spied a scene that had him questioning his own eyes. There in a secluded corner was Simmons, deep in conversation with a pugnacious looking fellow, whose tidy uniform was made even more resplendent by its direct contrast to his visage - so much so that Potter was sure that the original owner of the bright buttoned blazer must be lying in a gutter somewhere with either a cracked skull, a blade between the ribs or both.

Potter was no fan of Simmons, who in his humble opinion was nothing more than their mistress's panting lap-dog, but he held enough grudging respect for the man not to want him to end up in some back jigger like the previous occupier of the officer's uniform. Potter traced a way through the throng to the table.

"Simmons, it is you, I thought my eyes deceived me," he said brashly, interrupting their consuming conversation. Simmons' shock caused him to look up before he had fixed his customary mask in place. Potter didn't miss the concern etched across Simmons's face before he managed to gain control of himself.

"Potter, my good fellow, I had an idea our paths might cross among the spit and sawdust. You haven't a drink I see, let me just part company with my cousin here and I'll accompany you to the bar," he smiled, his eyes attempting to read anything Potter's features projected.

"Farewell then, Sam, my regards to Aunt Beryl, tell her I hope her gout becomes more manageable," he said as he stood, proffering his hand. Potter almost laughed at the pretence as the rogue in the uniform sat slack-jawed, gaping at the open palm in obvious confusion.

"Take care, Sam," said Simmons as he withdrew his hand and guided Potter away from the table. "Dropped on his head as a child, a terrible burden to my Aunt Beryl," he said from the side of his mouth.

Potter woke a little later than was his custom. The only impairment he suffered from the previous evening was a cracked tongue and a parched throat, his usual reaction to a night of excess. He reached for the jug of water on the bedside table and surveyed the room Simmons had procured for him as he filled his glass. It really was top notch, in fitting with the evening as a whole. On draining a second glass he settled back on to his pillow, reflecting on the previous evening. Simmons had been on excellent form, remaining with Potter until the landlord had called last orders and then insisting they visit a club that he claimed was so exclusive he'd warrant Potter had never heard of it. To Potter's amazement, Simmons was right. The club was a stark reminder of just how powerful and influential their mistress, Rebecca Warburton was when even, Simmons, no more than an employee of hers could access such grandeur in her name. He had walked past the merchant's office that took up the ground floor of Sir Thomas' Buildings a thousand times, never suspecting its basement was a gilded hideaway where the rich and well-to-do of the town enjoyed fantastically late suppers and some truly bizarre cabaret which had climaxed with a purring bout, the most anticipated and main attraction. Potter remembered tales from his childhood of the rough men of the mills and mines who took part in purring, kicking at each other's legs and shins while wearing their traditional wooden clogs. The art had been made illegal decades before, although he'd heard whispers that it continued in the deepest parts of Lancashire. His jaw dropped and the clientele erupted as two naked women walked on to the stage. The contrast between the two was stark and Potter watched as a bookmaker began dissecting the tables, his arms a blur as he accepted bets. Simmons laughed at Potter's incredulous gape.

"Care to make a wager?" Potter looked back to the bookmaker.

"We'll leave him out of it, you wouldn't believe what his minimums are. Choose your horse," he added with a nod to the stage. Potter appraised the women. One was an enormous specimen. Her giant breasts spread across her massive stomach and under her arms forcing them up into the posture of a pugilist, which was in keeping with her features. The other was much more pleasing to the eye, a fraction of the other's size with everything in proportion. Potter feared for her.

"Bit of a mismatch wouldn't you say? But if you insist I'll have the navvy there, shall we say a pound," he said proffering his hand. Simmons laughed again.

"I didn't realise our mistress rewarded you so well! A pound it is."

The bookmaker held a hand up to a man standing between the two women. The main candelabra's hanging from the ceiling were dimmed and those on the main stage brightened, intensifying the fog of cigar smoke that idled around them. The man between the two women stepped backwards and a heavy clacking of wooden clogs echoed around the now silent basement as the big woman, Sally of Stockbridge, and the smaller girl, Willow of Wavertree, began to dance around each other. Sally seemed content to allow the smaller Willow to catch her with lightning strikes to her shins and calves. Even with the slight frame powering them, the blows caused considerable damage and it wasn't long before blood began to flow freely from Sally's shins. Willow's clogs soon developed a sheen of blood that matched the glaze of perspiration on her naked, sweating body. With each kick flecks of blood flicked off her shining clogs, speckling those on the tables nearest the stage, who, to Potter's amazement, pawed at the blood with the tips of their fingers and sucked it off with obvious delight. Willow landed blow after blow on her static opponent and Potter was resigned to losing the wager. He watched as Sally finally made a move to defend herself, holding up her right leg in an attempt to evade the constant blows. Willow sensed victory and stepped in, aiming three quick kicks at the standing left leg. The third didn't land. Sally of Stockbridge brought her right leg crashing down onto Willow's shin. The crowd gasped at the sound of breaking bones. Sally's first assault leaving her opponent writhing on the floor, the screams of pain drowned out by the cheers of the jubilant crowd, Potter amongst them. Sally bent down, grabbed a handful of her prone opponents hair and wiped her bleeding shins with it before approaching the front of the stage; both arms held aloft, her still bleeding legs spread wide.

Potter had allowed himself to enjoy the evening thoroughly, changing his estimations of Simmons by the hour. He would have no qualms about proposing a repeat, and soon. He accosted himself for allowing his perception of Simmons to be defined by the relationship he shared with their mistress, after all, hadn't he been prepared to walk over hot coals for their master while he lived.

Potter was disturbed from his thoughts by the knock of the chambermaid. He permitted her to enter but remained stretched out on the bed.

"Any response from next door, is my colleague awake?"

"The room's empty sir, I'll warrant the bed hasn't been slept in."

'Cousin Sam' sprang into Potter's mind and he brought his hand to his forehead. The whole night had been a sham, an exercise in concealment. He recalled his initial impression that Simmons had been in danger from the miscreant. That was well wide of the mark. The concoction of simple cousin Sam as a cover story illustrated as much. The offbeat location of the meeting reminded him of his own clandestine meetings with Albert from a different age and he could almost feel the silkiness of one of his mistress's intricate webs. He jumped out of bed, intent on finding out whom it concerned and what it involved.

Simmons paid no heed to the remonstrances of the landlord as he rifled along the upstairs of the Saddle banging on doors. He'd already called at half a dozen pubs where he knew Wilkes took rooms when he had leave from the *Akbar*. His nerves were frayed. He was on the cusp of failing his mistress for the first time. He wouldn't allow it to happen.

"Wilkes! Wilkes!" he yelled as he stomped from room to room. His presentation and countenance remained immaculate, numbing the landlord into inaction. There was not a sign that Simmons had been up all night, drinking for the majority of it. Or that he had crossed the river, twice, and traversed half of the Wirral peninsula. He had not even entered his room in the Atlantic, instead hurrying to the pier as soon as he had bade Potter goodnight, closing the door as he did so. He had paid a bargeman to carry him across the river and wait for his return. The Karl Benz motorised car was parked in a well-maintained coach yard and he waited impatiently while the driver sleepily cranked it to a start.

His mistress appeared without a hair out of place, only seconds after being roused by Potter's wife.

"I'm afraid there is every possibility that the location of the boy has been breached," he stated. The muscles needed to deliver the news were the only ones that moved in his whole body. Rebecca remained unmoved.

"Albert?" she asked.

"As good as," replied Simmons.

"Potter! Damn that infernal man." As efficient as ever Rebecca simply stated her orders. "Put the contingency plan into place. Away from the *Akbar*, Simmons, have him put ashore under the guise of an escape, I want it carried out on land."

"Yes Ma'am."

"Your man on the ship also?"

"As soon as possible Ma'am."

"Goodnight Simmons."

The Sunday morning Dock Road traffic was only a token of its weekday counterpart and Potter enjoyed the relative peace along with the stiff breeze coming from the river. If, as he suspected, 'Cousin Sam' was on some kind of shore leave there was a chance he would have made a full night of it and sought out a hair of the dog before presenting himself back at his ship. The odds were long but, he decided, it would do him no harm to have a look while partaking in a hair, or two, from the same dog.

A junior brass band passed by Potter heading in the opposite direction towards the Pier Head landing stage. Potter half chuckled at the belligerent scowls that greeted his warm smile. The boys were spick and span in their spotless uniforms, but the phrase 'wolves in sheep's clothing' sprang to mind. He had walked another twenty paces before registering the officer who led them. He wore exactly the same uniform as Cousin Sam. Potter changed direction and followed the band to the landing stage.

As the officer bent down, fussing over a smear of soot on his toecap, one of the scamps in the group blew a loud raspberry on his trumpet. The officer, his face beetroot, straightened up and spun around searching for the culprit. His gaze found Potter and he eyed him suspiciously. Potter recognised the look.

"Excuse me sir, I was just marvelling at your fine young fellows. Where is it they're performing, might I ask?" he ventured as it dawned on him that the boys must come from one of the floating reformatories.

"I'm afraid you're out of luck, they've already performed," answered the officer.

"Ah, is that so? I would have liked to have heard them for myself, I've heard great things about the *Clarence* brass band," he exclaimed loudly enough for the boys to hear.

"Oi, we're no dirty Paddies," quipped one of the rascals. The officer spun around to hush the culprit.

"Apologies my boy, the *Akbar* then, I thought from the uniform…"

"The uniforms are quite distinct, the Clarence are a different hue of blue entirely," stated the officer.

"Again my apologies," Potter gestured towards Annie Garvey, a permanent fixture on the landing stage since Potter himself was a boy. The old shack she squatted in had never changed, and Potter must have eaten a ton weight of the apples and oranges she sold during his life.

"Allow me to purchase the boys a piece of fruit to enjoy on their crossing, they look so grand."

Potter distributed the fruit to the grateful boys. He had always hoped to assuage the grief that was eating Albert alive by reintroducing his estranged son back into his life but his surreptitious attempts at locating Jobe had come to nothing and Potter constantly rebuked himself for not having ensured the boy was safe and supported at an earlier date, perhaps then Albert would not have transformed into the cold husk he had become. Recognising the opportunity for redemption he quickly made the short walk to Covent Garden, saying a silent prayer to anybody who may be listening that Albert had stayed true to form in scorning his frigid wife and was lying with one of his favourite barmaids from the Pig and Whistle.

Albert was barely dressed as he bundled down the narrow staircase that led from the rafters of the pub. Potter half chased him down Chapel Street, passing him items of clothing as they semi-trotted to the landing stage. Potter was impressed at Albert's reaction to his theory. What had been a disinterested, indifferent form with a girl half his size draped around him was transformed into an efficient machine at word of his son. Hence, Potter scurrying at his side like a schoolboy relaying specifics of the theory that had resulted in his unseemly appearance in the loft of the Pig and Whistle while handing Albert garments to ensure he was fully dressed by the time they reached the pier. The handful of notes and coins Albert held out meant they had no trouble finding a craft to carry them across to the Sloyne off the coast of Rock Ferry.

Albert stood in the small boat and looked wistfully at the three square-riggers in the murky distance.

"Which of them is the *Akbar*?"

The vicar enjoyed the opportunity to breathe fire and brimstone over his congregation. His ninety-minute sermons were infused with carefully planned, sometimes rehearsed, stagecraft and histrionics. It wasn't his usual style of service but he had spent the whole of his childhood picking oakum in a Preston workhouse. The memory of his bleak existence, the ruthlessness of the regulations and the eternal merging of day into dismal day were etched on every face and reflected from every eye that he looked into. He hoped his weekly cameo was a welcome escape from their suffering and prayed that in later life the boys present would recall his dramatic interludes with fondness and associate them with the church and the true word of the Lord.

The boys sat content throughout, knowing that the twisted and tar-stiffened pieces of ancient rope, coconut husks and swabbing mops would remain locked away for the remainder of the day. After making repairs to any damaged clothes or boots they would be left, in a fashion, to their own devices.

Jobe heard the midday mess bell and laid down the dog-eared Old Testament he had borrowed from the *Akbar*'s minuscule library. He had already read and re-read both the Old and the New Testaments, the only books that were contained in the small chest that was unlocked each Sunday.

The excitement around the tables was palpable as the boys waited for their usually tar-black tea to be transformed by a luxurious splash of milk.

"C'mon Peters, get a move on with the cow juice would you, my tea's going stone cold here." A splash of milk wasn't the only luxury that the boys enjoyed on a Sunday and Jobe felt his stomach sink as an extra slice of bullock-head meat was placed on his tin plate. He couldn't look at either without a surge of despair and guilt flushing over him. The memory of Horatio's enthusiasm regarding his pint of milky tea and extra portion of gristly meat would settle on him like a weight, stripping him of his appetite. He had continuously warned his companion over the amount of the dried goods he consumed.

"Go easy H, the stock-take isn't over-exuberant but neither is it non-existent, besides you're going to make yourself sick!" H would look up at him, the half masticated food he was shovelling into his mouth escaping from the sides.

"Mnnmmn mnnom," he would reply, gesticulating wildly at the brimming shelves before setting his hands back to the task of cramming food into his mouth. To imagine him eating enough dried porridge to burst his stomach made Jobe feel as if his own was on the same course.

He looked down at the tin plate that clattered down in front of him, but unlike his peers, simply stared at the food, showing no attempt to eat. He could almost hear H's hopeful tone as he gestured to whatever remnants of food remained on his plate.

"What's that Jobe? You're not letting that go to waste are you?" Without looking up he slid his plate to the empty place beside him and patted the gaping space on the bench. It was wide enough to accommodate at least two of the boys who sat squashed around the table, their elbows knocking as they ate, but Jobe had decreed that the space was H's. It was a scant memorial but there would be no other paid to his memory.

He had earned the right to proclaim the space as H's memorial. Cameron had whimpered as he lay on the floor looking up at the possessed demon standing over him, clutching the bloodied paddle. He watched as his blood trickled slowly down the thick handle to the flat wooden blade. He could only nod his acceptance of the terms that were being spat at him.

"You can continue to be the officer's dog, I know the vile acts you participate in to gain your grubby perks, but if I hear tell of one beating carried out at your hands I'll kill you! This is my mess now!" Jobe remained standing over Cameron but looked at the wide-eyed crowd, he purposefully fixed gazes with captains of other messes, not looking away until they had lowered their gaze.

"D'you all hear me? This is my mess now!" He paused, inwardly praying that they would remain transfixed by the image of the toughest bully on board lying at his feet like a wounded animal. One voice of dissent would bring everything crashing down and he would more likely than not be lynched there and then. He turned his attention back to Cameron.

"Now I remember our first meeting. You spat on my meat, proving yourself a devout and pious

Christian, did you not?" Cameron lay in the foetal position unaware how best to respond. He hesitantly nodded confirmation. Jobe smiled.

"Good, good…Then like Jesus you can atone for the sins of your brothers who are gathered here today." He turned back to the crowd, the macabre look of fascination on their faces signalling their total deference.

"You have a saviour! One who will atone for your many sins! But beware, this is a one-time cleansing, anybody who repeats a sin will receive frightening retribution!" Cameron screamed and the blood that had traversed the length of the wood began to crawl back in the direction it had come as Jobe silently hefted the paddle above his head.

Wilkes cursed himself as he climbed the rope ladder back aboard the *Akbar*. He hadn't even slept off the drink before that jumped-up butler Simmons had stormed into his room above Ye Hole in Ye Wall and ordered him back to the ship.

"I've wasted the best part of the morning searching for you, you oaf! Up now, on your feet and back to the ship, there's not a moment to lose!" he had roared as he grabbed at the bed sheets. Wilkes had sat up, unsure where he was and unable to comprehend the intrusion, his mind still blurred from his excesses. The instructions imparted to him as he dressed had a more than sobering effect. He was to put the boy in a cutter and deposit him on shore with immediate effect. And that would be that! An abrupt end to his high living.

"But just last evening you were of the opinion his staying aboard was of no consequence? You said you had faith in my stock, my ability to ensure he remained nothing but Flynn?" Wilkes had become immobile as his frenzied brain attempted to retain his lucrative earner.

"The situation has evolved, now move, man! Time is of the essence!" answered Simmons, growing more animated. Wilkes remained stationary.

"I can see his neck snapped and have him found floating in the river," he whispered, his hushed tones an attempt to seduce his paymaster. Simmons froze and looked Wilkes in the eye.

"We've discussed it before, it can be arranged for a small fee, a final payment," continued Wilkes blithely. Simmons contemplated the idea for a heartbeat before dismissing it, his mistress had ordered that the act be carried out on dry land, away from the *Akbar* and potential recriminations.

"There's no time. I've already told you, the situation has evolved."

Wilkes had prospered by ensuring the runt kept his real identity to himself. It was money for jam and everybody knew jam could be preserved for as long as was needed. To that end he hadn't saved a single ha'penny with which to realise his ambition of retiring back to Bristol away from the northern filth he'd been surrounded by for over half his life. But there had been no rush, here was an opportunity to live fast and free before saving for his later years. The plan had been to keep the boy aboard the *Akbar* even after his three-year sentence was up. Violation after violation could easily be concocted to ensure the boy remained on the ship into his dotage if needs be, but now it had all come to nought. He hadn't even managed to get into the drawers of Lucy, barmaid in the Cotton Picker, although he was sure he was on the cusp with his big-spending ways.

He clambered up over the rail and made his way across the deck, passing the hogs head barrel that some shaven-headed scamps were filling with pails of river water ready for a new inductee. A sudden rage overcame him and he aimed a heavy boot at the barrel, which rocked back and forth before finally tipping, spilling its contents on the deck. The boys watched the water seep over the freshly swabbed deck and shot daggers into the back of the officer's head.

As was customary he had gathered to observe the inauguration of the last new cadet but his usual apathy at proceedings was further enhanced by thoughts of the inroads he was making to the defences of Lucy, his favourite barmaid on the whole of the dock road. He looked around the quarterdeck wondering whom he could bribe to take his watch that night, thus allowing him to continue his bombardment. The conservative demeanour of the crew had tugged at his conscience but it wasn't until the little emmet had walked the barrel and was standing naked before his peers that their silence hit him. Officer Daniels, charged with overseeing proceedings, was visibly shaken by the lack of response to the well-versed jokes and his patter tailed off so that the only sound was the wind whipping through the masts and the flapping of untethered canvas.

The Catholic counterpart of the *Akbar*, the *Clarence* had narrowly averted a mass mutiny just weeks earlier and the Captain had already given the order for pistols to be distributed to those who stood beside him on the quarterdeck. Wilkes rebuked himself as a loaded pistol was pushed into his hand; he had been so lost in his own fantasies that he had been completely unaware of the silent menace. Daniels brought proceedings to a close, ordering the new cadet to put on the uniform at his feet in hushed tones. Once he was dressed the officer dismissed the crew in as resounding a tone as he could muster, his voice breaking mid-sentence. Nobody moved and Wilkes was primed to face down a rebellion. The Captain stepped up to the quarterdeck rail and in a tone that was filled with authority demanded that all hands go below decks and lash hammocks. His order fell on deaf ears and Wilkes heard more than one pistol cock. Just as the Captain was about to be forced into the ignominy of repeating his order one boy stood and moved towards the hatch. As one his peers rose or climbed down from the rigging and followed him. In his disbelief and clamour to confirm what his own eyes were telling him Wilkes had almost bundled the Captain over the rail. It was Flynn who led the ragbag crew down the hatch.

He had contemplated keeping the information to himself but was aware that his paymaster's grapevine was a large one. Simmons, or whoever employed the jumped up butler, would no doubt find out that the boy had become a strong and uniting influence and he'd be for the chop. His cushy number on the floating reformatory would be over and he'd be thrust back into the hardships of life on the open seas. He'd rather forfeit his earner than risk that happening.

"Is midday mess over yet?" he shouted up to the officer on watch who stood at the quarterdeck. The officer's name was Brent, one who was always ready to cover his shifts if the price was right.

"Didn't expect to see you back until later this afternoon Mr Wilkes, shat in your bunk again, have you?" Wilkes ignored the lighthearted jape and disappeared down the main hatch.

The boys looking up expectantly waiting for their splash of milk were shocked to see Wilkes stomping down the steps with murder in his eyes. He scanned the mess for an instant before making a beeline for Jobe Flynn. Jobe remained staring at the plate he had just slid into the empty space beside him while patting the bench reverently. Wilkes came up behind and without a word lifted him bodily from his place on the bench.

Jobe had a strange sense of déjàvu. Wilkes had hoisted him up against his will in the past, throwing him on to a stinking, slime-covered rope ladder that had begun this whole nightmarish episode of his life. Without thinking Jobe rammed his head backwards with all his might, catching Wilkes plumb on the bridge of his nose. Wilkes, shocked by the impact, released his grip on the boy as he brought his hands up to his face in reflex. Jobe found himself free from the clutches of the man who had brutalised him these past months. He turned and aimed a kick at the privates of the prone officer. Again his aim was precise and the pain coupled with the shock brought Wilkes to his knees. Jobe became aware of the spoon in his grasp and manipulated it so the handle protruded from his hand. As he prepared to jam it into his nemesis's undefended eye a bevy of warning cries came from the tables.

"Beware Flynn, behind you!" Jobe spun - but too late to avoid the blow to the back of his head. Senses swimming, he sank to the floor. Before losing consciousness he looked up to see Cameron standing over him, a smile on his face and a metal platter in his hands.

★ ★ ★ ★ ★

"C'mon man, put your back into it," demanded Albert. Potter had already had to pull him back from the prow of the boat for fear of him falling in, such was his eagerness to reach the *Akbar*. When they were only a few metres away Albert began hailing the ship at the top of his voice.

"Ho there *Akbar*, I say *Akbar*!" The lack of wind meant that he was answered just as the small rowboat touched the hull of the square rigger.

"Ahoy down there?" came the response. Albert and Potter looked up at the face peering down.

"Let down a ladder at once. I demand admittance aboard," shouted Albert.

"Can I ask the nature of your business sir?"

"My son is being held falsely aboard that ship, I demand admittance!"

"This is the HMS *Indefatigable* sir, a training ship, nobody is held here. Why, it is a privilege to be aboard."

"The *Indefatigable*? The *Indefatigable*, you say? Is this not the *Akbar*?"

"No sir this is the HMS *Indefatigable*, The reformatory ship *Akbar* is the next ship along." Albert turned, red-faced, to the oarsman.

"You fool, quickly now, to the *Akbar*." The oarsman pushed off without looking up at the belligerent giant standing above him. As they approached the *Akbar* a small cutter came from around its prow, heading towards the city. Albert tapped Potter, bringing his attention to the cutter.

"You there, ahoy!" called Potter, just as a small sail was unfurled from the single mast.

"You there, coming from the *Akbar* what is your business?" Potter's voice carried easily to the other vessel.

"And what business is it of yours?" came the response of an officer standing in the prow of the boat. Albert ignored the officer.

"Ahoy, any boys in the boat, are there any boys aboard the boat? Jobe Warburton, are you aboard that boat? It is your father here!" On receiving no response Albert looked at the boatman, who had stopped rowing.

"To the *Akbar* man."

Potter unceremoniously pulled himself over the rail of the *Akbar*. Albert was already standing on the deck. He had made short work of the climb and was surveying the scene on deck. As Potter regained his legs he saw the officer from the dock road. He couldn't believe that the scoundrel truly was an officer. He raised his arm and pointed towards him. Within a dozen strides Albert had the man held by the throat.

"Where is my son?" he growled as he tightened his grip. The officer's face, which already bore the marks of a struggle, turned bright red as he fought for breath. Potter reached Albert's side.

"Perhaps if you release your hold he can answer your question, Albert." Albert looked at Potter before loosening his hold and returning his caustic gaze to the officer.

"My son?" Albert could see the man's mind turning. He was in no mood for procrastination. He dragged the officer bodily to the rail and tipped him over, holding him by the ankles like a rag doll.

"Where is my son?" he shouted. Wilkes felt the blood he had swallowed but which had refused to settle in his gut seeping back up his oesophagus. The sensation made him baulk and he found himself choking, his panic causing him to thrash about, and Albert struggled to maintain his hold.

"Are you Flynn's father, then?" piped a small voice beside him. The name caused Albert to suck in his breath.

"He was taken unconscious aboard that cutter there," Albert followed the boy's finger to see the cutter he had hailed halfway to the Liverpool landing stage. He dragged Wilkes back up onto the deck where he lay flapping, dragging lungfuls of air through his flaring nostrils as the Captain appeared on the quarterdeck.

"I say, what the devil is going on here?" Albert paid him no heed.

"I'll be back for you!" He snarled at the mess of a man he had left on the deck before swinging his leg over the rail and following Potter down the rope ladder.

Albert tore the oars from the boatman and began to row for all he was worth.

Jobe came to with a start, too late to avoid the second pail of water that was thrown into his face. He spluttered and fought for breath as he lashed out with arms and legs. His brain struggling to recall events. He had just been ready to turn out Wilkes right eye with the handle of a spoon. He regained his breath and opened his eyes, bracing himself for whatever reprisals were coming his way. He closed his eyes against the harsh blue sky. He had been brought up on deck. It would begin with a flogging then, he thought. The blast of a tugboat horn forced his eyes open and he registered the clamour of sounds around him. He was lying on the floor of a cutter, a clear blue sky above him.

"C'mon be off with you, up you get and begone!" Jobe recognised the voice of Officer Corrigan.

"What? What's happening?" he asked, struggling to his feet; one hand searching out the lump on the back of his head.

"Your privileges aboard the *Akbar* have been annulled. You're to be reconciled with this filth," the officer said as he swept his hand towards the town. He stepped towards Jobe with the notion of physically forcing him onto the landing stage, but hesitated as Jobe's body stiffened and he ceased rubbing the back of his head.

Jobe stood transfixed, watching from the southern end of the Landing Stage as the cutter pushed off and began to negotiate the river traffic. He fought to calm his whirring mind as it attempted to comprehend his situation. He paid no heed to the small skiff, a relative dot, heading towards the pier, in which a giant was rowing for all he was worth.

Potter feared Albert would burst his heart through his efforts. He also had one eye on the steamers and tugs that Albert was paying not the slightest attention to but which had the power to smash their little craft to kindling. They had already felt the full wrath of a ferry captain who, realising the small boat wasn't going to give way, had had to take evasive action.

"You're flagging Albert, let me take over." Albert sensed his strokes had slowed and moved over, pushing Potter into his place.

"Quickly man, don't lose the momentum," he said as he shielded his eyes and looked to the pier. He blinked shaking his head disbelievingly as he looked at a boy, no a young man, standing on the quayside. His heart quickened as he noticed how the boy held himself, his bearing reminded him so much of himself but he could also see his wife, his ex-wife, his dead ex-wife. He caught a moan in his throat, clearing it quickly. Now was no time for self-recrimination.

"He's there, we haven't lost him, row Potter, for pity's sake row man!"

The small boat continued inching towards the stage, the swell of other boats sending it off course and hampering its progress. Albert kept his full attention on the boy captivated by the river and suddenly fancied it was he who was holding his attention.

"He's spied us, Potter!" he exclaimed as he began to wave his arms above his head.

"Jobe…Jobe…Jobe Warburton!" he roared, in a futile attempt to conquer the sounds of the river.

"No Jobe, wait…Wait for me Jobe, I'm here!"

Simmons stood in one of the covered waiting rooms that spread the length of the Landing Stage. Detached from the cacophony of the crowd he watched as the boy began to retreat towards one of the iron bridges that connected the Landing Stage to the mainland before turning his gaze to the dogged skiff that was only metres from the pier.

Jobe unconsciously backed away from the uproar of the landing stage, seeking a refuge from the crowded quayside. All of the ideas and intentions he had imagined to while away the hours spent scrubbing decks, the fantasies he had conjured while swinging in his hammock had all centred around his freedom. The people he would see again, the places he would visit, the wrongs he would right. All of them seemed a million miles away and he had no sense of the liberty he had been granted as barrow boys, chandlers and the hundreds of people embarking on a liner that would take them to America, their luggage both physical and mental, lugging behind them cajoled and jostled him up the gangway in a dozen different languages. He uncorked from the bottle neck of the gangway in a daze and stood frozen in shock and awe at the city directly facing him.

★ ★ ★ ★ ★

Potter read Albert's mind. There was no way he could make the jump, not from a standing start.

"Wait, Albert, a few more seconds, that's all," he advised, his chest heaving from exertion. They had watched forlornly as the boy began to back into the crowd that was obscuring him from their sight with alarming rapidity. Potter physically felt Albert leap as he pushed down with all his weight and then sprang. The boat became instantly lighter and darted towards the stage with fresh impetus. Potter worried whether he retained the strength to pull Albert from the river and knew the opportunity to reunite father with son had gone, wasted by Albert's all too familiar impatience. He was astounded when Albert cleared the churning water and landed on the stage on all fours, before springing up and knocking a post-boy from his bike, the basketful of letters and parcels in his basket exploding into the air like oversized confetti.

"To your right, Albert," he shouted as the boat glided alongside the pier, guided to perfection by its pilot, so that Potter could hop off with ease before the pier-master could question the illegal drop-off.

"He was heading south," he bellowed with the last of his breath. He watched Albert scanning the crowd and, puffing and blowing, reached his side just as he dashed off scattering people like kindling.

★ ★ ★ ★ ★

The events of his life cascaded over Jobe like a tsunami and he fled to escape them, unknowingly following the path of his old dock walks, towards Mann Island and the Albert Dock with no destination in mind. He weaved in and out of the throng in a futile attempt to outrun himself, becoming more frantic with each stride, ignoring those who turned to curse him. He weaved right to dodge a cart full of coconuts, but unable to tear his gaze away from them thumped into a man standing wearing a sandwich board. He bounced back on to the seat of his trousers, still unable to drag his gaze from the hypnotising coconuts.

"Well, I've had plenty taking me up on my offer but none so eager as you, Sir," said the man with the sandwich board as he redistributed the weight of the board back on to his shoulders. He bent as much as his constraints allowed him, and was about to help Jobe to his feet when a man came from nowhere and smashed the boy across the head with a cobble.

"Aye aye, now…" The man cut his remonstrations short and eyed the five-pound note being waved in front of him.

"Take this and put the boy aboard your wagon. On its departure there'll be another one for you." It took a second for the man to step out of his sandwich board and drape Jobe across his shoulder. Simmons looked down at the legend on the chipped whitewashed board.

DOCK WORK in HULL

ALL MANNER of SKILLS

REQUIRED & RESPECTED

FREE PASSAGE

"Smallpox outbreak! Smallpox outbreak! Three quarantine hulks to be towed to the Mersey!"

"Smallpox outbreak! Smallpox Outbreak..." The words died on the newspaper seller's tongue as a huge man came bounding towards him. He closed his eyes, knowing that the collision, which would surely send him to his parents in Heaven, was unavoidable. When he opened them again he saw the man had somehow skipped around him and was approaching a man with a sandwich board. He shrugged his shoulders and carried on bringing attention to his papers.

Albert swivelled around, his head jerking as if he had some illness of the mind. At a loss he called to a man crawling under a stationary sandwich board.

"You, man! Excuse me! Have you seen a boy pass by? Thirteen years of age or so, he'll have been running...he's my son, my only son." The man brought himself from his knees, and fixing the board on his shoulders he surreptitiously looked over towards Mann Island, making sure the toff, who had a white fiver belonging to him in his possession, was there. A wagon driver waiting on the cobbles cracked his whip and clicked his tongue, two mares shuddered in the traces, pulling the coach off with a jerk.

"Nobody of that description has passed this way I'm afraid, guv'nor," he replied, spreading his arms. Albert hoped Potter had fared better but sank to his knees as he watched his friend heading towards him. He was alone. Potter looked at the man with the sandwich board before reaching down and helping Albert to his feet.

"C'mon Albert, let's see about getting you a drink." Albert allowed himself to be helped up but turned to Potter, his jaw set.

"There'll be no more indulging in drink Potter. My only aim is to be reunited with my son."

Chapter VIII

1893

Jobe groaned. The brilliance of the blue sky above him penetrated his eyes each time they flickered open, lancing deep into the recesses of his skull. He turned his head from the glare and opening his eyes fully was greeted by a row of filthy boots only inches from his face. He turned his head. He turned his head only to be confronted by the same view. He had the sensation of being back aboard a boat but registered he was being bumped rather than swayed.

"Hold up, he's coming round. C'mon, move along, give us room to get him up." The request was greeted by muffled groans and expletives.

"What's the matter with youse, don't expect the poor lad to remain on the floor, do you?" The owner of the voice bent forward and pulled Jobe up towards a row of seated men. Jobe's head swam as he rose and he baulked as if ready to retch. Those already seated, sidling along a fraction at a time so as to surrender as little space as possible, suddenly squirmed from his path, creating an ever-widening space that was big enough for Jobe to be pulled into.

"Charlie Doyle," said the man who had pulled him from the floor as he busied himself wrapping Jobe in a thin, greasy blanket.

"There's a warmth to the sun, but the wind is biting due to us being so exposed," he offered in explanation. Jobe glanced around the open-air wagon. There were a dozen, a baker's including him, men crammed on to the benches, which looked as though they were made to seat eight at the very most. The blankets that they wrapped around themselves did little to keep out the gusts of wind whipping across the open moor. Jobe's wits slowly returned as the man next to him finally seemed satisfied that only his face was exposed to the wind. He looked past the men facing him taking in the green expanse that surrounded them. He stood up with a start.

"Where am I? What's going on?" The blanket fell to the floor and he would have toppled out of the wagon if his neighbour's reflexes had not been so quick.

"Now, now, don't want another bump to that noggin, do we? C'mon Fred lad, down we come, there we go." Jobe was coaxed down into a sitting position. The man who had introduced himself as, Charlie was it, was busy fussing around him with the blanket again. He sat stoically trying to make sense of his situation, but couldn't. He calmly began to help the man who was busy covering him.

"Where am I?" he asked, the neutrality in his voice causing Charlie to look up at him.

"Well, I don't know where we are exactly, Fred lad," he answered despondently.

"But I know where we're headed," he added brightening up instantly. "We're on our way to Hull," he exclaimed as if it were the best news he had ever imparted to anyone.

"Hull." Jobe was indifferent.

"Now you've got it," answered Charlie happily, nodding his head to the other men as he gesticulated at his new partner with his thumb.

"There's a pretty penny to be made on the docks up there, the Humber's bottlenecked with ships queuing up to dock and not enough hands to unload them." Jobe looked blankly at the man.

"Oh," was all that he could muster, before another question formed in his still rattled brain.

"Why am I going to Hull? How did I end up on the wagon?"

"Well, you were lucky to make it - that's for sure! If those two beauties up front had been a bit quicker with their old nosebags, there's no telling where you'd be," said Charlie animatedly. Jobe looked at him, waiting for him to continue.

"Well, we kicked up a right stink when Ted hauled you on to the wagon." He looked to his surly travelling companions for an affirmation that wasn't forthcoming. He dismissed them with a wave of his hand.

"Pah, miserable buggers!" He turned back to Jobe.

"The fellow with the sandwich board, well, he doesn't exactly run this operation, but he makes sure there's enough backsides on the wagon before it sets off to Hull. Well, as I say, we were only waiting on the nags finishing their dinner when you flop at our feet. Oi, I says to him. Oi, what's all this then? Pressing now are we?" He rubbed his red nose, almost taking his own eye out, as the wagon went over a bump. Jobe's blanket flapped down exposing his throat and Charlie tucked it back in before carrying on.

"Well Ted, that's his name, says to me, to pacify me like, 'the lad's in peril, look to the bumps on his head if you doubt my word, his name's Fred and he needs out of the town he does.' Well, I has a look and your old noggin *is* in a bad way, the claret's not exactly flowing but there was a trickle all right." Jobe freed his hand and brought it to the back of his head. His hair was stiff and matted with dried blood and he traced his palm across not one but two lumps.

"By the time I'd put a bit of a rag to your head and laid you down there, old Ted was back at his board and we're pulling away, and do you know what?" he paused for effect, pushing his face closer to Jobe's.

"There's only a big toff talking away to him, all frantic like, massive he was! Well, unsure of Ted's resolve I shouts to the driver up front, hurry up then Bert, let's get up to Hull and don't spare the horses," he tapped his nose knowingly.

"A couple of these oafs, those that can form an opinion like, reckon you to be a runaway from one of the reformatory ships, judging by your attire like! But I says to them, who absconds from a ship in only a thin undershirt and no Guernsey! Whatever's been going on, I reckon you had a near miss, Fred my lad! A lucky escape and no denying!"

Jobe looked into the big mess of a face unable to make sense of the stream of words that were escaping from it.

Rebecca heard the heavy, purposeful footsteps of her son approaching the walled garden where she sat in front of a moon shaped pool. Composing herself she took a deep breath inhaling the scent of the Damask Roses that surrounded her, making a mental note to have a bunch placed in her rooms. Simmons had informed her of proceedings aboard the *Akbar* and in preparation of the confrontation to come she had dismissed all of the gardeners and informed all servants to remain indoors. Even so she had ordered the ornamental fountain to be turned on, ensuring that any raised voices would be muffled and distorted by their melancholic burbling.

Albert stooped through the arched entrance to the garden.

"I must congratulate you, Mother, this time you have really outshone yourself. Surely even you have never before woven such an intricate web of deceit and intrigue." He looked straight at his mother who, rather than meet his eye, watched him through his distorted reflection in the rippling pool. Rebecca, unaccustomed to being economical with the truth, had decided that refuting Albert's allegations would only debase her righteousness. Looking up she accosted him with her glare.

"You speak as one who is enlightened, yet you remain ignorant of everything barring the slightest strands of what you aptly name my web. You estimate it to be a recent undertaking? You have no idea of the magnitude of the interventions that I have made on your behalf, all of which I have executed in your best interests. What did you suppose, Albert, that I would allow you to renounce your legacy for the love of a Catholic slum-dweller? That my authority over you would be diluted by the width of a river? How could you have been so criminally callow?" the tone of her voice was mirrored by the caustic glint in her eye and, Albert, unprepared for such a frank admission, turned and took a seat on a stone bench. He looked at the gravel under his feet and shook his head as he attempted to formulate a reply.

"It is you who has committed the crime, Mother. Did it cause you such grief to think of me happy?" his head remained bowed and he didn't not see his mother's lip curl into a snarl at his words.

"Do not have the temerity to question me on the subjects of happiness or grief, is there not an ounce of respect in you for the black you see me wearing day after day?" Rebecca strode over to her son and grabbed him by the jaw, forcing him to look her in the eye.

"Ask yourself, Albert, whose fault is it that I am forced to wear these mourning colours day after day?" her meaning dawned on Albert and he grabbed her wrist, forcibly removing it from his face. He stood, his mother's translucent wrist still in his iron grip.

"Do not speak in riddles, Mother, explain yourself!"

"Did you imagine I was ignorant of the monthly stipends that encouraged you to remain in your squalor?" she shook herself free of his grasp and smoothed out her ruffled dress before looking her son in the eye once more. "That I would sit idly by and permit my only son to rot amongst the lowest classes of the toiling multitudes?"

"You killed my father, your husband, in order to restore your control over me?" Albert whispered the question, his tone muted through disbelief rather than any fear of being overheard. On seeing his mother roll her eyes at his bearing he stiffened his resolve, discarding the speech he had prepared, understanding that nothing he said could puncture his mother's callousness. His only power over her existed with himself.

"I came here only to inform you that I want you to arrange my divorce." He said. Rebecca illustrated her disdain by refusing to justify Albert's demand with any response, focusing her attention on the petal of a rose she had plucked and held between her forefinger and thumb.

"This is no request, Mother. You had my last marriage annulled within a week; my wife is a woman is she not? The law states that I can divorce of my own accord, and I will." Rebecca crushed the petal allowing it to drop into the pool.

"A woman yes, not that your uncertainty surprises me, but, Felicity is no Catholic whore from the slum, she is from a family of good standing. There will be no divorce, no further scandal." Albert's hand unconsciously went to his moustache, which he twisted.

"Speak of my departed wife in that manner again and I will see you hang for the atrocity you have conducted, regardless of whether I have to drape the noose myself." Albert's hand retuned to his side, the look of shock across his mother's features appeasing his temper. "But you speak the truth, Mother, and I will, like you, concoct and hatch, plot and plan, just like a common rough. My wife, hmm Felicity, I like it, will come to see my son as her own. Her wealth will be the vehicle of your destruction! Scandal, oh yes there will be plenty, and I assure you, I will continue to shovel it onto your grave long after you are dead and forgotten by all bar me."

* * * * *

As the sun began to set the stream of words
continued to spew forth from the shapeless face
and showed no sign of abating. The throbbing
in Jobe's head became more concentrated and
he wished that the sporadic complaints of his
travelling companions would have some effect on
his communicative neighbour.

As the last shaft of light disappeared from the
sky the wagon turned off the well-worn road that
intersected the bleak moor and began to bump
along what was little more than a dirt track. The
moor came to life and the calls of its nocturnal
inhabitants drove terror into the men in the wagon.
Even Charlie ceased his continual babble, better
to hear the approach of any wild animal intent on
snatching him from his perch.

It had been dark for a long time and a cacophony
of snores had joined the chorus of animal calls
when the wagon stopped. Jobe looked around, not
noticing the house that was moulded into the gloom
until a shaft of dirty light escaped from an upstairs
window. Somebody must have heard the wagon pull
up and was now holding a candle up to the glass. The
window returned to darkness and after a minute
or two the same candle lit the entrance as the front
door was pulled open.

Nobody emerged from the dingy entrance but a
scolding voice carried to the wagon.

"Arrived have we! Well, I hope you're not expecting hot food. There'll be bread and butter for supper!" The men in the wagon remained stationary. Following hours of griping at the wagon driver and straining their eyes in the hope of seeing their overnight billet, not one of them moved.

"What is it you're waiting for, an invite from the Lord himself? Some of us have work to do!"

The men trailed out of the wagon and, as one, traipsed up a gravel path to the barely illuminated front door. Charlie looked back to the wagon. Bert had climbed into the back, busy gathering all of the blankets together.

"You coming, Bert?" Bert looked up from the wagon.

"Horses!" he called by way of an answer.

"Besides I like to take advantage of the night air," he muttered. Charlie shook his head and followed the waning glow of the candle that was proceeding through a narrow hallway and into a kitchen. The candle, the only source of light in the room, was placed on a long table. The men took their place on the benches around it. Without any audible conference they arranged themselves exactly as they had been positioned in the wagon.

"I won't bother remaking the fire as it'll be bed following supper." Jobe looked towards the grate that didn't have even the slightest glow of dying embers.

"Well, what about the tea?" asked Charlie from beside him. "It's all that's got me through that bog and all the hooting, the thought of a nice cup of tea."

"Yes, yes, there's a pot on the table there. Here I'll light the lamp shall I!" The solitary candle was finally supported in supplying some illumination as the landlady lit an oil lamp from it and banged it back on the table. Jobe was sure he saw something scurrying from the light and back into the safety of the shadows but his head was still spinning and he was loath to strain his eyes. The lamp temporarily illuminated the landlady's face. Sharp cheekbones accentuated sunken, eyes and a puckered mouth lent to an overall look of shameless brutality. The smell that permeated the room thickened with her proximity and Jobe gagged.

The man nearest to the pot grabbed at it and filled a jar that was next to him, not bothering to pass the pot on to his neighbour, he slammed it back down and after a haphazard journey around the table it reached Charlie.

"Pah, it's not even lukewarm and it's thick as treacle but weak as piss," he spat, wiping his mouth with his sleeve. The response was caustic.

"Take it or leave it, you city folk coming up here with your fancy ways!" Charlie nudged Jobe.

"Our fancy ways? Tell you what, happen we're lucky that we're blinded by this gloom, Fred lad, I wouldn't like to see what lays behind it." Jobe found himself unable to do anything but nod. A platter of bread and butter clattered on to the table. As with the teapot, courtesy was abandoned and the platter skittered across the table as hands from all directions descended on the mound of sparsely buttered bread.

"I've cut it extra thick and there's more than a slice each," Charlie's hand shot out and grabbed two slices, one of which was proffered to Jobe. Jobe folded it, conscious of the indents caused by fingers and thumbs that didn't belong to him. He hoped they were Charlie's. He bit into it, immediately feeling a sharp pain in his mouth. He manipulated his tongue and worried a piece of grit free of his molars, a sure sign of the cheapest of bread.

"It's almost snapped my tooth!" shouted Charlie, experiencing the same thing. He brought a hand to his offended mouth.

"Pah, I'll not bother with this. I think I'll retire if you don't mind," he said, half rising from the bench.

"No, you don't! I'll not have you all lumbering up the stairs one at a time disturbing my other guests. They're well-to-do gentlemen, local, loyal customers. I'll not have you waking them." Charlie was forced to sit in simmering silence until the men had eaten their bread and drank the cold tea. Realising there was no form of recreation on offer they began theatrically to clear their throats. The landlady approached from wherever she had been lurking in the shadows.

"I suppose it'll be bed for you now, will it, well some of us have work to do. I'll show you up and then I'll be back down to clear your mess shan't I. Quiet mind, I don't want my regulars disturbed."

The whole staircase shuddered as the men tramped their way up it. The landlady led the way carrying the candle and the oil-lamp, loath to relinquish either. Those directly behind did their utmost to angle their heads from her wake. She stopped in front of a closed door. Hanging the lamp on a rusted nail protruding from a scorched patch of the wall she unlocked the door. The smell that emanated from the room caused the most hardy of the men to turn their face as if in response to a slap from an invisible hand.

"Well, are you planning on staying the night on the landing? In with you," she barked as she reclaimed the oil lamp from its hook. She had lost all interest regarding her loyal guest's peace.

"All of us in the one room?" contested Charlie.

"Come on, in you go, some of us still have work to do, can't afford the luxury of sleep, never mind complaining of the machinations of it." The landlady remained outside the room jealously guarding both sources of light. The men, heads bowed, had already begun to file into the pitch-black room. A startled shout came from within the darkness.

"'Ere, there's folk already in these beds!" The landlady hung her oil-lamp back on its hook and entered into the room, beating her free hand down on the beds with venom.

"Shove over you bleeders, haven't I warned you about spreading yourselves!" she screeched, before turning her ire on the men crowded around the door.

"Don't tell me you haven't shared a bed before, c'mon in with you, some of us have work to do." Charlie grabbed the oil-lamp from the hook and shouldered his way into the room. He held the light to each of the half dozen double beds squeezed against the walls, paying no heed to the landlady's protestations. Bleached white faces blinked in the feeble glow of the lamp, the marble orbs of their skeletal knuckles almost popping with the effort of pulling the tattered bedclothes further up to shield their eyes.

"Bless us and save us! What is this place! These men would be better off in their graves!" The words were only uttered, shock muting the usually booming tones. The landlady snatched the oil-lamp from Charlie's limp hand.

"Well I never...in all my time running this establishment...in the lot of you now!" Jobe and Charlie were the only two who did not respond to the order. Charlie hadn't even registered it. He stood in a state of dread.

"And the door locked to boot," he mumbled as he shook his cannonball of a head.

"And it'll remain locked! I'll have nobody creeping around under the guise of answering a call of nature. There are two chamber pots." Charlie came to as if waking from a nightmare.

"Yes, and doesn't the smell tell you that both are in desperate need of emptying! Sod this, I'm off to the wagon! It's no wonder Bert opts for the night air! You coming, Fred lad?" Jobe followed Charlie down the dark unsteady staircase, his hand reluctantly but frequently brushing against the greasy wallpaper for balance and direction.

The landlady, gripped between following the two down the stairs and leaving those milling about the room to their own devices, settled on crouching on the uppermost steps to ensure the two renegades left the house. On reaching the front door Charlie spun around and addressed the flickering glow of the candle.

"And another thing, missus...you wanna try wiping that arse of yours with sandpaper!" he crossed the threshold into the clear night air, noisily filling his nostrils with it. Bert sat up when he heard the commotion at the front door.

"What's the matter?" he asked as Charlie gave Jobe a leg up into the back of the wagon. His wide frame, topped by wide rising shoulders that expanded to his huge head, gave the impression of a man who would struggle to drag his bulk, but his movements were lithe and graceful and he pulled himself into the wagon in one fluid movement.

"We've all grown up sharing beds, if we were lucky, but asking fit and able men to sleep with the infirm and bedridden, I've never seen the likes. That hag must be on to a pretty penny locking them poor blighters up and cashing in their settlement bonds and savings," he paused in reflection.

"I'll tell you what Bert, there's nothing much that's endearing this trip to me thus far, apart from making the acquaintance of young Fred here. If we get to Hull and the promise of work is as farfetched as everything else there'll be hell to pay for those who've sent us." He made his declaration as he pulled Bert's covers from him; ignoring the driver's remonstrations he counted them before handing him a third of them back.

"Don't get up Bert, you stay on your bench, the lad can take the front seat, he's got littler legs than us, that ok with you Fred?" he asked as he placed another third of the blankets on the driver's bench.

Silky fingered the heavy iron poker in his hand. His favourite weapon, his belt, with it's three sharpened brass buckles that, when whirled about, would gather one by one next to the fastening buckle to create a vicious instrument of violence would be of no use in the confinement of the Den. He closed his eyes, sensing the rest of his boys lurking with intent in the darkness.

Everybody who had a right to know, knew about the jars. Even the lads who came home, their heads muddled by Laudanum, opium mixed with water, which he strictly forbade, remembered the jars. Nobody ever knocked one down accidently, they knew that sending a jar crashing to the floor would alert the whole gang and could well result in them getting knocked unconscious or worse. Silky could tell by the huge forms of the two that had entered the room that it wasn't members of the Canal Bankers or Bridge Boys carrying out a midnight raid, neither one of those maggots would dare, nor could it be the Logwood Gang, they'd disbanded when the need for their vigilantism had passed. The invaders must be aware that they had set off some kind of alarm or warning system, but judging by their confident movements paid the fact little heed. If they weren't from another gang they could only be coppers. Silky was smart enough not to launch an attack against coppers, spending the rest of his life behind bars didn't appeal to him. He struck a match, holding the flame to an oil-lamp. The room was instantly lit. The two men standing before him weren't fazed by the sudden illumination. Silky drew in a breath. He hadn't looked into the peculiar green eyes that stared at him now for what seemed like a lifetime. Memories of penny pies and a hot air balloon rolled into his mind. He lowered his poker.

"You haven't come looking for your sixpence have you, 'cos I'm afraid it's been well and truly spent." Albert instantly recognised the urchin from Georges Dock. How long had it been, six perhaps seven years previous? The boy hadn't grown a great deal but had filled out adequately. He was obviously doing well for himself judging by his attire. Silky didn't register the recognition in the green eyes.

"You don't remember me?" he asked.

"On the contrary, I'm glad to remake your acquaintance, and that you have the good grace to recall the pie and sixpence I furnished you with that day."

"Perhaps," replied Silky noncommittally. His mind was racing through recent jobs the gang had carried out, trying to create a link between any one of them and the man in front of him. It was useless. He could have been a victim of anyone of a score of recent jobs they had carried out. Silky looked into the green eyes searching for a clue of the man's intentions. There was no trace of the humour that had put Silky at ease on their initial meeting and he involuntarily swallowed as his mouth flooded with saliva, his Adam's apple betraying his concern.

Albert noted the reflex and moved to put the boy, no the young man, at ease.

"I have no malicious intentions here. I simply come in search of my son, Jobe Warburton."

"Jesus it's the Giant O' coming looking for Jobe!" The outburst from somewhere behind Albert was quickly repeated by the dozen or so gang members around the Den, and whispers of 'the Giant O' traversed the room, the boys repeating it in awe rather than to inform their comrades. Silky threw the box of Lucifer matches to a boy facing him and made his way to the Chesterfield, giving no indication of the rising panic he was feeling. The Giant O' in his Den! He sat down ignoring the urge to take the gold-rimmed monocle from his embroidered waistcoat lest his hands shake and betray his fear.

"We've heard no news of Jobe since he was taken aboard the *Clarence* almost eighteen months past. We're expecting one of our members to be released a fortnight from now, he's sure to have news for us." Silky noted the pained look that flashed across his impromptu visitors features. "I've no concerns for his wellbeing though," he added quickly. "Jobe was sentenced with my lump of a cousin, Tommy Molloy, and he'd fight the devil himself to stop any harm coming to Jobe." Albert gestured to a three-legged stool.

"May I?" he asked. Silky provided permission with a curt nod of his head. He looked up at the Giant O's companion and, his confidence returning, made a pharaonic gesture with his left arm inviting him to be seated also. Potter watched the boy who was busy lighting the remaining oil lamps before sitting.

"Jobe was not confined on the *Clarence* as you suggest, he was placed aboard the *Akbar*," explained Albert. Silky recoiled from the news.

"Then I'm afraid it's more than likely he's dead, no Catholic could endure aboard the *Akbar,* populated as it is by treacherous O's," Silky remembered who he was addressing and fought to control his Adam's apple while retaining eye contact.

"You're mistaken, I'm delighted to say. I've been looking for him these last two days, since Sunday afternoon in fact, when he was put ashore from the *Akbar,* I last observed him racing toward the Albert Dock but since then have neither sight nor sound of him." Silky shook his head.

"But it makes no sense, he hasn't served even a half of his three year sentence…" Albert turned to Potter who inclined his head slightly. Albert was in agreement with his friend's unspoken endorsement of the boy's reaction. For the second time in two brief meetings Albert decided Silky was telling the truth. He had no knowledge of Jobe's whereabouts. Albert pulled a five-pound note from his wallet and gave it to Silky, along with a card.

"My address is on the card, furnish me with news of my son's return, or his whereabouts, and there'll be more money than you and your gang can count together, said Albert standing. Silky stood with Albert and brought himself to his full height, still not coming to Albert's chest. He handed the five-pound note back to Albert but retained the card.

"If Jobe wants you to hear of his return, then you'll hear."

Jobe didn't immediately realise he had woken. Each breath felt cold and pure in his lungs. He lay vacuously watching the stars play out above him. He had never known that they were so numerous or that they could shine so bright. The sense of serenity he experienced was a new sensation.

"Jobe Warburton!" he said out loud. The name caused him to sit bolt upright as if a jolt of lighting had coursed through his body.

"Jobe Warburton," he said again, more loudly this time.

"What's that...who...what?" Charlie's arms flailed as he attempted to sit up.

"What's the do, Fred lad?" he asked as he finally steadied himself.

"I'm not Fred, I'm Jobe, Jobe Warburton." Charlie looked across at Bert who was snoring blissfully. He looked over at Jobe before rubbing his face with both hands as if dry-washing it.

"What's this you're saying, Fred? You're name is really Jobe?" he asked.

"That's right Charlie, Jobe, Jobe Warburton," he shook his head.

"That's the first time I've said my name out loud for over a year!" he whispered to himself. He cupped his hands around his mouth and stood.

"My…name…is…Jobe…Warburton!" he shouted at the top of his lungs. Charlie sprang forward, finger on his lips.

"Shhh, all right Jobe lad, don't want to rouse the whole of Yorkshire now do we?" he grabbed his blankets and gestured over to the front of the wagon.

"What say I have a seat up front with you, eh? We'll have a good chinwag and wait for the sun to come up."

They pooled their thin blankets producing a thicker layering, which they sat under in silence looking up at the stars. Charlie fully concentrated on them, broke the silence.

"So, Jobe eh? I like it! Better than Fred. I thought you had a bit more about you than a plain old Fred." The silence continued, as did their vigil of the stars.

"I can remember my mother telling me his story," said Jobe.

"He was the most pious man in his village, good and holy. But God took everything from him, his herds, his land, his family and finally his health. Stripped him of everything in a wager with the Devil. He was persecuted mercilessly but throughout it all he never lost his faith, remaining good and pious,"

"The Book of Job," said Charlie.

"I remember it from Church," he declared shaking his head in wonder, as if amazed by the power of his memory.

"I think it was a gibe at my father's mother, my grandmother," said Jobe. "She ostracised my father when he married my mother, kept him from his birthright and me from my legacy."

"You've lost me now, Jobe," said Charlie, after taking in a deep breath.

Jobe started from the beginning. The house in Everton, his father, the descent into the slums, the death of his mother and downfall of his grandparents, the gang and finally his term on the *Akbar*. All the while looking up at the stars making their arc across the night sky. When he was finished a silence settled between the two again; Bert's snoring and the odd animal call the only sounds.

"I accused Ted of pressing you," Charlie said after a while. He sensed Jobe take his eyes from the sky and look at him for the first time since they had sat down. He didn't return the look but continued.

"You know, like in the old days. The Press Gang used to hunt down men, mostly drunks. Any who had the misfortune of crossing paths with a Press Gang would wake up far out to sea with a head resembling yours." He felt Jobe return his gaze to the sky.

"No, I don't think I was pressed. I think someone followed me off the *Akbar*, Wilkes or whoever was pulling his strings on shore. I don't know. It makes no sense. But at first light I'm heading back to find out." The determination in Jobe's tone made the hairs on Charlie's neck stand up. He didn't doubt the lad's conviction but was of the opinion that a passage of time would help his situation.

"Why not let a layer of time settle on it, for now at least. It sounds to me like your feet haven't touched the floor. Continue to Hull. Think. Plan. Work; fill your pockets with a bit of brass, it'll make things a lot easier when you do return. C'mon now what about some shuteye before the cock is crowing?"

★ ★ ★ ★ ★

Jobe's knees cracked as he jumped from the wagon. His headache had almost abated but it protested with a jagged wave of pain as he looked back at Charlie, who remained seated pawing at his eyes and cheeks. He brought his hand up to the back of his head and traced it over the still prominent but diminishing bumps as he made his way around the house in search of some privacy in which to answer his ever more urgent call of nature.

He wondered at the piles of rubble as he picked his way among them, assuming that they were remnants of an old storehouse but gasped in the realisation that they had once belonged to the boarding house itself. The back portion of the house consisted of interior walls, the exterior was gone, dilapidated, as if a giant hand had swiped it away and scattered it over the moor to serve as proof that a full house had once existed. Jobe could make out the pattern on the remnants of wallpaper that doggedly clung to the exposed walls. Weather-beaten interior doors now served as part of the exterior wall. Jobe wondered if the landlady ever opened them to provide much needed ventilation, but judging by the smell of the place he doubted they had been opened in years. No wonder the sleeping arrangements were so cramped, had anybody 'creeping around during the night, under the guise of answering a call of nature' ever wandered through one of the doors and found themselves on the lonely moor with two broken legs. Jobe shook his head in disbelief as he wiped his hands on his the seat of his pants.

On his return to the wagon Charlie was placing a blanket on each of their travelling companions' perches. Jobe doubted they would be needed, the sky was a perfect blue and the sun already had a warmth to it. He turned toward the house on hearing a loud rapping to see Bert hastily scuttling back up what served as a path before the front door could be opened.

"Soon be setting off, Jobe lad. If we make good time we should be able to get half a day's pay in, more if the light lasts," Charlie said as Jobe climbed back aboard.

The silence was total and even Charlie seemed absorbed in his own thoughts. The moor suddenly turned into the outskirts of a town without any warning. The two piebald mares took a small crest in their stride and on breaching it found that the dirt track became cobbled and a flurry of low grey housing sprawled down towards the River Hull which they could see meandering through the town before feeding out into the Humber. The attention of the men was pricked by the change in terrain but they remained tight-lipped and in possession of their own counsel.

They hadn't travelled far through the town when, nearing midday, the wagon came to a halt outside a rundown public house. A trio of burly men lounged on a bench against its poorly whitewashed wall, paying no attention to the men in the wagon. The landlord appeared as if he had been expecting them, hurriedly buttoning a bottle-green overcoat that he wore over a pair of brown buckskin breeches.

"Welcome to Hull," he said in a thick Yorkshire accent as he cast his eyes over the men.

"Goodness, you're a scrawny one," he stated in astonishment as he noticed Jobe, who was busy taking in the garish attire he wore. Jobe realised the landlord must be their ganger. He turned his attention from Jobe and ducked in order to pop his head inside the pub doorway calling instructions to someone inside.

"Thirteen halves if you will, Trudy," he ducked back out beaming at the men.

"We know how to treat our guests in these parts! A quick stretch of your legs, a wetting of your whistles and then we'll see about squeezing in half a day, shall we? You'll be needing the price of a pint when we get back!" he collapsed into a fit of coughing and wheezing as he shook his head, enjoying his own joke, alone. A thin girl appeared through the doorway holding a tray with half a dozen pint pots. Jobe thought back to the commotion caused by cold tea and grey bread in the guesthouse, he didn't fancy the girl's chances, but the sombre tone that had been a constant companion across the moor remained prevalent and the men waited quietly for their glasses.

"Is there any chance of a cup of tea, mister?" asked Charlie hopefully. The landlord looked at him quizzically before noting that the girl still had one full glass on her otherwise empty tray. Bert looked expectantly but the landlord paid him no heed, instead ushering the girl through the small doorway. He followed re-emerging with a silver canteen and two cups.

"You'll never drink tea again! I'm not usually so free with my Colombian beans but seeing as you're a guest." Charlie took the proffered cup, examining the ink black contents. He took a sip and with a shrug of his shoulders held up the cup to the landlord in a toast. Jobe didn't relish the half pint he found himself holding but such was his desperation for something cold to drink he drained the glass in one, to the delight of the landlord.

"Ha, there mightn't be much of you but you drink like a true Liverpudlian. Let's hope you can work like one as well, eh! C'mon then, muckers…" He entered into one of his laughing, coughing fits with this utterance and could only wave them towards the wagon, his bottle-green sleeves shimmering in the sun.

The thoroughfare they followed was a busy one. Trestle tables lined both sides of the street, creaking under the weight of the fresh fish that was piled upon them. The sight of a group of working men in a wagon was certainly not a peculiar one and Jobe wondered at the baleful stares of those that stopped their appraisals or turned from their wares to watch them pass. He was relieved when the wagon turned into a narrow, relatively unpopulated side street, coming to a stop next to a set of rusted gates. The men dismounted from the wagon, the last one down being the landlord who had sat next to Bert for the trip. Bert turned the wagon around and without bidding farewell to anyone started back on the long journey to Liverpool.

The landlord took a heavy key from his pocket and unchained the gates, which creaked open. The dock itself and the surrounding warehouses were deserted. The array of weeds and vegetation lent the whole wharf an aura of long-term disuse and abandonment. Jobe looked at Charlie, who raised his eyebrows. The scene didn't fit with his original description of ships cramming the Humber waiting to unload. The landlord noted the disquiet etched on every face.

"Why the long faces? Don't worry the work's here! Hull's a busy port but it's not Liverpool. Docks are abandoned now and again, now c'mon, let's be having you," he breezed as he led the group to the wharf's edge. Looking down into the undisturbed water Jobe saw a barge tethered to a rusting ladder, which was only precariously bolted to the quay. Jobe's stomach sunk as he realised why ship-owners with a town full of dockers to employ had sent to Liverpool to recruit.

"This has a bad feeling to it, Charlie," he said. "What's all this about?" he called to the landlord.

"Don't suffer seasickness do you, the dock we're working is on the other side of the river," he answered innocently.

"Don't you have bridges in Hull! I've never sailed into a pitch."

"My apologies, button, we're not so enlightened in Hull as to have a railway to ferry dockers about like royalty. Dockers from these parts rely on their legs to get to work. Our pitch is t'other side of the Hull, feel free to swim,"

"He obviously doesn't know the prices they charge on the overhead railway, but to be fair it does serve as a decent umbrella," said Charlie in an attempt at breaking the tension.

"Times a-ticking, men," continued the landlord, pointing up at the sun. All tones of virtue had left his voice and there was no doubt the sentence was an ultimatum. Jobe watched as the tightly huddled dockers approached the ladder as one. He wondered whether it was just habit that they grouped together like sheep or something darker and more depressing born out of generations of servility. He shouted at the group, anger straining his voice.

"Listen, we've all seen boats like this unloading knobsticks on the dock! They're the worst kind of scab, if scabs are worthy enough to warrant a pecking order that is!"

"Hark at him! Bright little union button I've been saddled with here," smiled the landlord through gritted teeth.

"There's nothing untoward here, those that want an honest day's work, with plenty following, look sharp. Those that don't…" The men began to file towards the ladder, disappearing down it one by one.

"Jobe, lad?" Jobe forced himself to look into Charlie's mishmash of a face.

"Did you know, Charlie?"

"Well, I had an inkling but was hoping it wasn't the case. I'm sorry," he said, unable to meet his eye. Jobe paused before taking hold of one of his massive hands, clasping it in both of his. Charlie pulled the boy to his breast.

"I won't ask you to come or understand," he said as he hugged him.

"Don't do it Charlie, never mind what kind of shoes you find yourself in today, they'll be walking a new path tomorrow, this decision will taint your steps forever, you're a good and honest man, to good to become a scab." Charlie broke the embrace. A man who was about to broach the descent called to Jobe.

"What about the likes of us what've been blackballed by your union? Shut out because we're happy to pick up a day's work when it's available, you can't expect the bosses to pay us for sitting on empty crates using our last coppers to send for beer." It was the first time Jobe had heard the man utter a word.

"Down the ladder with you, gobshite, looking for a boy to redeem you from your nefarious doings," Charlie turned back to Jobe.

"Go home lad, go now, reclaim what's left of your family, see if you can catch Bert and the wagon. If he tries to stop you getting on board tell him he'll have me to answer to!" Jobe turned and ran without looking back.

The landlord had locked the gates but there was enough slack in the chain for Jobe to push the gates and squeeze through the gap that appeared. He jogged up the quiet side street, slowing to a walk as he entered the busy thoroughfare. The malevolent looks its occupants had shot at the group of knobsticks in the wagon made sense to him now and he quickly retraced its route being sure to give a cursory glance at the pubs he passed in case Bert had tethered the mares outside one of them.

He arrived at the landlord's pub out of breath. He hadn't caught sight of Bert and his heart sank when there was no sign at the pub. The three men remained lounging on the bench; Jobe guessed they were heavies employed by the scab-ganger to protect his interests. They supped at the foaming mugs they now held, paying him no attention until he made to enter the pub.

"Oi, weren't you on the scab wagon?" asked a thickset man without getting up. The peak of his filthy cap covered the top half of his face so all Jobe could see was a dirty unshaven mouth and chin.

"Has the wagon that brought us passed back this way?" Jobe asked hopefully.

"Off with you, scab!" came the unhelpful reply.

His race to retrace his steps had left Jobe tired. He had been hoping for at least a glass of water from the thin serving girl. Without the landlord's eagle eye he was hoping to charm her out of something to eat as well.

An image popped into his mind, Bert licking his lips in the hope of a half pint that wasn't forthcoming. Of course he wouldn't stop there. He ran from the pub leaving the final rows of squat slum housing behind him. He struggled up the small rise the wagon had rolled up earlier that day. Reaching the crest he took in a breath. Everything that stretched ahead, for what seemed like an eternity, was green. He never appreciated how expansive the space was from the wagon. There was no sign of Bert and his piebald mares on the road and his Adam's apple bobbed in reflex to the enormity of the journey that lay ahead. The sense of exposure added to his discomfort and he had half a mind to turn back into the shelter of the grey anonymity he had just left. He could scrape along in Hull as well as in Liverpool after all but images of Molloy and Silky, Fergus and even the Giant O' his father, crowded his mind. There would be no replacements for them in Hull. Scattered though they may be, they were all at least somewhere in his home town.

The memory of the suppliant men he had left behind steeled him. They had led a life of servitude. They would be better as serfs, at least then their lord would prosper from them and have a reason to keep them alive and fed. These men had given the best of themselves, for little reward, to employers who used and discarded them like rubbish. Memories of their appeasement of the landlady, tolerance of the wagon drive, and complete compliance to the scab-landlord filled him with a burning rage. They watched as animals were given better treatment and yet they still responded to the whim of their employers, usually to the disadvantage of their fellows. Jobe took in a lungful of the fresh Yorkshire air. He wouldn't capitulate. He would crawl back to Liverpool if need be. He would maintain his liberty. The gang would become an avenging force, taking from those who prospered from the burdens faced by his class. If the gang no longer existed he would simply form a new one. One that would target the ship-owners and strike fear into the hearts of their ilk.

Charlie must have deposited the coins during their farewell embrace. He hadn't held money for a long time and the selection of coins felt heavy in his hand. He tried to recall if they had passed any kind of house or farm on their journey but couldn't recall anything that had disturbed the barrenness following their departure from the grisly guesthouse.

He wished he had been able to persuade Charlie from the clutches of the scab-ganger and the stain that he would never be able to cleanse from his conscience. His easy manner and light-hearted banter would have provided a welcome aside from the bleeding soles and yearning stomach that were sure to be his companion the whole route. In his haste to catch up with Bert he had not even had the sense to pilfer a few apples or a loaf of bread to see him through the first miles of his long journey. He realised the only thing he had eaten or drunk in almost three days was the grey piece of bread in the digs and glass of ale outside the pub. Once his mind became conscious of this it persecuted him by sending constant messages to his stomach. The pangs of hunger were almost unbearable but he retained the hope of coming across fellow travellers that he could hitch a lift with or a farmhouse where he could purchase some food, perhaps even rent a room for the night. But the moor extended unbroken as far as he could see.

He absent-mindedly counted the money over and over as he walked. The novelty of having it in his possession soon diminished and he would gladly have swapped it all for a piece of bread and cheese to placate his rumbling stomach.

As the light began to fade he thought it better that he should stop rather than stumble through the dark and risk losing the road. He ventured on to the moor, finding a small trough in the ground. He couldn't imagine that it was natural. It seemed that a heavy rock had been left there for a long time, or that it had been dug out. Even in his exhausted state Jobe couldn't help but wonder. Regardless, the grass was long, soft and served as an excellent mattress. He fell into a deep, dreamless sleep, waking just before sunrise, his legs and back stiff, but his mind refreshed.

The sole of his right shoe, which he had mended on numerous occasions while aboard the *Akbar*, only remained attached to the upper leather by a few tenuous pieces of thread. He had brought it to the attention of the stores officer on numerous occasions but was always ordered to mend it. The pitted, uneven track had decimated what was left of the thread and the sole flapped open, allowing pieces of debris in and constantly threatening to trip him. He shivered as he did what little he could to secure the sole before making his way on to the desolate road.

Hull was a gateway to the continent and the east. The flow of goods in and out was considerable; he couldn't understand the dearth of traffic on the road in either direction. The sun had reached and passed its midday zenith and he still hadn't encountered a living soul. Keeping his head up became a struggle and he was powerless to stop it from sagging to his chest. The effort of placing one foot before the other became his own personal purgatory. He developed a limp in an effort to protect his right foot, only serving to place added pressure on his left leg. It became impossible to judge his progress. On lifting his head from his chest he found that the terrain remained monotonous and unchanging.

His stomach gnawed at him, the rumblings seemingly keeping time with his step. He thought of H and how he had become a martyr to his stomach. The pangs evolved into spasms that had him clutching his stomach with each sharp contraction. His energy waned and his once-confident strides were now reduced to shuffling. His hand rubbed at the two lumps on his head. He tried to gauge whether they were growing, imagining his dehydration was causing them to swell. The remnants of spittle in his mouth were a curse, the stale redolence of the ale he had drunk the day before causing him to retch.

He took out the coins that Charlie had secreted in his pockets. He didn't bother to count them but held them in both hands like charms. Intermittently he would place his hands together and jingle the coins within them.

"Ey up, looks like a few bob thee's got there, petal!" Jobe was startled into opening his hands and spilling his coins. He looked at them scattered around his feet but made no attempt to pick them up. A dozen or so men had appeared in front of him. He had developed a keen instinct for danger aboard the *Akbar*. Encountered enough belligerent boys to detect when the threat of violence was imminent.

His senses now tingled with foreboding, but there were no boys among this group, each one of them was a grown man. He looked around, whether for an escape route or to fathom where they had appeared from he didn't know.

"Has thee addled so much that thee can afford to go throwing Godspennie's into the dirt to get all clarty like they're nowt but trammel?" said the man who had first addressed him. He was shorter than Jobe but was so stockily built that he resembled a cube. He was the only one not wearing some kind of hat. His mane of blonde hair flowed and merged with his side-whiskers; hanging well below his jaw-line they resembled large muttonchops. A blade of grass hung from the side of his mouth and vibrated when he spoke. Jobe could barely decipher the thick slang or brogue he spoke and was forced to answer intuitively.

"No, it's not that, I just got a fright that's all," he stammered, kneeling to retrieve the coins. Taking his eyes from the men was excruciating but he forced himself to scan the track for the fallen coins.

"I can well imagine my ansum, thee must be capt to encounter owt on this dwine of a road?" said Muttonchops, an air of sympathy in his voice. The sarcastic tone helped Jobe dissect the sentence and it became clear why he hadn't seen a soul. He had been following an uninhabited back road that Bert had used to cloak their arrival into Hull. Why hadn't he considered as much? He felt like crying for his aching feet, stomach and head. How many miles had he wasted following a winding unpopulated dirt track across the moor?

"It's known as the Scab Road these days," confirmed Muttonchops matter of factly. He was the only one who had spoken and obviously the leader of the men who bristled behind him, barely able to contain themselves. Jobe knew there was only one conclusion to the encounter; there was no chance of escape, but if he could just engage his tired mind there may be a chance of rescue. Muttonchops seemed to be enjoying the game and Jobe's only hope, no matter how slight, was to keep him enjoying it until somebody came along the road; hopefully it would be a wagon full of scabs. He struggled to gather his senses.

"We call them knobsticks in Liverpool. Scabs who travel in from other towns to break the pickets," he said, as he furtively deposited the coins into his pockets.

"Knobsticks is it? Happen we should rename this snicket into town the Knobstick Road!" The blade of grass dangling from his mouth reverberated as he laughed. Jobe waited until he had stopped, squeezing every second from the exchange

"I'm no scab. I didn't earn this money, it was given to me," he said trying to keep his voice even. Muttonchops turned to the men gathered behind him.

"By all his blether happen our new ansum here is of a mind that we're all gauvies." Jobe wasn't sure what was said but knew by the resentful looks shot his way that it couldn't be good. His energy was fading fast and he was too tired to feel relief when Muttonchops turned and continued the conversation, his countenance remaining cordial.

"Think on petal, you'll gain nowt for thissen by trying to marlock us," he smiled.

"A lot of these men are in a right mullock. They, me an' all, have watched a lot of friends clutter up in the Bastille because of thee and tha knobsticks!"

The stress of the situation coupled with the exertions of deciphering what was being said to him drained the remnants of Jobe's energy. His head began to thump. Lights danced before his eyes. His confidence waned; he knew there was no chance of redemption.

"I'm going back to Liverpool, I'd never scab," he tried to explain, the words sounding hollow in his own ears.

"Always a bad job when good Yorkshire silver leaves the county in the britches of fugglins…I dassent allow it to petal, these taistrils wouldn't abide it, they'd have my entrails for their snap if I let so much as an 'aporth aht." He took the stem from his mouth, shaking his head as he examined it carefully. The act was an unspoken sign and before Jobe knew it the men were rushing at him, obscuring Mutton-chops who stood aside engrossed in his blade of grass.

The sun was still in the sky when Jobe woke. Dry blood clogged his nostrils and, panicking, he began to choke as he became aware that he couldn't breathe. His lungs almost burst until some sense of self-preservation caused him to simply breathe through his mouth as he had for the time he had been unconscious, bringing a sudden end to his self-suffocation. He lay gasping as his lungs filled and deflated, becoming aware of a sharp pain in his chest, his rib cage. On realising he had broken or cracked his ribs he recalled the beating that had taken place before he lost consciousness. As one, his pain receptors flared, opening the floodgates to a wave of pain that engulfed his body, causing it to constrict in agony.

Jobe touched his swollen hands to his puffy and blackening eyes, before rubbing them carefully over his thumping head. His tongue protruded limply from his mouth, swollen and numb. He attempted to run it over his teeth but couldn't ascertain if any were broken. Rolling on to his back caused him to cry out in pain and he began to suffocate again and so painfully rolled on to his left side where he remained entering in and out of consciousness.

The light was beginning to diminish and he forced himself to half crawl, half roll underneath some bracken at the side of the track. His chest rose quickly and a cold sweat broke out all over his body with the exertion.

The sun was directly above him when he woke. The foliage he lay under shielded him from the worst of its glare but the tongue that he played over his cracked lips was still swollen and dry as sand: he tried to swallow but his throat wasn't functioning properly. He knew he had to get up and move on but felt he had expended all of his energy by simply licking his lips. He closed his eyes, just for a second to clear his head. He felt better with his eyes closed. Images of his mother played behind them. Scenes of Liverpool viewed from his father's shoulders caused the corners of his lips to curl into something that resembled a smile, the effort involved registering as a grimace of pain across his swollen, black eyes.

"'Its the bloody Trades Council that's bringing all the Liverpool men up here Jim, I guarantee it."

The words entered into Jobe's conscious mind but his eyes remained closed and he remained prone.

"I tell you when we find proof we'll flay them with it," the voice continued. Jobe peered through the bracken, seeing a man standing with his back to him filling his pipe. He was addressing a pair of legs that were poking from underneath a carriage. Jobe squinted and could see that there were two men under the coach repairing something under it.

"Will you give it a rest James! Why is it I'm on my back in the mud and you're there enjoying the scenery, no doubt filling your pipe as you do? Wasn't it you who didn't want to take the train?"

Jobe rolled on to his front, a small army of insects abandoning their temporary resting place, and began dragging himself through the bracken, grunting with the pain and effort. Dirt clung to him and the bracken scratched his already damaged face and hands as he crawled through it. The man with the pipe turned at the rustling and grunting, letting out a scream as he set eyes on the picture of horror emerging. The contents of his freshly stuffed pipe flew through the air. Before they landed one of the men working under the carriage rolled out and was on his feet in one fluent movement. The man with the pipe manipulated himself so that he stood behind him. The man was huge and held a spanner in his hand but on seeing the figure of Jobe dragging himself towards them dropped it to the ground.

"Water James, now! Are you soft in the head, it's just a boy," he admonished his companion, as he ran towards Jobe.

"Grab the flask also," he called over his shoulder.

"Here, you're all right, son? Can you understand me?" he asked as he knelt and supported Jobe's shoulders. The boy's eyes were so heavily bruised and swollen that it was impossible to tell if they were open or not. He cleared the dried blood from the boy's nostrils and then brushed the leaves and twigs that nestled in his hair before lifting him in his arms. Jobe's body draped listlessly across the man's strong forearms and his head lolled to one side as he was carried to the carriage.

"James...the water! Quickly now!" He held the water to Jobe's lips and after the first few drops escaped from his mouth Jobe grabbed weakly for the bottle.

"That's the way, easy now, a drop at a time," he said as he gently lifted the bottle from Jobe's grasp. Commotion over, James the man who had thrown his pipe in fright, busied himself refilling it. He watched as his companion ministered to the boy as best he could. Bringing his pipe to his mouth, he struck a match and began sucking and puffing on it. He blithely threw the match over his shoulder. The big man immediately admonished him.

"Haven't I told you this whole journey you need to be more careful with your matches, James, you could cause a heck of a fire."

"Ah behave would you, Jim, did you not see me blowing it out?"

As Jim looked through his friends billowing smoke for a tell tale sign of the match he spotted a man running toward them. Something in his manner immediately put him on guard. He lay the boy down on the ground as gently as possible.

"Get behind me and watch over the boy, James, I don't like the look of this fella!" James looked over his shoulder and quickly followed Jim's advice. They both watched the sweating man advancing, his pace, if anything, growing.

"Do you think it could be our boy's assailant?" asked James. Jim didn't answer but absentmindedly began to roll up his sleeves before realising he had already done so to work under the carriage. The man stopped a dozen or so paces before the coach. The sweat that streamed from his brow mingled with the dust that covered his entire front but his breath was steady and even. He looked past the two men in front of him to the broken boy that lay on the ground.

"Have you run him down?" he asked. Jim picked up on the menace in the man's voice, sensing that he was on the edge of violence.

"We found him like this, or rather he found us, he crawled from the bracken there," answered Jim pointing to the side of the road.

"We were just in the process of cleaning him up and finding out how he came to be in this shape."

Something in the man's demeanor changed and Jim felt no threat as the man began to approach him.

"You're from Liverpool!" stated the sweating man. "So is the boy there, his name is Jobe," he stated as he passed the two men, wafting pipe smoke from his face.

"Who did this to him then?" asked James, in between puffs of his pipe, he received no reply as Jim and the newcomer knelt over the boy.

"He's suffering from exhaustion, as well as the beating but I think he'll be ok. Are you from Liverpool as well then?" asked Jim tipping water on to his handkerchief and wiping at Jobe's face. He wet the handkerchief a second time before passing the container to the man next to him. The man nodded his thanks and took a huge draught of the water before replying.

"Yes, I'm from Liverpool. My name is Charlie, Charlie Doyle." He said holding out his hand which Jim and James shook in turn.

"Me and the boy were taken to Hull to scab, but he refused to do so, preferring to attempt the walk home, I stayed to work…to scab, but it proved harder than I imagined." James and Jim looked at each other.

"Who brought you to Hull?" asked James, his pipe forgotten.

"All right, James, enough with the questions, let Charlie rest, we know enough for now, there'll be plenty of time on the way home for questions," he said, as he picked up Jobe and placed him in the carriage.

"We're taking him with us?" asked James, a horrified look on his face.

"Well, we're certainly not leaving *them* here," said Jim.

"I'm Jim, Jim Larkin. The pleasant chap there is James Sexton," he said holding open the carriage door so Charlie could clamber inside.

The wind battered the side of the coach as it made it's way across the dark moor. Jobe's head rested in Charlie's lap who was at pains to stop it bouncing with the creaking coach. Occasionally he put a handkerchief to the neck of the water flask squeezing drops onto Jobe's cracked lips. James and Jim sat opposite listening as Charlie related every event, leaving nothing out, from Mann Island to Hull. On the ending of the tale the three men sat in silent reflection. It was the first time silence had dominated the coach and the driver could be heard encouraging the horses through the dark night. Charlie focused all of his attention on the window although it was so dark outside that all he could see was his own reflection flickering in the lamplight.

"Charlie?" Charlie looked down to see Jobe looking up at him through eyes that were no more than slits in the puffiness and bruising. Charlie smiled although his eyes betrayed his guilt at allowing Jobe to leave the dock alone. Jobe attempted to sit up but couldn't.

"Yes, it's Charlie, Jobe, shush now, save your energy."

When Jobe woke the sun was streaming through the open window of the carriage and the three men were eating bread and meat from a small hamper. Jobe made no sign that he had woken, instead choosing to observe Charlie and the two men opposite him.

The man they called Jim was speaking animatedly about the burgeoning support of the workers for representation and organised labour, sometimes remonstrating with his colleague, James, or defending his own points from James's remonstrations. The clear blue eyes that shone from dark heavy brows were quick and Jobe imagined they observed everything, missing nothing. Prominent cheekbones and a powerful, stubborn chin framed the fleshy nose that housed cavernous nostrils. Jim, feeling he was being watched looked in Jobe's direction.

"Ah, we've woken our young friend with all of our blather," he said reaching across with the contents of the basket. Charlie took the basket and ripped up small pieces of bread and meat, which he then gave to Jobe. Jobe resisted the urge to bolt down the food, several of his teeth and his whole jaw ached with the effort involved. He chewed both meat and bread deliberately and felt almost human once he had eaten his fill. The men let him break his fast in peace but on finishing it asked him to relay the events of his time on the moor. Charlie had ground his teeth as Jobe recounted his run in with the Hull dockers, but held his peace. Jim broke the silence on Jobe's story ending.

"I hear from Charlie here that you were willing to walk all the way back to Liverpool rather than scab the dock!" he said, with something like admiration in his voice.

"What a lad." He stated wistfully. "Having said that, d'you know I walked to London when I was nine!" he said with a grin.

"Nine, and alone!" he nodded, his smile growing. James Sexton snorted.

"I feel like I walked it with you the times I've heard the tale! Now what are we to do with their information?" he demanded. Jim looked from his colleague to the two passengers in the coach.

"Well I'm of the opinion that we should pose he of the sandwich board a few questions. I'm certain young Jobe here has more than a few of his own he'd like answering."